Your Fierce Love
(The Bennett Family, Book 7)

LAYLA HAGEN

Dear Reader,

If you want to receive news about my upcoming books and sales, you can sign up for my newsletter HERE: http://laylahagen.com/mailing-list-sign-up/

Cover: RBA Designs
Cover Photography: Sara Eirew Photographer

Copyright © 2017 Layla Hagen
All rights reserved.

CHAPTER ONE

Blake

"To another Bennett wedding," I exclaim, clinking my glass against my baby sister's. Summer sips champagne, her gaze scanning the packed venue. Our sister Alice got married today, and almost three hundred guests are in attendance. Weddings are big affairs in our family.

"Look at them. They're so happy." Watching Nate and Alice, Summer sighs, a dreamy expression on her face.

"You're daydreaming about your own wedding, aren't you? I bet you already know where you want to do it."

"Don't be silly. I know the theme and type of dress too." She grins, tapping a finger to her right temple. "Have all the details in my mind. I just need a groom."

Chuckling, I lace an arm around her shoulders, kissing her forehead. It's so good to have her back. She's been working at a museum in Rome for the past few years, and for a while, I feared she'd move there permanently. "I'm sure a certain member of our family will happily lend you a hand."

Summer wiggles her eyebrows. By certain, I mean our oldest sister, Pippa. She's quite the successful matchmaker. Proof: We're nine siblings in total, and six are married. Single people are a disappearing species in my family. Summer, my twin brother Daniel, and I are the last remaining musketeers.

"Let's go mingle with the guests," I say. The party is still young, and I've yet to greet many members of our *very* extended family, and close friends. The dance floor is already full, but given the sheer number of guests, that still leaves plenty of candidates to rope into a conversation.

"You're right. Divide and conquer?"

"Yeah."

Summer heads straight to one of our cousins, but I stop by the kids' playground corner first. The best part of having married siblings is that I've got a whole bunch of nieces and nephews to spoil. At the rate everyone's shooting out babies, the group is going to reach double digits soon. As far as I'm concerned, the more the merrier. Not to toot my own horn, but I have reasonable evidence that I'm everyone's favorite uncle.

Because of their different ages, things tend to get out of hand when we group them together. I'm expecting action tonight since the group is large—many guests brought their kids too. We've hired sitters for the event, but I want to get a feel for the situation, see if there's a war brewing. So far, it seems not.

"Uncle Blake, I want more sweets," says my four-year-old niece Mia.

Her identical twin, Elena, drops the doll she was holding at the word "sweets". "Me too."

They press their hands together as if in prayer, looking up at me with wide, pleading eyes. Now, I know for a fact that Pippa doesn't allow her daughters to eat sweets this late in the evening, but... eh... I never can tell these angels no. This weakness is probably why I'm their favorite uncle.

"Right away, girls."

I cross the enormous ballroom along the edge of the dance floor, which is getting more crowded by the minute. At the sweets cart, I run into one of my favorite people: Clara Abernathy. I met her more than two years ago, around the time Nate and Alice started dating. She's not just a close friend of Pippa's, but what we affectionately call an *adopted Bennett* in my family. Wearing a red wraparound dress, she hovers in front of the cart, inspecting the offerings.

"Fancy seeing you here, Clara." I grab a plate, trying to guess what Mia and Elena would like.

"You know me. If there's sugar in a room, there's a good bet I'll be gravitating to it. The hazelnut cake is to die for, by the way."

"Wouldn't be my first choice."

"Excellent. More for me." She grins, loading her plate with cake, then turns her attention to a plate in the center containing one lonely cupcake. "Please tell me you don't want that, or I'll have to fight you for it."

I'm tempted to tease her, but growing up with three sisters taught me that you don't get between a woman and her sweets unless you're prepared to suffer the consequences.

"I don't want it. Be my guest."

"My, what a gentleman you are tonight."

"I'm dressed like one, might as well act the part."

"Have to say, for someone who seems allergic to suits, you sure wear one well. Should try it more often."

"Let's not get crazy." I wink at her. Suits and cuff links are not my usual style. I'm a jeans man through and through. She laughs softly, her dark brown hair bobbing down her back, a whiff of her flowery and feminine scent reaching me.

"Why aren't you putting anything on your plate?"

"I'm actually on a bounty hunt for Mia and Elena. Not sure what they want. Help?"

"Oooh, but the girls will love the cupcake. And the hazelnut cake." She glances once at her plate before handing it to me, and taking the empty one from my hands. "Take this to them."

"You don't even bat an eyelash at giving up the cupcake for my nieces, but you wanted to fight me for it? Good to know."

"I can't resist any of your nieces and nephews, and don't judge me. Since you cater to their every whim, neither do you."

"Guilty."

"Know what? I'll eat sweets later. Let's make plates for the rest of the kids too. Taking sweets to just part of the group is a recipe for war."

It didn't occur to me, but she's right. "Thanks for saving my bacon."

"It's good bacon. Deserves saving."

I can't put my finger on it, but her tone sounds off. As we head over to the kids' corner carrying loaded plates, a subtle shift in her body language convinces me that something is definitely awry. She hunches her shoulders, sighing. Usually, Clara has an energy that lights her up from within, but that vibrancy is melting away right in front of my eyes. Time to find out what's bothering her, and either fix it or make her forget about it—for tonight, at least.

***

Clara

The kids attack the plates the second Blake and I place them on the low tables. We move a few feet away from the group but watch for any signs they're about to attack each other.

"What's wrong?" Blake asks, and I wince.

"That visible, huh?"

"Yeah, to anyone who knows you."

Oh snap! I don't want to be a Debbie Downer. I have all the time in the world to worry about my living situation once the wedding's over. I have one job tonight, and that is being happy for Alice and Nate.

Before moving to London with Alice, Nate was my boss, and a great mentor and friend. He also introduced me to the Bennett family, and they've become a huge part of my life. They're warm and close, and I adore them. Last year, they threw a surprise birthday party for me, and whenever I'm sick, someone from the family—usually Blake's mother—brings me food.

Long story short, I owe it to Nate big-time, and the least I can do is smile and push my current predicament to the back of my mind.

"So, what's wrong?"

"Nothing that can't wait until after the wedding," I say with determination.

Blake lifts a brow. I should've known he wouldn't be satisfied with that nonanswer. He can be intense when he wants to. Now he definitely wants to. He leans in a tad too close, pinning me with his dark eyes. I won't lie, my resolve cracks a little under the weight of his attention. My flight instinct kicks in because being in sniffing distance of Blake is dangerous. It usually sends my pulse into overdrive, messes with my senses. Tonight, his proximity seems to affect me less—

Wait, I spoke too soon. There is pounding in my ears... Yep, that's my pulse spiking. My heartbeat accelerates. Blake is still holding my gaze captive. I stubbornly look back but give in when I feel the heat rising to my cheeks.

"You know I was supposed to receive the keys to my apartment next Monday?"

I'm still over the moon about the *my* bit. This will be the first home I will own. A tiny box, but it will be mine. Eventually.

"Yeah."

"Well, turns out the construction crew found some issues, and they're delaying the project completion by ten to twelve weeks."

Blake sets his lips into a grim line. "Let me guess. You already put in the notice where you live now?"

Shifting my weight from one leg to the other, I cross my arms over my chest.

"Exactly. I'm supposed to move out by the end of next week. Called the landlord, asking if he can extend the contract, but he's already rented the place to someone else, so his answer was something along the lines of *chop, chop, move it, move it.*"

"I'm gonna take a wild guess that house hunting isn't going well?"

"Not easy to find something on such short notice in San Francisco."

"Especially for only a few months."

Blowing out a breath, I nod. Ever since the construction company notified me of the delay two weeks ago, I've been browsing apartment listings and emailing with a real estate agent, but so far nothing. The short lease time is a deal breaker for all the places I can afford, so my options are rather bleak.

"I'll have to suck it up and look for a room in a shared apartment. Those are more flexible." The prospect of sharing my space with strangers is daunting. I grew up in group homes, sharing a bedroom with five, sometimes seven other girls. Only half were friendly at any given time.

"You're not going to live with strangers, Clara." He sounds a little concerned, a lot protective. In the background, the music changes, and I tap my foot against the floor to the rhythm of the new tune, watching as a crease appears on Blake's forehead and he runs a hand through his almost black hair. "You never know what weirdos you'll end up with."

"Trust me, I'm not a fan of sharing, but I'm out of options."

"I have an idea." He pulls himself to his full height, which I estimate to be at six foot two or three. Despite his height, he appears strong, not massive. His muscular build and tapered waist make him look athletic. Scratch that. They make him look the definition of sexy and sinful.

"Do tell, because I'm completely out of good ones."

"The apartment next to mine above the bar is empty."

It takes a moment for his meaning to register. Blake owns a bar, and while I did know he owns the entire building and lives on the upper floor, I had no idea there were two apartments there, but it makes sense. The building is huge. There's just one hitch in this plan. Considering the size and location....

"I don't think I can afford that kind of rent."

"I wouldn't charge you."

This stabs at my pride. I make it a point to take the chances that are given to me, but this feels like charity. I deliberate my answer for a moment because I don't want to come off as ungrateful when he's going above and beyond to help me.

"I wouldn't feel comfortable with that, Blake."

"Look, that place is empty anyway, and I'd never rent it out."

"Why not?"

"I don't want neighbors," he says simply. "You're a friend, that's different. And it would only be for twelve weeks tops."

Emotions clog my throat, but I muster a smile. Even though the Bennetts have been a constant in my life for the past two years, I'm still surprised every time they offer to help me. Still, this doesn't feel right.

As if sensing my doubts, he adds, "You can pay me what you're paying for rent now."

"That's more reasonable, even if not fair to you."

"It's fair." His eyes crinkle as he offers me a wide smile. "Now, since the kids seem peaceful, let's return to the realm of grown-ups." He leads me away, resting one hand on the center of my back, splaying his fingers wide.

"Do you want to come see the apartment?"

"Sure. When do you have time?"

"Tomorrow would be good since it's Sunday, but I'll probably sleep like the dead after this. Monday? Before happy hour begins at the bar?"

"Deal. And Blake? Thank you. You're the one saving my bacon now. Big-time."

His fingers press gently into my back, and he leans in *dangerously* close. "I'll be a fun neighbor, I promise."

Is it suddenly hot in here, or is it just me? I glance sideways, inspecting Blake. Yep, just me. He isn't even breaking a sweat, while it's all Niagara here under my dress. I wish I'd had the good sense to style my hair up in an elegant bun instead of loose waves, though I suspect the flash of heat has nothing to do with my hair sticking to the back of my neck and everything to do with the man next to me.

As we make our way to the center of the ballroom, I notice the hook holding up Alice's long train has come off, and the fabric is cinched behind her at her feet. Since she's engrossed in a conversation with Nate, it's possible she hasn't noticed. She could trip on it if she doesn't know.

"See you later," I mouth to Blake and head toward his sister. "Sorry to interrupt you lovebirds, but the hook holding your train has come off."

Alice glances downward. "Oh, crap. They warned me this would happen because the fabric is so heavy. I have safety pins in a small white bag under our table."

"I'll go get it, and then I'm going to fix your dress."

"Always the savior, eh, Clara?" Nate asks good-naturedly.

"That's how I roll." Ah, I miss having him as a boss, or at least close by. I have no siblings, but while I worked for him, it felt a bit like I had an older brother.

Five minutes later, Alice and I are in the bathroom, and I'm trying to replace the hook with the safety pin. Alice, bless her, is talking my ear off about everything.

"I just can't rein in my grin," she confides. "Every time someone says "smile for a photo", my face just explodes with happiness." Her happiness is infectious, and I can't help wondering how it must feel to love someone and to be loved back so fiercely. "I think my face is going to hurt from so much grinning tomorrow."

"There, all done," I exclaim, finally. "I think it'll hold, but I'll keep an eye on it anyway."

"You're my hero. Now let's get out there and have a blast."

We do have a blast. I dance my feet off, but my mind keeps circling back to one thought—especially whenever I'm dancing with a certain Bennett brother. If Blake's proximity affects me this much, how on earth will I pull off living next to him?

CHAPTER TWO

Clara

"I am going to frame this and look at it every day." I'm hugging a magazine to my chest while doing a bad impression of a *cha-cha*. This is one of the best things about having my own small office at the studio. Inside here, I can be as ridiculous as I want. No one can see my antics, which often leads people to not take me seriously. As if having a sense of humor and a tendency to overexpress my joy means I can't be serious when the situation requires it.

But whatever, I'm not going to change anyone's minds, so I've learned to only let my crazy out around people I trust. Once I've danced the energy away, I lay the magazine on the desk, smoothing it out. I've crumpled it a bit in my display of affection. It's a stellar review on one of the last segments I've worked on with Nate as his assistant producer. It only came out last week. I like my job, but I'm not crazy about it, and sometimes a good review is exactly what I need to keep pushing.

I know that I'll never make it to executive producer, but that's fine with me. I have no such aspirations. I want to transition out of TV at some point, because work-life balance isn't a thing in the industry. I hope to have a family of my own one day—kids to love, a husband to dote on. I also want a job that will allow me to contribute financially while not taking over my life. Maybe I should wish for calorie-free ice cream while I'm imagining impossible things.

For now though, I'm doing my best to be the most kick-ass assistant producer. I work on a local TV show, and they pay me a salary that is just enough to buy my own tiny apartment just outside the city.

Today I'm being sneaky instead of kick-ass, tiptoeing out of the studio at four o'clock so I can meet Blake before happy hour begins at the bar. Thank heavens my boss is on a set on the outskirts of San Francisco today, so he's not privy to my shenanigans.

After parking my car a block away from the bar, I walk at a brisk pace, soaking in the energy of the Pacific Heights district surrounding me. It's a bright, if chilly, evening, perfect for the second week of May. I've been here before, but now I'm seeing things through a different lens.

The bar itself is in a three-story building, on the ground floor. The apartments are on the top floor. He uses the floor in between for storage, which means no noise from the bar reaches the apartments. I clap my hands in excitement as I survey the building once more: fresh, energetic, promising a good time if you step inside.

The bar is already buzzing with customers, despite it not even being five o'clock. Then again, most tourist guidebooks or websites list it as a recommendation, so chances are many of the customers are tourists who aren't bound to their work schedule. Two bartenders are behind the counter, but Blake sits at one of the high, round tables right next to the bar. He's with two other men and a woman who are wearing suits, and from what I can see, they are pointing to some papers on the table. He's in serious business mode, and it's a damn good look on him. Even though he's talking to a group, he dominates the space and, as far as I can tell, the conversation.

I wave discreetly at Blake, then hop on one of the stools in front of the bar in a move I hope conveys that I'll wait for him to finish the conversation. But Blake nods at the three strangers and heads toward me. The crowd parts for him as he stalks through the room. Blake emanates power and confidence in a subtle way. Everything about him makes you stand taller and pay attention.

"Hello, future neighbor. I'm wrapping up things with the group there, and we'll go up in a few minutes, okay?"

"Sure, take your time. I'll wait and have a glass of whatever in the meantime."

"Great." Blake motions to the closest bartender. "Whatever the lady here drinks is on the house."

"Blake," I admonish. "No way—"

"When you drink in my bar, you don't pay."

He smiles, but his tone leaves no room for argument.

Before I even have time to open my mouth and argue, Blake leaves, returning to his group. I order a glass of ginger lemonade and, while sipping from it, inspect the bar closer.

Before I know it, Blake is ushering his conversation partners toward the entrance. Quickly, I try to pay for my drink, and I'm smart about it, approaching the bartender Blake hasn't instructed to provide me with free drinks. I almost manage to hand him ten dollars when Blake catches my forearm midair.

"No," he says simply. The bartender's eyebrows climb into his hairline but he steps away, finishing the cocktails he was mixing when I approached him.

"I want to pay for my drink," I insist.

"Family and friends don't pay in my bar."

His voice holds equal parts domination and determination, and it sends my pulse into overdrive. He holds my gaze captive, and my forearm, his fingers applying a gentle pressure on my skin. The contact sends waves of heat through me. *Oh crap.* Any day now, I will grow immune to his charm. Any day now. But today is not the day. At least the attraction is one-sided, thank goodness.

Licking my lips, I pull back my arm, placing the ten-dollar bill back in my bag. "Okay. Thank you." I down the last few gulps of lemonade.

"Let's go upstairs. Unless you want another drink?"

"No, I'm good. Let's go."

"Follow me. There's a separate entry though the back, so you wouldn't have to walk through the bar every time. I'll show you."

Blake leads the way, opening doors for me and tucking me into his side as we step outside on the street and round the corner. His protective streak is most endearing. When Blake pushes the door to the apartment open after we climb two flights of stairs, I smile. It's love at first sight. The place, at least what I can see of it, is even better than I imagined, even though a blanket of dust covers it.

"I've done improvements," Blake explains as we step inside. "But the building has an old infrastructure."

"I like old things. They have a soul, a history."

"True."

The apartment is a lovely blend of old and new. Blake gives me a quick tour. The living room is spacious and the bedroom a little on the small side, but I love it. It's quaint.

"My bedroom is on the other side." Blake points to the wall. "The two apartments used to be one single unit, but the owner before me divided them by a wall and made a separate entrance."

Briefly I wonder how thick the wall is and barely manage to keep myself from asking out loud. That's a rabbit hole if there ever was one. I suppose I'll find out as soon as Blake has a lady friend over.

My stomach churns unpleasantly at the thought, which is ridiculous. I have no business being jealous. No business at all.

"It's dusty, but I'll call a cleaning company before you move in," he says as we return to the living room.

"No need. I'll do it myself."

"I'll bring in a cleaning company."

"Is there any point in contradicting you? You're extra bossy today."

A grin lights up his face. "You can always try. It's good for me to be challenged now and again. Keeps me grounded. Otherwise I'd buy my own hype."

"You're one of a kind, Blake."

"Are you trying to kill me with kindness?"

"Is it working?"

"No. Just so we're clear, I'm still bringing in a cleaning company. Feel free to give me a hard time for it."

"Nah, I'm saving up the hard time for another occasion. Choosing my battles and all that."

"Smart. Any changes you want to make?"

"What am I allowed to change?"

"Anything except tearing down walls."

"I'll buy a floor-to-ceiling bookshelf for the southern wall. I already know which one it'll be."

Excitement coursing through me, I take my phone out of my bag. I've bookmarked the page with my dream bookshelf, but have yet to be able to buy it because it's huge, and it couldn't have possibly fit in my old apartment. I turn the phone, showing it to Blake, who seems a bit taken aback by my enthusiasm. I make a mental note to dial it down a notch or two. I know I can come across a bit manic when I'm excited about something.

Blake zooms in on the size of the bookcase. "That will fit right in."

"Exactly."

I do a full turn and see dust motes playing into the light streaming in through the windows. The window is immense with French doors that open onto a balcony. The place will be bathed in sunlight on clear days.

"If you don't mind, I'd also paint the southern wall."

"Sure, what color?"

"The one you have in your bar. You're going to have to tell me the exact color code because I love it." It's somewhere between champagne and peach. "I know I'll only be here for a little while, but I like... personalizing my spaces."

Blake nods. "Want to see the balcony? It's the only downside."

Before I have time to ask how on earth a balcony can be a downside, Blake opens the French doors and we both step outside.

"We'd have to share it."

"Ah, so this is why you don't want to rent out this place."

"Yeah. I could have it remodeled and split it in two. It would take a shitload of permits, but it could be done."

"It'd be such a shame, though. Besides, maybe one day you'll want to tear down that pesky wall between the bedrooms, and then you'd have a split balcony."

"My thoughts exactly. I was thinking of doing something with the balcony, get rid of the beanbags." He points with his thumb behind him to the two bright green beanbags stacked in a corner. They look comfy, but this balcony deserves more love and attention.

"Hmm, some nice lounge chairs. Oh, and a swing would be nice." I animate at the thought, bouncing back and forth on my toes. "Just imagine sitting out here and watching the sunset, drinking a glass of wine. I bet it's beautiful."

I could also see myself sitting out here and sketching illustrations, which is hands down the best hobby in the world. Keeps me afloat when things get too cray-cray at the studio.

"Lounge chairs and a swing," Blake declares.

"You don't have to buy them just because I want them," I say reasonably, even though the thought of a swing makes me bounce back and forth from my heels to my tiptoes again.

"I asked for help, you shared your ideas. I like them."

"Okay." I'm trying to rein in my excitement, I really am, but I can't help grinning widely at the thought of lounging on chairs on sunny days and curling up in the swing with a book, looking up over the roofs when I need to rest my eyes.

I move over to the edge of the balcony. The railing is sturdy black metal curled in intricate patterns. A little low, but the pattern is thick enough that no one can see on the balcony from the street. It offers privacy while not obstructing the view. I love it. At least I do until I accidentally catch my skirt in said railing. In my efforts to free myself, I lose my balance. My stomach churns horribly as my upper body lunges over the railing. For a split second, I'm convinced I'm about to hurtle two stories to the ground, before two strong and sturdy arms pull me back to my feet. I don't protest when Blake pulls me against him, wrapping his arms around me. I just inhale his manly scent, losing myself in the safety of his strong and muscular frame, my eyes firmly closed.

"Shit!" I mutter into his chest. To my horror, I realize I'm trembling.

"I've got you." Blake's voice is soothing but tinged with unease, and I discover I'm not the only one trembling. I scared the living daylights out of us both. "I've got you, Clara. You're safe." I remain in his arms until the last of the tremors subside and my heart is in the right place again, no longer in my throat.

"I'm okay," I whisper. "You can let me go."

"As soon as you stop tugging at my shirt."

I blink open one eye and then the other. Sure enough, I'm fisting his black polo shirt like I'm planning to sink my claws into his chest. I unclench my fingers right away, my hands hovering awkwardly just above his pecs. I can't exactly lower my arms because Blake hasn't let go of me. I'm still pressed against him, my breasts squished against his granite chest. Our bodies are aligned, touching in more points than I want to think about. Blake is looking down at me, his pupils a tad more dilated than before as they search my face, resting on my lips. I lick them, almost unconsciously, and he exhales sharply, his hot breath landing on my mouth. *Sweet baby Jesus.* What's happening here? Am I imagining things? Have I misread Blake and my attraction isn't quite as one-sided? That's a dangerous thought if I ever had one. I must have imagined it. Wouldn't be the first time I mistake people's attention for affection.

One of the group home supervisors once explained that orphans sometimes grow into adults with attachment issues because the lack of parental love in the formative years leaves a huge hole. I certainly fit that pattern. As a rule, I'm careful with the people I let in, but those I do let in? Oh boy, they'd better brace themselves for excessive displays of affection. There might be a lot of pampering involved, even surprise cuddling sessions if I decide to go crazy, which I often do. Some aren't that keen on being showered with affection. Past boyfriends, in particular, haven't been. The words "clingy" and "suffocating" popped up during a break-up fight or five, which make my hope of a husband and kids as likely to happen as world peace, but that's an issue for another time.

Back to my current issue. I'm still wrapped in

Blake's arms, and his gaze is still zeroed in on my lips. Right... time to face the music and either confirm or eliminate my suspicion. Slowly and deliberately, I lick my lower lip again. Blake's reaction is almost primal. Another sharp and hot exhale lands on my mouth while his fingertips press into my skin. *Sweet baby Jesus on a unicorn.* What am I supposed to do with this? As I extract myself from his arms, I can barely wrap my mind around this shift between us. I knew from the start that moving next to Blake is a risky business. Even when I thought the attraction was one-sided, I was dabbling in dangerous territory.

But if it's not one-sided? This just turned into a minefield.

"You sure you're okay?" he asks as I step back.

"Yeah, it was just a scare. Won't go close to that railing again anytime soon." I back away from it, heading back inside, with Blake hot on my heels. "Let's talk rent. Where I live now I pay—"

"You're not going to pay anything here."

I cross my arms over my chest, turning to face him. "Yes, I am."

"This place is empty, and if you don't move in, it'll continue to be empty."

"We already talked about this at the wedding."

"About that... I was just shutting you down, telling you what you wanted to hear so you could relax and enjoy."

I open my mouth, then close it, unsure what to say. "I feel like I should be mad at you for being sneaky."

"Feel free to be mad."

"I can't," I admit. "I happen to abide by the rule that sneakiness is allowed for a good cause."

"That's my girl."

"Look, I know you don't need the money."

"I *really* don't, and I'm not saying it to be a prick."

Right, how do you negotiate with someone who doesn't need anything? Blake doesn't just own this bar but also co-owns three restaurants with Alice. I saw the profit they make about two years ago. Nate helped them get featured on the *Delicious Dining* show, and I worked on the pitch for the network with him. They make a truckload of money and then some. The entire family is well-off. More than half the siblings work at Bennett Enterprises, one of the most successful players in the high-end jewelry market.

"Doesn't mean I get to stay here free. It's not right."

"It is if I say so, and I'm saying so."

He steps closer, towering over me like he's determined to dominate the conversation. Dominate me. He should really stop because everything about this pose is alluring.

"Stop being so stubborn."

His face breaks into a Cheshire cat grin. "Why, am I wearing you down?"

"No." I pull myself up straighter. Unfortunately, this doesn't do much, seeing how

Blake is more than a head taller than I am, even if I'm wearing heels. "But I'm running out of good arguments. Just so you know, I will circle back to this topic again."

"Excellent. Warning you though, I can hold my stubborn."

"So can I."

"So, what do you say? Willing to take this very bad deal?"

"Oh stop, Blake. You know you're doing me a huge favor. I'll be out of your hair as soon as possible. I promise I won't impose while I'm here."

"You won't *impose*, Clara."

"Wait until you have a lady overnight and she realizes you're almost house-sharing with a woman. That won't go over too well."

He jerks his head back, clearly not having considered this. "Don't worry about that. You're a friend. Practically family. Anyone who has a problem with that isn't welcome in my home."

His words touch me deeply, make me feel important. I'm unbelievably lucky to have him and his family in my life. I try not to think too closely about his future overnight guests. He's not dating anyone, which is why he went alone to the wedding, but during our numerous girls-only outings, Pippa and Summer let slip that Blake enjoys... variety. As he should, considering he's twenty-nine and sinfully attractive.

"What about you?" he asks. "Do you date much?"

"I try, but I keep meeting men who want different things than I do. They're looking for fun or just hanging out in a friends-with-benefits sort of way."

"What are you looking for?"

"I want a family, so someone nice and dependable. Someone safe and not argumentative. Trustworthy. I know some people think safe is boring, but I don't think that at all. I think it's just...safe."

"Clara, relax. You don't have to defend your choices." His eyes search me for a brief moment before he adds, "I mean, starting a family right now is the last thing I'd want, but...I don't think I've ever heard someone speak so openly and honestly about what they want."

I've never voiced these thoughts, and now that I have, I suddenly feel very vulnerable, which I hope to mask with a joke.

"Well, I *am* one-and-a-half-years older than you. Wait until you hit the thirty mark—hormones go haywire, though it might have something to do with being a woman. Biological clock and all that. Anyway, don't worry about any sexy nocturnal activities on my side of the wall. I don't plan for any until I'm with someone who at least seems to want the same things. Speaking of...nocturnal activities, can you give me heads-up when you plan to bring someone home? Not to pry, but I have to know if I should have ear plugs on hand... that's a fake wall between our bedrooms and bathrooms. Can't be too soundproof."

Shit! If I were any more transparent in my prying efforts, you could see right through me. Placing the glass on the counter, he leans into me slightly. Not in an intrusive manner, but close enough to make me wish simultaneously that he'd step back *and* lean in closer. I'm officially losing my mind.

"We'll figure this out as we go. We'll improvise."

He steps away from me. Thank heavens for small mercies. I nod wordlessly. What is there to say? The man is right, and I'm great at improvising. Seeing how most of my life has been a big improv all in itself, I'm a pro at it. I don't know why I'm getting all up in arms about this.

"Okay. Just...as I said, I don't want to impose."

"That's a terrible word. I don't want to hear it again."

"I'll make a mental note. Anyway, no need to worry. I won't walk in on you romancing anyone on the balcony. I know how to be invisible when the situation requires it."

***

Blake

She almost shrinks into herself, and I instantly see red at the thought that others made her feel small or wish she'd be invisible. My first instinct is to ask who made her feel that way and make them pay, but I don't see how that would make this any better. So, I follow my second instinct—reassuring her that I won't ever make her feel small.

I close the distance to her, placing my hands on her shoulders, pressing one thumb at the base of her neck. Her pulse is erratic.

"I *want* you here, Clara. I wouldn't have offered this place otherwise."

"Okay."

I value my privacy, which is why I didn't rent out this apartment, not even to friends.

For the longest time, I had zero hesitation about letting people in my life. I'm a very sociable person; I like being surrounded by a crowd. The more, the merrier. Making friends has always come easy for me. It took me a long while to realize some people just hung around because I provided them with luxuries—free vacations, free everything. I was young when my family came into money, which had positives and negatives. I had everything I needed and wanted, but I also didn't learn the value of caution or mistrust. It took many mishaps for me to realize some people only stuck around for what I gave them, and when that wasn't enough, they showed their ugly side.

So now I'm more cautious, but Clara is one of the few people I feel comfortable around. I can be myself with her, just like with my family. She's fun, smart, and no one who openly admits that what she wants most is a family can have a mean or traitorous bone in their body.

There's that small detail of me being unable to stop touching her, especially since she's so responsive. The pad of my thumb is still at the base of her neck. Her pulse is, if possible, even more frantic.

"Any general house rules?" she asks, her voice uneven.

"None that I can think of. Except...I usually go to sleep very late and then wake up late in the mornings."

"Makes sense, since the bar and the restaurants open and close late."

"Yeah. I'm a light sleeper in the morning, so if you sing in the shower—"

"I don't."

An image of Clara in the shower pops in my mind. Christ, what I wouldn't give to see that, to join her. *Not going there. Not going there.*

Lowering my hand, I skim it down her arm. Her skin turns to goose bumps under my touch, and she sucks in a breath. Her reaction to me is intoxicating, makes it hard to keep my thoughts in line, even harder not to touch her more, see what other reactions I can provoke.

Jesus, this is escalating far too easily. We've spent time with each other before, so why is this spinning out of control so fast?

We're saved by the bell—in this case, the sound of a message on my phone.

"The bar manager needs me," I tell Clara, reading his message. "Have to go downstairs. When exactly do you have to move out of your apartment?"

"The end of this week."

"Okay. You can keep this set of keys, I have another one."

"Thanks."

I lean in to kiss her cheek, and because I can't help it, I linger with my lips on her skin a beat too long. She shudders lightly, her breath coming out almost on a moan. The things I'd do to this woman. I'd taste every inch of her skin, every—*fuck me*.

I step back right away.

"Come on, I'll walk you to your car, almost-neighbor."

As we leave the apartment, I have a eureka moment and a plausible explanation for the sudden shift in tension between us. Before we mostly saw each other at family events; we were rarely alone. As neighbors sharing a balcony, we will rarely *not* be alone. Turns out it's a dangerous move to ask a woman you're drawn to far too much to move next door.

CHAPTER THREE

Clara

"Clara, Quentin is asking for you." Mona motions with her head in the direction of our lunch buffet. My boss, Quentin Meyer, is hovering in front of it, loading his plate.

"Thanks, Mona."

She shudders almost imperceptibly, then heads to the buffet herself, keeping her distance from Quentin. Nearing his forties with a nasty smile and permanently wandering eyes, most of the women at the studio do their best to avoid him. But alas, he's my boss, so I'm the one person who can't do that. I make a point to never wear anything even remotely sexy at work.

"Hey, boss," I say, loading a plate for myself. "Mona said you need me."

"Yes, yes. How well do you know the Bennett family?"

I pause in the act of biting into my burger. Maybe it's because Quentin watches me with his trademark nasty smile, but I don't feel like volunteering the truth.

"Not well at all, why?"

We move toward a corner of the room because it's getting crowded over at the buffet.

"You were at Alice Bennett's wedding. Someone tagged you on Facebook." He bites into his own burger, and my stomach plummets. I take a big bite, using the excuse of chewing so I don't have to answer right away so I can form a plan. Damn Facebook. I thought I had my settings on private so only friends could see what I post or what I'm tagged in.

"Of course I went. Nate and I are good friends, but that's all."

Quentin grimaces as if he accidentally swallowed lemon juice. "Damn shame. Ran into one of the heads from Entertainment Central, Ryan Shepperd. Pitched him our show for *Our Picks*, but he's not giving us the time of day."

Our Picks is a show that spotlights and reviews other shows. It pulls in incredible numbers for such a segment. Truth be told, it's pulling about ten times the numbers our flailing show is. If we'd be featured on it, our viewership would skyrocket.

We're barely scraping by in the rankings, but with a lot of hard work the show will climb up the charts...eventually. It's been on air for four months, and I've been here for two.

After Nate moved to London, I kept working on his show with the new executive producer, but then he left too, and the one who took his place wanted to bring in his assistant. I wanted to stay with the network because the pay is above what I'd get somewhere else. Quentin here just had his fifth assistant quit on him in two months, so they gave me the job.

"So anyway, Shepperd said one of his people saw you tagged on Facebook in the wedding. They've wanted a scandal about the Bennett family for years for their *We See You* segment. Said he'd trade me: Juicy story on that family for a feature of our show on *Our Picks*."

My body goes cold.

We See You is nicknamed *Gossip Central* in the industry—a weekly evening show where they tear apart whoever is their subject, flaunting dirty laundry and scandals for the entire country to see. It pulls in even better numbers than *Our Picks*.

Over my dead body will the Bennett family ever be a subject on their show.

"Was hoping you'd know something about their skeletons. Have you heard anything juicy from Nate?"

He says Nate's name with disdain, and I grit my teeth. I don't know why he dislikes Nate—probably because he's made a name for himself even though he's younger than Quentin. And Nate never got ahead by selling anyone out.

"No," I say calmly. "From what he says, they're great people. No skeletons."

As if I'd tell you if they had.

"Please, everyone has skeletons. The press is dying for some dirt. A scandal."

Blake told me once that as time passed the press became more interested in their personal life rather than the company, and that they're always fishing for scandals.

"You sure you can't get closer to them?"

I don't think you can get any closer than living next to one and attending all their family events, but I shake my head, my hackles rising—no one is going to mess with that family.

"I have many press leads." I work as much positivity in my tone as I can muster. "We'll climb in the rankings, you'll see."

Quentin pays no attention, instead eying the ass of a passing assistant. I bite into my burger to hide my groan. I *loved, loved, loved* working with Nate. He was a great boss and mentor. More than a mentor, he was almost like a brother, *and* he accepted my crazy. That's always a bonus. Of course, lightning never strikes twice, so I wasn't dreaming I'd get another boss like him.

But is it too much to ask for a decent boss? One who does his job and doesn't look for shortcuts that involve selling people out? One who doesn't make my skin crawl?

Part of me regrets taking out the mortgage because I'll be stuck here for a long while until I can find something better. But then I think about how great it'll be to have my own place. That puts everything into perspective. When Quentin leaves, I take out my phone, pull up the Facebook app, and change my settings to private.

***

Blake

"Mr. Bennett, the earliest we can deliver is next Monday," the vendor repeats for the fifth time. Her voice is just as friendly as it was the first time but just as unhelpful. If I were at the store, things would move much faster. I work my charm better in person than on the phone. "The bookshelf version you requested is a custom-made piece, so it's not just about the delivery. We have to make it first, and we take great pride in our craftsmanship."

Time to sweeten the offer. "I'll pay double your rush fee if you deliver it on Friday."

"We have no rush fee."

Well, now that's just bad business, but to each his own. I pace in front of Blue Moon, our flagship restaurant, growing impatient. The meeting with my location manager was supposed to start three minutes ago.

"Call it a thank-you fee if you want."

"What's the rush? Birthday present?"

"No. Someone moves in on Saturday, and she wants the bookcase. I want to surprise her by having it here already."

"Oooh, a romantic gesture. Right. Hang on, let me see...Yes, I can shift another order until Monday and move yours into its slot. Then I will personally make sure it's delivered on Friday."

"Thank you. Appreciate it."

"Look out for the confirmation e-mail and message with the new delivery date. Have a nice day, Mr. Bennett."

"You too."

Hanging up, I shake my head. Ten minutes of sweet-talking and bribing got me nothing, but the assumption that it's a romantic gesture wins the game in five seconds flat? Maybe I should put more stock in romantic gestures, though I've never been one for them. I didn't correct the assumption because I suspect that explaining it's for a "friend" doesn't have the same impact, even though it's true. At least eighty percent true, anyway.

At the wedding, I tried not to focus on how beautiful she was in her red dress. Yesterday I tried not to notice how perfectly her skirt fit her, or imagine what's underneath. I failed on both accounts. Truthfully, I've been failing at not noticing every detail about Clara for a long time. If there's ever been a time to succeed, it's now. Until Saturday, I'd better become a pro at it.

She's a family friend, an adopted Bennett, and those are off-limits for good reasons. Clara is more off-limits than anyone else. She doesn't have any family, damn it, and it's clear how much she loves being close to mine. I'm not going to make a mess of that. When it comes to women, making a mess is my specialty. I will be the best neighbor and friend I can be, make sure she's comfortable here.

Ross, my location manager, is waiting in the

kitchen. It's the down-time between lunch and dinner, but we're still half-full, so the chefs and sous-chefs are buzzing around.

I co-own this place, two more restaurants, and the bar with Alice. Since she moved to London when Nate was made the executive producer of a famous TV show there, I'm in charge of overseeing day-to-day operations, and she focuses heavily on the business side that doesn't require her presence— mostly marketing and strategic planning. I say mostly because she still keeps a close eye on operations here at Blue Moon since it's our flagship location. She promised that she'd take a break while on her honeymoon. She kept her promise for all of two days.

"The meeting will be short," I tell him. "As you know, Alice is on her honeymoon. We already discussed that she'll be off the grid until she's back in London, but a mishap occurred today. Apparently, she exchanged fifteen e-mails with you. I want you to set an auto-responder to your e-mail for any messages coming from her address, saying,

"You are currently on your honeymoon. All your emails will be forwarded to Blake Bennett, and you will only receive an answer once you are back from your honeymoon.

Kind regards,

Your Faithful Team Who Insists You Need Time Off"

Ross looks somewhere between skeptical and terrified. For God's sake, has he no sense of humor?

"In a nutshell, don't answer any of Alice's e-mails, and under no circumstances will you *send* her any. I'll handle everything."

"What about the weekly report?" he asks in a timid voice. Yeah, Alice promised me she wouldn't request said report because she knows herself and will start firing off twenty e-mails the second she finishes reading it. I'm just saving my sister from herself with these measures.

"Don't send it to her."

"But what if—"

Right, the laid-back way isn't going to work today. Luckily, I'm not only excellent at laying the charm thick in person, but also displaying authority. "No ifs. Under no circumstances will you bother my sister. I'll handle any complaints from her. Understood?"

Ross nods quickly.

"Excellent. This meeting is over unless you have other open points."

***

After a few minutes of working through minor issues, I head inside the restaurant, where I find my brother Christopher at one of the tables. He's the chief operations officer at Bennett Enterprises. Smart like a whip, I like to pick his brain about ways to make our own structures more efficient.

"You brought Chloe. What a surprise!"

Chloe is his wife's much younger sister.

Victoria's parents died in an accident a few years ago, and she raised her teenage sister Sienna as well as the much younger Lucas and Chloe. Without her stepping up to the plate, they could have ended up in group homes, like Clara.

"Victoria couldn't make it to pick her up today, so I did. Brought her by for a treat. We just arrived."

"Do you want your usual, Chloe?"

She nods decisively, and I ask a waiter to bring her chocolate cookies.

"School better?" I ask, dropping in the chair next to her.

"Lessons are okay, but a boy put a grasshopper in my backpack today."

"And she wants revenge," Christopher explains.

"If you need any tips, I'm the one to ask. Growing up, I was the master—"

"Master of disaster," Christopher cuts in. "You want to be sneaky and get away with it, I'm your contact person. This one's creative but always gets caught." He throws his thumb in my direction.

"Says the one who once had his twin brother kiss his girl on a scheme he masterminded."

Christopher cocks a brow. "That happened one time when I was sixteen, and only because the logistics were too complex."

"What's *logitis* mean?" Chloe asks with a lovely frown.

I ruffle her hair. "A fancy way to say details."

"I like details better."

"So do I. But some adults like to use big words to cover up their messes."

My brother narrows his eyes. I love giving him shit, especially when he provokes me.

"I am going to wash my hands before I get my cookies," Chloe exclaims. She rushes off to the restroom, and I point my forefinger at Christopher.

"Everyone knows you and Max were the successful prankster duo. Daniel and I were a lousy competition, and I have no problem giving you credit where credit is due. But don't make me lose face with the kids. It's a matter of principle."

Christopher grins. "Duly noted. Now let's talk business."

"Yeah. I appreciate you taking time for this. Let's mastermind together."

They are constantly improving operations, introducing better reporting systems and whatnot at Bennett Enterprises. Of course, the company is a mammoth compared to what Alice and I are doing, but we can learn a lot from them.

We're deep in debate whether it makes sense for Alice and me to implement one of their more complex pieces of software, and Chloe's already on the second serving of cookies, when my phone pings with a notification. It's from the bookshelf company, confirming delivery on Friday. I can't wait to see Clara's reaction.

CHAPTER FOUR

Clara

Next Saturday, on the morning of my move, I wake up with an infectious energy.

I double-check every corner of the apartment, making sure I haven't forgotten anything. Everything I own is packed in ten large boxes, not including the furniture, which is lined up against the wall. It's all from IKEA, so it's easy to disassemble and then reassemble in the new apartment. The couch will be a little more challenging to move. It's modular, and I separated each section, but it's still rather large and cumbersome to get through doors.

At ten o'clock sharp, there's a knock on my door. I scramble to answer in a flurry.

"Morning, almost-neighbor," Blake says.

"Come in."

He insisted on helping me move, and I enjoy his company too much to turn down the offer. Now, surveying him from head to foot as he enters the apartment, I wonder if it was a bad idea.

He's wearing jeans and a burgundy polo shirt that reveals his muscle-laced arms. The memory of those arms keeping me tight against him after my almost-fall is still too fresh on my mind.

"Let's start. Here are my prized possessions." I open my arms, pointing with one to the stack of furniture against the wall and with the other to the boxes.

"That's all you got?"

"Yep. Told you I didn't have much. I also have a skateboard we can use to put the boxes on, and even the furniture. That way, we only have to balance the load, not carry it. So don't worry, you won't break your back."

"Darling, it would take a lot more to break my back."

I don't know if it's the "darling" or the "a lot" that has me breaking out in a sweat, but I barely swallow the urge to ask *A lot of what?*

"Okay, let's start."

It takes all of four trips to get my boxes downstairs. However, it takes quite a few more to get my furniture out.

We load the furniture in the moving van Blake brought, the boxes in my car, and drive separately. An infectious energy fills the space, and I sing out loud to the music blaring from the radio and clap my hands to the rhythm while I'm waiting at a red light. I know I'm being ridiculous, but I don't care. I'm enjoying this too much. My life is too damn good not to be celebrated every step of the way.

When Blake pushes the door to the apartment open some twenty minutes later, I'm prepared to see a cleaner version of the same apartment, but instead

I'm flummoxed. The southern wall has a new coat of paint, in the exact shade I've told him. And my dream bookshelf is exactly where I want it too.

I turn around. "Blake—"

"Stop right there."

"What?"

"Sounds like you're about to admonish me."

I chuckle. "Not at all. Thank you for the paint and the bookcase. Let me know the costs, and I'll reimburse you."

"No need."

"Ah, see, but then I have to admonish you. You can't—"

"No arguing." His tone is strong, and his body language can only be described as intense. Never in my life have I equated intense with sexy, but Blake makes it sexy. I have a hunch he can make anything seem sexy as all get-out.

"I see. I'll have to put this on my list of things I still need to negotiate with you, which includes rent. For now, thank you. You really shouldn't have gone through all this trouble."

"No trouble at all. I wanted to do this for you. I was going to order what you said for the balcony too, but I'd rather you help me pick them. I'm not good with furniture."

"Of course."

"Good. Let's bring in your stuff."

There are two flights of stairs and no elevator here, so my skateboard isn't of any use. Having Blake help me has its perks. Chiefly, the irresistible manly sounds he's making while we carry the furniture. Several times I have to stave off the urge to ask him to move something just for the sake of it so I could hear more of those sounds.

We join forces when we're down to the planks to my bed because damn, those things are *heavy*.

"Okay, you grab that end," Blake instructs while we survey the load, side by side. "I'll take this one. Shout if it gets too heavy and we'll stop on the way."

"Can we take a small break first?"

"Sure."

Before I get the chance to say anything else, my phone beeps. I pull it from my back pocket. Predictably, it's a message from Quentin.

"Wait, I have to text back. It's my boss who doesn't understand boundaries or weekends."

"How did you end up working in television?"

"Luck."

Blake tilts his head, shifting into a presumably more comfortable position against the van and shielding his face from the sun by holding up a hand.

"Mind expanding on that a bit? I've known you for two years, but there's so much I don't know about you. I'm at a distinct disadvantage. You know much more about me. Come to think of it, given your close friendship with my sisters, you probably know a lot more about me than I'd like you to."

I smile coyly to escape having to either confirm or deny his suspicions. Yes, Pippa and Summer do talk *a lot*, and I love fishing information out of them. We're a match made in heaven. Blake is looking at me with genuine interest.

"Once I turned eighteen, I was out of the group home. Needed to pay for food and rent, so I took any job that came my way. Had zero skills, so I started at the bottom with waitressing and cleaning. That lasted a couple of years. I got a bit desperate because I wanted to move on to better paying jobs but didn't know how. College was out of the question."

"Why?"

"I didn't have the grades, extracurriculars, or the money. I took a few classes at a community college, but that was it."

I took bookkeeping and data organization, basic computer programming and, on a whim, children's book illustration. That last one turned out to be an unexpected gem. "Then I got very lucky, and one of the companies I was doing cleaning for needed a back-office assistant for the week. The one they had was sick, so I helped them for a while. Then they offered me a job. A few years later, I met Nate. His assistant had just ditched him, so he asked me if I'd like to work with him. See? Luck."

"And a lot of hard work."

"I only get lucky when I work very hard."

"Hats off to you for working your way up. Be proud of it."

"I am."

"Do you like your job?"

"Yeah. I don't love it, but the point of a job is

to pay bills, and it does that just fine."

"Very practical."

Yep, that's me. Practical could be my middle name. Ain't nobody got time for dreams.

"Should we finish carrying these inside?" I point to the bed planks, and he nods.

We take them inside, and then we both breathe with relief.

"Thank you." I look at the unopened boxes and still-disassembled furniture, whipping up a plan. "I'll get started right away with setting up the bed and the couch."

"I'll help you."

"I can handle this."

"I know. But you don't have to. You have me. Use me," he offers.

Ah, what an image that conjures. Blake on his back on my couch. I'd start with those arms, tracing the contour of his bicep, then lifting his shirt, applying the same treatment to the ridges of his six-pack (I have not seen them yet, but I have a wild imagination).

What is it with me today? I've been near him before.

"Okay. Thank you. When do you open the bar?"

"Four o'clock, but I need to be down at three for a meeting. Plenty of time."

We get to work right away, and I'm surprised by Blake's assembly skills. Between the two of us, this will look like home in no time.

"How did you decide to go into the bar business? Why not join your siblings at Bennett Enterprises?"

"I wanted to. I majored in finance in college, so I figured I'd work with Logan."

"Logan is the CFO, right?"

He nods. "I spent a couple of months there, but it wasn't panning out. Everyone treated me like their younger party brother. Hard to do your job when you constantly have to convince people to take you seriously."

"That I can relate to. People at work sometimes think I'm a joke because I'm so...." I wave my hand in the air, trying to find the right word.

"Exuberant?"

"Yes."

"Us weirdos must stick together. Anyway, striking out on my own seemed like the better decision."

"Why bars?" I continue my interrogation as we move to the bedroom, assembling the bed.

"I had contacts in the scene. Since I couldn't escape my reputation, I decided to use it to my advantage."

"Smart. You were a tabloid darling a few years ago." Not since I befriended the family, but I pulled up his history online. All for research, of course, when the network featured his and Alice's restaurants on *Delicious Dining* the first time. They'd wanted to know if Blake's past would turn viewers off. But the search history hadn't brought up anything scandalous, merely portrayed a man who liked parties and women, and even that was old news.

"I'm not that man anymore."

"Hey! I'm not judging," I assure him, nudging him with my shoulder.

"It was time I got my head out of my ass. Anyway, working, building something, feels right. It was time to make the Bennett name proud. And I get to work with Alice, which is a bonus. Between you and me, I think the best thing that happened to Alice was that she moved away and I took over operations. She was working twelve to fifteen hours a day, that little workaholic."

Female solidarity is one of my cardinal rules, and I deeply admire Alice—she could take the world by storm if she put her mind to it, but I'm with Blake on this one. She was overworking herself.

Sighing, I remember my own family. They passed away in a car crash. I lost them so long ago, that sometimes when I try to reach back to a memory, I realize it's gone. I don't want to forget them.

We keep talking about everything under the sun while we assemble furniture, and I take snapshots of the apartment, wanting to document every stage of the move. After we're done, I scroll through the pics, and my jaw hangs. Blake appears in almost every picture. I don't remember consciously doing so—clearly my subconscious is trying to prove a point. And I have to give it to Blake, he'd make an excellent model.

Guilt gnaws at me, but what do I do? Do I put the phone down? No, sir, I do not. Instead, I snap a new pic of Blake, who is currently checking whether the screws fastening the legs to the top of my dining table are tight enough. It is, in my humble opinion, the best shot yet.

His bicep is flexed, and the contours of his muscles are delicious eye candy. Great, not only am I a shameless Peeping Tom, but I also harbor dirty thoughts for a man who is not for me. I am the worst. *The worst.*

He's a Bennett, for the love of God, and I'm determined for them to be a constant in my life. That means no crossing boundaries with Blake. He's not the man for me anyway.

"All done," Blake says seconds later, straightening up and startling me. "At least I think so." His eyes sweep across the room as if checking whether anything is unfinished.

"Yeah, all done. I just have to unpack my boxes."

"Speaking of boxes, I just have one mailbox. I can put a second one for you."

"No need, I won't put this address anywhere. I already gave Penny's address at work. The emergency plan was to camp on her couch for a few days until I found a better place. No sense redoing the paperwork since I'm moving into my condo in three months max."

"Okay."

Come to think of it, it's far better for my work file to display Penny's address. I wouldn't put it past Quentin to check where my address is and realize I'm living next to Blake.

"Do you want water?"

He nods, and after I take two glasses out of the box labeled *kitchenware,* we both walk to the kitchen.

Handing him a glass full of water, I say, "I'd thank you again, but I sound like a broken record even to my own ears. I'll make it up to you, promise. Delicious dinner coming your way after I settle in."

"Looking forward to it." He gives me a wolfish smile and a wiggle of his eyebrows, and my body reacts instantly: rushed breath, weak knees, racing heart. Check, check, check.

While Blake helps himself to a second glass of water, I carry one of the boxes labeled *bed linens* to my bedroom. When I return, Blake is hovering dangerously close to an unlabeled box. As surreptitiously as possible, I lift it, intending to carry it to my bedroom as well. Several mishaps occur before I'm even halfway there. A strange sound cracks through the air. I can't place it, but a few seconds later, two loud bangs—metal on wood—follow. Two batteries fell from the box, but how is that possible?

The cracking sound returns and I realize what's going on: the bottom of the box is giving out. *No, no, no. Not this box.* Panic shoots through me as Blake seems to realize this too and hurries my way.

"Here, let me help—"

"No need." I run to the bedroom, two more metallic bangs following me. With a relieved breath, I set the box on the floor. Straightening up, I'm startled to find Blake right next to me, holding out his hand, the four batteries in his palm.

"Why in such a hurry to get that box out of the way? What do you have inside, battery-operated friends?"

My cheeks flush, and I can't form a comeback. Blake, who was probably only joking, looks from one cheek to the other, then to the batteries in his palm, finally lowering his gaze to my box. My mouth turns dry as dust, and I think I could melt butter on my cheeks right now. I swear the air between us charges. Suddenly, the room is too small, and there is not enough air. Hastily, I reach out to take the batteries. Our fingers touch, and *holy hotness*. The skin-on-skin contact is so charged, it sends my senses into a tailspin. My eyes meet his, and there is no mistaking the intensity of his gaze—or the heat in it.

Why, oh why didn't I pack my vibrator in my suitcase? This was an accident waiting to happen.

"You're killing me, Clara," he says, my name almost a groan. "The wall between our bedrooms has no phonic isolation."

It takes me a second to realize what he means, and I blush even more violently. Then I drum my fingers against my thigh, plotting my revenge. He could have been a gentleman about this and pretended nothing happened, but instead he put me on the spot. Well, well, this just begs me to turn the tables on him. After all, he did say he likes being challenged.

"Don't worry, I have pillows. They're a good enough buffer."

He exhales sharply, his eyes zeroing in on my lips. "Sweetness, if pillows are enough it means your battery buddy isn't doing a great job." Advancing slowly, Blake pushes a strand of hair away from my face. The contact zings through me, an almost imperceptible shudder traveling throughout my body. Hold that thought!

Blake's lips curl up in a smile...yeah, my shudder was everything but imperceptible to him. Instead of taking his hand back, he moves it down to my earlobe, tracing the contour of my jaw. *OhmyGod*. It's all I can do not to press my thighs together. An ache's formed between them, so sudden and so intense that I don't know what to do with myself. How can his proximity affect me so much?

A smarter woman would back down, but I'm determined to go toe-to-toe with him. Some small part of me wants to know if I affect him as much as he affects me.

"Oh, it's doing a great job. I just need the right inspiration." Wiggling my eyebrows, I add, "I have an excellent imagination. And I'm not afraid to use it."

Blake breathes out on another sharp exhale, and this time he's so close to me that the rush of hot air lands just above my upper lip. My pulse jackhammers, and I bite into my lower one, painfully aware that the ache low in my body has intensified. He swallows hard, his Adam's apple dipping in his throat. Up close, I can see the beginning of a five-o'clock shadow on his chiseled features. How would it feel against my fingers, my lips? Oh God, everything about Blake is too masculine. Too potent. Too much.

My pulse ratchets up even more. Distance. I need distance. Ever so carefully, I tiptoe around him, just as his phone chimes.

"Have to go downstairs to the bar."

"Right. Thanks for all your help."

He quirks up a corner of his mouth. "My pleasure."

Ah, no! How can he pack so much sensuality into one word? No fair. Not at all.

"See you around, Clara." Taking my hand, he brings it to his lips, kissing my knuckles with a feather light touch. The gesture would ordinarily be gentlemanly, but sometime between him realizing what's in my unlabeled box and me trying to outwit him, he lit a fuse inside me. Feeling his lips on my skin is torture. The rhythm of my pulse is now at an all-time high, and a wild pounding is in my ears. Which is why, when he brings his mouth to my ear the next second, I almost don't catch his words. Almost.

"You'll forgive me if I won't try too hard *not* to listen, Clara."

With a smile and a wink, he leaves my apartment. It takes me almost an entire minute to calm down, and I swallow a few times until the rush of blood in my ears subsides somewhat. The rhythm of my pulse is almost normal, but then I hear three knocks from the other side of the shared wall in the bedroom and it ratchets back up, even wilder than before.

CHAPTER FIVE

Clara

"Mmmm...delicious."

I'm elbow deep in preparing my "thank you" dinner for Blake.

I called Jenna, his mom, to check what Blake's favorite dish is. From the numerous Bennett meals I attended, I gauged that it would be either spaghetti arrabbiata or pork chops, but I wanted to double-check, just in case. Jenna confirmed my guesses, which is when I realized I pay far more attention to Blake than I thought. I haven't memorized anyone else's favorite dishes.

Shortly after six, I hear footsteps in the corridor, and then Blake's door opens and closes. Ten minutes later, I'm done with dinner. My palms have started to sweat, which is ridiculous. Just as I finish setting the table, there is a knock at my door. I open right away.

"Hello, Clara."

His hair is mussed, and his skin has a thin sheet of moisture—he probably just popped out of the shower.

"Come on in."

He steps in, running his hand through his damp hair, sending sprinkles of water everywhere. A few land on my shoulder, and I shiver lightly. His T-shirt sticks to him slightly, as if the skin is still damp.

"Wow, this place is barely recognizable."

"I wouldn't say that, but it looks lived in." Since moving in a week ago, I put up decorations and ordered twinkle lights, which arrived two days ago. I hung them around the window and have lit them up for this occasion. It's cloudy outside, and they make a nice contrast, casting a warm glow over the living room.

"Sit down. I'll bring dinner right out."

As I dash from the living room to the kitchen, I feel his gaze following me. When I serve the dishes, his entire expression brightens.

"This is my favorite food."

I nod proudly. "Called your mom to make sure."

"You did all this for me?"

"Yeah."

"You're amazing."

We dig in, making easy conversation over dinner. After we eat, he inspects the changes I've made.

He approaches the bookshelf with a frown. "You have three sets of the Harry Potter books...why?"

"They mean a lot to me," I say simply. "Besides, each set has different covers."

"Different covers," Blake mumbles to himself, as if that isn't a good enough a reason to own different editions.

"If you tell me you aren't a fan of the series, I might seriously reconsider our friendship," I warn jokingly.

"I saw the movies, but I'm not a big reader."

"Ugh, stop right there."

"I liked them. But obviously, there are fans"—he points to himself—"and *fans*,"—he points to me and winks.

"I think I felt a big connection to Harry because he was an orphan too, and his life with the Dursleys was very shitty."

Shit! Why did I open the can of worms? I usually avoid any reference to my childhood. People react weirdly when they find out I grew up in group homes. Some pity me, and some simply don't know what to say. Blake knows, of course, but it's still not a pleasant dinner topic.

Blake straightens up, training his eyes on me. "Hadn't thought about it like that. Makes sense. Dreamed of going to Hogwarts and all that?"

I nod enthusiastically.

I discovered the series shortly after arriving at the group home. I devoured it, feeling a deep kinship with the orphan boy. I desperately wished for something or someone who would take me out of that place where I was surrounded by loneliness and bullies. No such luck. Sometimes I wished I'd ended up in foster care as a baby because then I wouldn't have experienced the warmth and love of a family, wouldn't have known what I was missing. But then I chastised myself because I cherished those years I had with Mom and Dad.

"Where did you go just now?" Blake asks, and I snap out of my thoughts. He closes the distance to me, leaning against the shelf a mere foot away from me.

"Old memories."

"Want to share them?" His voice is unusually soft, but I don't detect any pity. I never can take pity.

"Nah! There's nothing quite like enjoying the present day."

"I can help with that. I'm all about enjoying life."

"That's right. I don't think I've ever seen anyone eat with quite so much gusto."

"All your doing. That dinner was delicious. Your arrabbiata sauce is even better than Mom's, but don't tell her I said that."

"Don't worry. Your secret is safe with me."

Turning around to face the bookshelf, I rearrange the copies of the Harry Potter series because they're out of order. I barely register Blake is moving until I feel him right behind me.

"Now I'm considering other ways to help you so you can thank me often. I'm really good at maintenance: changing lightbulbs, the batteries for your battery-operated buddy, that sort of things."

I freeze in the act of pulling out the sixth volume. Blake brings one hand to my waist, and the contact stirs something deep inside me. Ever so slowly, he skims his hand upward, sliding it along my ribs to my back, then inching up on my spine. It's all I can do not to lean into his touch. What is he doing to me? And why am I enjoying this so much?

Warmth radiates through me everywhere he touches, but when the fabric of my sweater ends and his fingers touch the bare skin at the back of my neck, a small gasp tumbles past my lips. Blake presses his fingertips slightly into me. Then he inches closer until the tip of his nose is in my hair, his breath landing on my scalp. One deep inhale and his hand travels from the back of my neck down my arm. He moves with exquisite slowness, stopping for a breath after nearly every inch downward. It's almost as if he's waiting for my reaction, testing how far he can push. Well, if he is testing me, I'm failing spectacularly. By the time he reaches down past my elbow, I'm positive I will combust. But then he cinches up the sleeve, running his thumb along my forearm right down to my wrist, cuffing it.

"Your pulse is wild," he murmurs.

"You think?" I ask in a strangled voice. He knows what he's doing to me. He knows it exactly. This man turned me into a ball of need without touching me intimately, or even kissing me. When he moves his thumb in a little circle over my pulse point, I press my lips tightly together. This is too much. How we went from zero to one hundred in the span of seconds, I don't know, but I need fresh air to clear my thoughts.

I inhale deeply, gathering my wits. It's no small task, considering Blake has me under his spell again. When I pull away, turning around, his molten gaze holds mine stubbornly, and I can't look away, hard as I want to.

"Want to watch the sunset on the balcony?" I manage eventually, stepping back, putting some much-needed distance between us. "I have a bottle of wine too, and some sweets: Turkish Delight."

"Sure."

While I get out the wine and the sweet treat, Blake hovers in front of the bookshelf again.

"What's with all these albums? Can I look?"

"Yeah."

Those albums contain my illustrations. I like to print them out and look at them in albums. I feel like I can track my progress over the years better that way.

"Are these illustrations for children's books?" he asks.

"Yeah." I put the wine, glasses, and candy on a platter but leave it on the counter, heading to Blake instead.

"Wow. All these albums are full of them? There must be hundreds."

"Lost count over the years." While I was traveling with Nate on the job, I kept the albums in storage, but since I relocated to San Francisco I've kept them in my living room.

"When did you start?"

"At eighteen. Took a class at the community

college, and since then I buy random kids' books that are text only, and I make up illustrations."

He looks up from one of the albums. "I know a children's book publisher. I'd have to double-check, but I'm sure they do illustrated books too. Do you want me to set up a meeting?"

"Oh no, no, it's just a hobby."

"That's a lot of work for a hobby. I'm no expert, but I think you're really creative. I collected comic books growing up—not the same as children's books obviously, but you're good. He could at least give you feedback."

"No, it's really fine. I'm part of several online communities, and we give each other feedback. That's all I need." Also, the prospect of a publisher looking over it and saying "No, thanks" is terrifying. Yikes.

"Let me know if you change your mind."

Taking the platter, we head outside, settling on the two neon-green beanbags. I showed Blake a swing online, and he ordered it, but it hasn't been delivered yet. For now, we have the beanbags, and they are plenty comfortable. We also have two thick blankets because May in San Francisco isn't exactly balcony weather, not even in the second half. Blake pours us wine. The sky is cloudy but the sun shines through, casting a beautiful glow—a color I can't name, something between pink and orange.

"Where did you see the best sunset?" Blake asks.

"London Eye," I answer without a doubt.

"You know, the Ferris wheel? I went on it once at sunset, and it was a spectacle. It made me fall in love with that city even more."

"How come you didn't move with Nate to London, then?"

"I grew up here. I always wanted to return. I have many nice memories with my parents. Walks in Golden Gate Park, lunches in Fisherman's Wharf. The occasional trip to Alcatraz. Even though I moved a lot, this has always been my anchor point, my home."

"Makes sense. I didn't know you grew up here."

Afterward, we fall into a comfortable silence, watching the sun disappear from the sky. We chitchat about his family. I'm not sure how long we stay out on the balcony, but it's pitch-dark by the time the wind starts blowing so powerfully, it chills me to the bone. The empty glasses and wine bottle are on the floor between the two beanbag chairs.

"I'm cold," I declare when I can't ignore the fact anymore.

"Me too. Up we go."

Blake rises to his feet and holds out his hand for me. I gladly accept the help because climbing out of a beanbag is serious business, especially after half a bottle of wine. I'm as unsteady on my feet as a toddler. But the moment my hand touches Blake's, a bolt of heat singes me. It travels through my limbs, making my toes curl and my nipples tighten. In the span of a few seconds, my body has gone from relaxed to wound up. Blake hauls me up so close our chests touch. Our noses are dangerously close too.

The proximity makes me light-headed. The wine isn't helping either. I pull my head back a notch so I can see Blake better. I make the mistake of looking him directly in the eyes. The intensity in them is overwhelming. I've been on the receiving end of his hot looks before, but this is different. There isn't just lust here, but downright hunger. A little too late, I realize it's probably because he can feel the tight peaks of my breasts pressing against him. He drops one hand to my waist, and his fingers are pressing against my flesh possessively. I become aware of every single point of contact—there are far too many.

We're close enough that I can sniff the scent of his shower gel. Crisp. Masculine. My mind immediately supplies images of Blake in the shower, rubbing gel on himself. I imagine he does that job thoroughly, not leaving out even one morsel of skin. I wonder how he looks with only a towel wrapped around himself. Now that we're neighbors, there's a distinct possibility I might see him in that scenario, especially with the shared balcony and everything. Shit, my Peeping Tom tendencies are getting out of hand.

I try to whip my thoughts into shape, but they're jumbled together and become more jumbled still when I feel Blake's hot breath on the lobe of my ear, then the tip of his nose on my cheek. When the corner of our lips touch, he presses his fingers into my sides, a low sound reverberating in his throat.

"Blake, I..."

"You look so kissable right now, Clara."

His voice is low and rough—his bedroom voice. I haven't heard it before. It's sexy and inviting, just like the rest of him. Great. I won't be able to unhear it.

I draw in a sharp breath. Wanting to diffuse tension, I try to joke, but under the influence of the wine and his intoxicating proximity, the best I can come up with is, "So I usually don't? Careful, Bennett, I take offense easy after drinking wine."

"Always do. First time I saw you, I wanted to kiss you."

"You did?"

"You have no idea how much you affect me, do you?"

Blake is looking down at me with so much intensity my knees nearly buckle. He skims his thumb along my jawline, moving to my earlobe, rubbing it gently between his thumb and forefinger. I clench my thighs together almost involuntarily. My ear is *not* a sweet spot. It really isn't. But I have a hunch Blake can turn any body part into a sweet spot.

"Blake...I...oh God, how did I end up in your arms?" I'd blame the wine, but that would make me a hypocrite.

"Because you can't help this either. I can't stop thinking about you, Clara. When I'm working, when I'm at home. You've been on my mind since we met, and I thought I could pull it off, living next to you and not wanting to make you mine, but now I know I won't."

I can't wrap my mind around what he's saying, but I hang onto his every word, melting against him.

"I want to kiss you, all night long. Just kiss you."

"Please don't."

"Why not?"

"You know why. I care too much about your family and—"

"You want safe and—what was that word? Nonargumentative. Don't think anyone ever used those words to describe me." Leaning even closer, he adds in a low baritone, "But you want this—us—even *more*." He cups my face, his thumb pressing on my lips, his fingers splayed on my cheek and jaw. A current races through me, white-hot and intense. When he drags his thumb from one corner of my mouth to the other, my hips shift, my entire body arches. Blake is pulling me to him like a magnet.

"God, you're intense," I mutter.

"You have no idea." To my relief, he steps back, and after picking up the glasses and bottle, we head inside. "I'm going to go now, before we end up in kissing distance again."

"Blake—"

He holds up his hand. "I know what you said, but it doesn't stop me from wanting what I want."

There's no mistaking his meaning. He wants *me*.

"You want this too. I know you do, and you know it too. But you won't be able to resist. I'll make sure of it."

I walk him to the door in silence. When we reach it, he kisses the tip of my nose and then lets himself out. Rooted to the spot, I'm still reeling from the intensity of it all.

***

Blake

I can't wind down after leaving Clara's apartment. I'm wired up, energy coursing through me. I end up descending to the bar. The closing time is two o'clock, and the bar is still buzzing with people. I hop behind the counter, giving a hand to my trusted bartenders on shift, Jack and Alex.

"Blake, didn't know you were joining us tonight," Alex says. Since I'm overseeing three restaurants and this bar, I rotate between the four locations. I'm not one for tight control or surprise visits, making my schedule available to my employees so they know when to expect me.

"Wasn't planning to."

But I have too much energy to sleep, and working behind the bar is the best way to burn it off. Years ago, I used to burn off my energy by going out with friends, but this is a much better use of my time. Not to mention I've drastically cut down the number of friends since one tried to sell details to the press about Pippa's divorce from her asshole first husband. Details I'd told her, never thinking they'd leak out. I spent a lot of money shutting her up and killing the story before it hit scandal magazines. It still makes me angry that she walked away with money, but at least no harm came to my sister. I can deal with moochers to an extent, but I draw the line at people going after my family.

After being used to the kind of bone-deep loyalty running in my family, I can't and won't settle for less. Maybe the standard is too high, but I don't give a damn. I don't hesitate to put my neck on the line for the people I care about. If they don't want to reciprocate, they have no place in my life. There are enough Bennetts to fill my time with, especially now that we have a whole new generation to raise.

"Quite a crowd you have here tonight, Blake," Arthur says. He's been one of my earliest clients and is a regular. Back then, his wife of more than thirty years had just died. He never drinks much, and my theory is he comes here more to socialize than drink. Once he let slip that his house was too empty without his wife. I always find him a spot right at the bar when he stops by, no matter how full it is.

"We had a group of tourists for a wine tasting earlier, and they stayed after it was over," I explain. Having Napa Valley close by is good for business. I even thought about buying a vineyard or two, go into wine production.

"This is fantastic," Arthur comments, sipping one of the wines we had at the tasting.

"It is. Starts out a little strong, but it opens up in a rich bouquet."

"Reminds me of my wife," Arthur says, tipping the glass back. "She spent the entire first year I knew her turning down my advances. But when she finally gave in..." He raises his glass, as if that's explanation enough. I understand. I also take Arthur's words as a sign. Mind you, I'd take anything and twist it into a sign right now.

Here I am again, thinking about Clara, wondering if she's asleep, replaying in my mind the way she *leaned in* when she asked me not to kiss her.

She was so responsive to me, I wanted nothing more than to push her against the kitchen table and kiss her. I wanted to do more than kiss. I wanted to drive her insane with pleasure, bring her over the edge again and again. I want her, and not just in my bed. I can make her laugh, but I want to learn how to make her *happy*. She beckons to me on a visceral level, her sweetness and passion pulling me in like a magnet.

I will make this woman mine.

CHAPTER SIX

Clara

Over the next few days, I constantly run into Blake. On our balcony, on the staircase, in front of the building. There is no reprieve, and the tension between us escalates with every encounter. I'm positive the next time I see him I'll spontaneously combust.

Which is why Tuesday morning, I go for a run. I'm only an occasional runner (with the occasion usually requiring me to fit in a tight dress for a special event), but my body has been humming with tension for days, and I need to shake it off.

My battery-operated friend will remain out of commission for the time being, considering wall thickness and all that.

The morning is pleasantly cool as I start my run, and there isn't much fog even though wisps of mist do seem to linger here and there. It's early enough that dew still covers the greenery.

It's a great neighborhood for a run, what with all the mansions and manicured lawns lining the streets. As I approach our building, Blake infiltrates my thoughts again.

I slow down to a brisk walking pace about one hundred feet from the entrance, but I'm still panting as I climb the staircase.

"Morning!"

As if I've conjured him up by sheer force of daydreaming, Blake appears at the top of the staircase, which has never seemed narrower. I always get the impression that any space instantly shrinks when Blake is inside it. I don't know if it's because he takes up a lot of space anywhere, or because I'm so consumed by him that everything else fades around him. Probably a combination.

"You're up early."

"Bank meeting."

Ah, that explains the suit. I lick my lips. Sweet heavens, this will not bode well for me. On any given day, I'm having trouble keeping my thoughts in check around him. Now, with Blake in a suit... call me shallow, but I'm a sucker for a man in a suit. That goes double when the man in question is Blake.

"Thought you weren't a runner." He descends two steps until we're level, and in my clumsy attempt to put some distance between us, I back into the wall of the staircase.

"I'm not, but I wanted to clear my head and." *Shake off the crazy sexual tension.* Yeah, that's a thought best kept to myself. "Had some extra energy to shake off." Licking my upper lip, I taste salt. I need a shower stat. My tank top clings to my back, and to my chest, a detail that does not escape Blake.

"I have to go shower. I'm a sweaty mess."

"I disagree." He brings one hand to my face, his finger skimming across the skin over my upper lip, where I licked before. "You're sexy as hell. I love your smell." Leaning forward, he rubs the tip of his nose against my temple. "So feminine. Sweet."

He places his hand to my bare shoulder. The fine hairs on my arms instantly stand on end. When he runs his thumb along my clavicle, I shudder. "I'm dying to taste you, Clara."

His voice is low, gruff, and so full of intent it sends an arrow of heat straight through me. It's all I can do not to clench my thighs together.

"You're being intense again," I inform him, struggling not to melt right here in his arms.

"I plan to keep that up until you *relent*."

"I... you're... sweet baby Jesus, it's too early in the morning for this," I mutter. "Can't a girl have her coffee before you try to melt the panties off her?"

Blake throws his head back, laughing. "You're one of a kind, Clara. Unfortunately, I do have to go or I'll be late for the meeting. I'll leave you to your coffee, and your shower."

He steps back but still fixes me with that molten gaze of his. "And by the way, there are much better ways to release sexual tension than running."

Damn this man and his wicked way with words. Shaking my head, I bid him goodbye, hurrying inside my apartment. My body is so alive and tight with tension, I feel like I'm about to implode.

Well, that was a waste of a run.

YOUR FIERCE LOVE

***

Tuesday is, as usual, the worst day of the week, because the final ratings for the show come in.

"If we don't improve, we're gonna get axed." Quentin paces the small balcony of the studio later that day, smoking his fifth cigarette in twelve minutes. Yep, I'm counting the minutes, because I have a million things on my to-do list today, and wasting time by keeping Quentin company while he chain-smokes and complains isn't one of them. But when the boss is about to have a mental breakdown, it's my duty to point out the positives so the entire show doesn't go to hell in a handbasket.

The problem is I can't contradict him. If the numbers don't improve, we're not going to get another season.

"I booked our lead actors on a number of talk shows. That'll bring in new viewers."

Executive producers and their assistants don't typically get involved in marketing and PR, but this case requires all our efforts.

No two shows are the same, but there are several patterns. Some shows start on a high and then maintain it for one or two seasons before sliding down the rankings as their prime time passes.

Others begin on unsteady feet, trudge along for the first season, then pull in better numbers in the second, when their viewership solidifies. We're in the second category, but here's the crux: the show needs to be renewed for a second season first.

"What we need is a boost from *Our Pics*."

Red alert! His watery and wandering eyes narrow. I swear to God, if he's going to bring up the Bennetts and *We See You* again...

Clasping my hands behind my back, I steel myself.

"Noticed you've changed your Facebook settings to private. Anything to hide?"

I set my jaw. "No, but I don't like strangers snooping around. It creeps me out."

He narrows his eyes, clearly not believing me. I unhitch myself from the balcony railing, heading toward the entrance door.

"I'm trying to book our stars on the big dogs. Late-night shows and such."

"Right. Like they're gonna give us the time of day if not even *Our Pics* does. Set your sights on something achievable."

With persistence and hard work, we can get the top dogs on our side. But Quentin is not about persistence or hard work. He's all about shortcuts.

"Nate always said—"

Quentin snickers, stepping closer. "I am not Nate. You got used to him blowing smoke up your ass, that's your problem. I'm gonna need you to perform."

I pull myself up straighter, crossing my arms over my chest. I will not let this prick put me down. But he's also my boss. *Handle this with grace, Clara.* I wonder if my slapping his cheek would be considered graceful. It would be an improvement over kicking him in the groin, which I'm seriously considering.

"I'm doing a very good job, whether you admit it or not. Getting a show up and running is teamwork. I'm trying my hardest."

"Try harder." As he passes me on the way to the door, the smell of cigarettes mixed with garlic on his breath almost gags me.

***

"Don't you dare crap out. Come on!" I exclaim the next morning

My coffee machine makes a loud, shrill noise, and then muddy water spills out of every crevice, landing on the kitchen counter, dripping to the tiled floor. With a sigh, I unplug the machine, then clean up the mess. I'll just have to stop by a coffee shop on the way to work. Typically, I like to drink my coffee every morning outside on the balcony, enjoying the view. Drinking it this early also means the caffeine has time to kick in by the time I reach the studio. After my infuriating exchange with Quentin yesterday, I need my eyes open and my brain functioning at maximum capacity.

"What's wrong?"

Blake's voice startles me. He stands in front of the French doors, which were open. I assume his balcony doors are open too, or he wouldn't have heard me.

"My coffee machine crapped out," I explain through a yawn. "Almost done cleaning. Sorry, didn't mean to wake you up."

He shakes his head. "Was already awake. Be back in a minute."

Just as I finish cleaning, Blake appears on the balcony, holding a cup of coffee, motioning with his head for me to join him. Butterflies roam in my stomach as I step outside.

"Thanks," I say, taking the cup from him. Our fingers touch briefly, and I swear every cell leaps up with attention at the contact.

"Welcome. Thought it would be a bad start if you skipped your morning coffee on the balcony."

I sip from my cup, trying to hide my surprise and delight that he noticed this tidbit.

"Why are you up early again?" I ask, taking in his appearance. He's not wearing a suit today.

"Haven't gone to bed at all, actually."

"Oh?"

"Two pipes broke at the Blue Moon, whole kitchen was under water. Been there all night overseeing repairs."

"I'm so sorry."

Blake waves his hand good-naturedly. "No major harm done. We'll forego lunch, but we'll be ready to open for dinner today."

"You should go to bed."

"I'll crash after you leave. Right now, I'm exactly where I want to be. With you."

Shifting my weight from one foot to the other, I grip my cup tighter, chuckling. "Not even a sleepless night dampens your drive, eh?"

"Not a chance."

Blake's eyes snap fire, but I hold his gaze stubbornly, even though I feel like I'm melting under the weight of it, not to mention the intensity.

"Blake, our friendship—"

He silences me by pressing his thumb to my lips. "Our friendship is one of the best things in my life. But I can't think about you just as a friend. Not anymore. When I'm home, I'm looking for any opportunity to be around you. When I'm away, I think about you nonstop."

"Blake," I whisper against his thumb, but I have no comeback. His words wrap around me like a soft, warm blanket. He pulls himself to his full height, leaning in slightly, towering over me. Determination is etched on his handsome features. His gaze is a little possessive, a lot dominant, and I suddenly feel as hot as if I submerged myself in a bathtub.

"I know how to fight for what I want, Clara. And I've never wanted anything as much as I want you. So I'll wait. And I'll fight."

CHAPTER SEVEN

Clara

I'm reeling the entire day from the exchange with Blake. At seven o'clock that evening, I nearly fly out of the studio to meet my two best friends, Kate and Penny. It's a rather windy evening, and I button up my coat completely. I can't wait for June to officially be here. Just one more day. Not that June is much warmer than May in San Francisco, but it helps to at least mentally think *summer is here*. Plus, there are dahlias right outside Blake's building, and I can't wait for them to bloom.

As I step inside the coffee shop where we agreed to meet, I see the two of them have already arrived. Kate has changed her hair, her usual waist-long hair now cut in a stylish bob. She's also dyed it a brighter shade of brown. Penny's platinum-blonde hair is in a tight bun, as usual. They are sipping drinks, laughing, and my heart swells. I adore them.

A waiter brings cheesecakes, and as I approach, Kate exclaims, "This is an enormous portion. I'll never be able to eat all of it."

"No worries, I'm ready to lend you a hand," I say. The girls whirl around in surprise. They hadn't seen or heard me approach. They leap to their feet and hug me. Not for the first time, I wish they both lived in San Francisco. As it is, Penny lives here, but Kate is in Seattle and is in town only for a couple of days, attending an education fair. She's a kindergarten teacher.

After I order a drink, I take my phone out of my bag and show the girls pictures of my temporary home.

"This is insane," Kate exclaims, thumbing through the pictures.

"Girl, when are you inviting me over for a housewarming party?" Penny asks. "Your view is to die for." When she found out about my housing conundrum, she offered for me to crash on her couch, but Penny's one-room apartment is too small for two.

"As soon as you make time for me in that crazy schedule of yours. You really should take it easier."

I refrain from saying more because I can quickly become meddling, and I'm making an effort here not to. Penny doesn't appreciate it—but it's for her own good, really.

"Can't right now, but as soon as I get promoted, I'll have a life outside work."

Kate sighs. "No, then you'll set yourself another goal, then another, and before you know it, life will pass you by and you'll be old, alone, and full of regrets."

Penny gives her the evil eye. "Are you trying

to be especially depressing today?"

"No, just telling it like it is. You're an uber achiever, which is admirable, but don't forget to live a little."

I'm with Kate on this one. I'm afraid our friend will burn out. Penny is brilliant, but even badasses need time to recharge. She and I have been friends since we were four years old. I lived next to her parents' house. Even after I moved to the group home, we kept in touch, sending letters, then later e-mails. I met Kate in the group home and we developed a close friendship, had each other's backs. As best as we could, anyway. I introduced Kate to Penny via letters first. We'd been breathlessly waiting for each of Penny's letters, hanging on to her every word and living vicariously through her. Now as adults, the roles are somewhat reversed.

"Is this hottie the infamous Blake?" Penny asks when a picture of Blake pops up on the screen. I deleted almost all the pics I took of him the day I moved in, except the one where he was bending to fasten the legs to my table. The shot of his flexed bicep is so perfect, if I say so myself, that I couldn't bring myself to delete it.

"Yes, girls, that is Blake. Best eye candy I've ever seen."

"Talk about a *view*." Penny whistles, looking at the screen in admiration.

"There is some seriously hot male real estate in this city," Kate says. "I can't believe this is your neighbor."

"He looks like the type of man who knows his way around a woman's body," Penny chimes in.

"Oh, I'm sure he does."

Kate wiggles her eyebrows. "Planning to find out?"

"It's complicated." In quick words, I relay the pros and cons—mostly the cons. I really need some perspective on this. Some non-Bennett perspective. I love the Bennett girls, but if there's one thing I can't talk to them about, it's my crazy attraction to one of their own.

"So, you see, this isn't the best idea," I say. "But bad ideas are so delicious and tempting."

"Like cheesecake," Kate states, nodding to her half-eaten cake and pushing her plate toward me. I dig in right away.

"The real question is how will you resist him while you live next door?" Penny pushes.

"Excellent question. My rational side says he's a great friend, and his family treats me like one of their own, so I'd better not mingle. My dark side says he's hot and single, and he'd know how to make my lady parts tingle."

The girls roar with laughter, and I join them.

"I think your dark side should win," Penny says after we calm down. "I mean, worst-case, you jump his bones and things get awkward. You'll move out anyway, and you can avoid him whenever you hang out with the Bennetts. Or you just hang out with them less."

That wipes the smile right off my face. Kate

only offers a cautious smile and a shrug, and I know why. The two of us grew up without the safety net of a family, a group of people who'd love us and support us no matter what. People, who have that, like Penny, take it for granted. But I never will. The Bennetts might not be related to me, but they're as close to family as possible.

When the waiter brings us another round of drinks, I hold up my glass, and the girls follow suit.

"To hotties who make us suspect we have double personalities," I exclaim as we're toasting. Since the conversation hasn't helped my conundrum in the slightest, I'm eager to change topics, so I ask Kate about her job and her husband. Josh is truly the loveliest man on earth. Kind and gentle, perfect for my friend.

We stay out for so long that by the time I climb the staircase to my apartment, it's past midnight. I'm nearly at my door when I see Blake unlocking his.

"Fancy meeting you here again," he remarks with a smile, moving closer.

I shake my head. "This is so inconvenient. The corridor is too small, and you're far too hot."

Blake cocks a brow. "Did you drink any cocktails?"

"Nah, just estrogen overdose. I've been out with two close friends, Kate and Penny. Outings with the girls give me a high, and I'm usually prone to making rash decisions and bad choices afterward."

"Excellent news. There's a festival tomorrow

evening. I want to take you to see it."

"Oh, I don't know."

"Just come with me, Clara. You'll have a great time."

"It's not a wine festival, is it?"

"No. Why? Are you afraid of drinking when I'm around?"

"You make me lower my guard even when I'm sober. So yes, I'm afraid."

"Good. You should be."

Why, that sounds like a sinful promise, and my cue that I should say no, which of course, I don't.

Instead I ask, "So what kind of festival is it?"

"Local food and crafts."

"Oooh, forgot it was so soon. I actually wanted to go."

"I know. You mentioned it a few times."

Emotion rushes through me, just as it did when I entered the apartment and found the wall painted and the bookcase in place. He isn't seducing me. He's charming me. I don't know if he's doing it on purpose, but he's thoroughly and efficiently attacking my defenses.

"I'm taking you." He says this with such determination that I have no idea how to counter. As if sensing that I'm scrambling to strengthen my defenses, Blake moves even closer, stepping right in my space, propping a hand on the door behind me. All of this is too much. The determined glint in his eyes, the arm on the wall, his closeness. I can feel the heat radiating off him. "I'll pick you up at seven, okay?"

Licking my lips, I nod. "Seven."

His eyes glint with joy and triumph. "I'll see you tomorrow."

CHAPTER EIGHT

Clara

The next evening, I'm on pins and needles as I'm preparing for the outing. I'm wearing dark jeans and a bright red sweater that molds to my curves nicely, showing just enough cleavage to entice.

Great! I'm telling myself we're going as friends, but I'm dressing to *entice*. I want to kick myself. At seven o'clock on the dot, Blake knocks at my door. I try to ignore the way my heart squeezes and excitement courses through me.

When I open the door and come face-to-face with Blake, I have the distinct impression someone sucked the air out of the room. Damn him! Why isn't it illegal to be this hot?

He grins. "Careful. It's too early to undress me, even with just your eyes. But I like a bold woman."

I inhale deeply, snapping my eyes up to him. I'd been admiring his torso. He's wearing a dark blue coat and a gray sweater that clings to him almost shamelessly, highlighting the ridge of his abs. I like how he called me bold. If a man were ogling a woman as blatantly as I did him, he'd be called a pig. I'm all for double standards tonight.

"Let's go," he says as I shrug into a coat.

As we step outside, I smile, taking in the beautiful evening. The sun will still be up for almost an hour. Inhaling deeply, I admire the expanse of blue streaked with orange sunrays. First day of June.

"Do we have a plan?" We descend onto a steep street.

"Yeah, we do." Blake pulls a folded piece of paper from his pocket. When he unfolds it, I'm surprised to find a detailed itinerary. Itinerary is perhaps the wrong word, but there's a list of booths and stops on it, with keywords next to every stop: names of people, food, or drink types, sometimes accompanied by a note such as *invite over* or *seal deal* or *remind about delivery*.

"You're cheating," I accuse him. "This is for work, isn't it?"

"What's on the list, yes. But we have plenty of time to sneak in other visits." He leans in to me. "For our own pleasure."

A white-hot current races through me because he said that last word on a lower octave, and it came out *very* seductive.

"I didn't peg you as the list-maker type."

Blake grins. "I wasn't, but since I started working with Alice, it's become a vital skill. Learn fast or die trying."

The perimeter of the festival, set in the shade of Presidio Park, is absolutely full. As we step inside it, he places his hand at my lower back, warm and protective, guiding me to a booth labeled *Trifecta*, displaying all kinds of pastries. My mouth is watering already.

"This isn't on your list."

"No." He presses the pads of his fingers into my flesh as he steps right next to me, pinning me with his dark gaze. "This is for your pleasure, Clara."

Hearing my name and "pleasure" in one breath is messing with me. Or maybe it's the way he's saying it. With a little intent and a whole lot of double entendre.

"Blake, you're here. Just in time."

A grinning chef greets us. He has a thick dark brown mustache that almost makes up for his lack of hair. His prominent belly hangs slightly over his apron. Blake takes his hand away from my back, shaking the man's hand. I miss the contact already.

The chef winks at me, and as he lowers himself under the counter, I feel like I'm watching a secret mission unfold. Straightening up, he shoves a tray with sourdough bread—a treat San Francisco is known for—in front of us. When he places it on the counter right in front of me, I bring my hands to my face, bouncing on my toes.

"For me?" The question is superfluous, but I have to make sure before I attack the goodies.

"Yes," the chef and Blake say in unison. I immediately shove a slice in my mouth. It's divine. I barely bite back a moan as I munch on it.

"Delicious."

"Glad you like it," Blake says. "We should be going."

"Lots of stops on the list," I agree. After saying goodbye to the chef, we move on.

"Thank you," I say simply as we walk side by side.

"You're welcome."

As we walk deeper into the festival area, Blake places an arm across my back, resting his hand on my shoulder, lightly tucking me into him, as if I belong to him. I'm in terrible danger next to this handsome man who is feeding me delicious goodies and making me swoon. He's exploiting my weaknesses, and he's doing a thorough job of it.

The festival buzzes with people of all ages: professionals who clearly just got off work, retired couples, groups of teenagers, and even the occasional parents pushing a stroller. Everyone is enjoying the city, celebrating it, and I'm soaking in all that infectious energy.

We stop at the first booth on Blake's list, and I'm surprised by the instant change in his posture when he talks to the vendor. He seems taller somehow. In charge. It's the same body language I saw when I first went to visit the apartment. It's a *very* sexy look on him.

We finish the stops on his list surprisingly quickly.

"What do you want to do now?" Blake asks. "What looks good?"

Everything looks good. I peer around, trying

to decide on a booth.

"That one." I point to a booth that boasts having the best Dungeness crab in the city. "Since they brag, let's go try it out."

Blake and I go wild. At the end, when I pull out my wallet, Blake catches my hand midair.

"No!"

"Blake—"

"Clara—"

"I wanted the crab. I'm paying for it."

"Absolutely not. You're not paying for anything when you're out with me."

The vendor is looking between us with an amused expression. I'm not having any of this. I yank my hand away from Blake's grip because his touch is melting my resolve, and I want to be firm.

"You're not letting me pay for stuff I want inside the apartment, or drinks I have at your bar." I cross my arms over my chest. "I'm not having any of this man-must-pay nonsense."

He holds up his hand. "It's called being a gentleman. Never let a lady pay. You have an issue with that, then take it up with my parents. That's how they raised me."

He disarms me, of course, and Blake pays in the next moment. I briefly wonder if he likes to take charge in the bedroom as well. Nope, not going there. But I already did, and the question is on the tip of my tongue. I swallow it down.

The scenario repeats itself several times. By the time we're done, the button of my jeans threatens to pop, and I feel like a stuffed teddy bear. I suck in my tummy, which shows a small beginning of a muffin top even on an empty stomach. I cycle to work twice a week, but that isn't doing much for my tummy. Eating less carbs would help, but where is the joy in that?

The sun is setting by the time we finish our round, and more people seem to have spilled into the festival.

"This is getting claustrophobic," I comment, and Blake nods in agreement. "Hey, I have an idea. Can we walk up the Lyon Street steps back home? They should start somewhere nearby and lead us right up in the Pacific Heights district."

I do one full turn, trying to guess which direction Lyon Street might be, but I feel lost.

"Great idea," says Blake. "Come on, I know the way."

"Do you know there are some four hundred stairways in San Francisco?" I rattle off as we head out into the night.

"No, I didn't."

"Yeah. Some are so well hidden, it's like they're a secret."

Blake nods, impressed.

"I have the habit of memorizing random stuff I read in city guides," I explain. "Honed the skills years ago, when Nate and I worked on that international show. Even though we spent a few weeks, sometimes even a few months in each city, the work schedule was so Draconian that I had time to cram in visiting. Tried to make the most out of the time I had, which included reading city guides thoroughly."

Ah, but the Lyon Street stairs and their surroundings are a thing of beauty. As we climb them, I wish I had three more pairs of eyes so I could take everything in. Past the hedgerows are luxurious old mansions (some resemble small palaces), perfectly trimmed lawns, and lush plants. Far behind us, I can see the Palace of Fine Arts dome, and further still the Golden Gate Bridge. If I focus intently, I can even make out Alcatraz Island out in the distance on the water, clouded by mist. The only downside to this scenic climb is the three hundred steps or so. At some point, I feel as if someone is stabbing the left side of my belly.

"Let's stop for a bit." Blake merely smiles as I lean against the railing, panting. Have to say, I would've expected the steps to be crowded, but we've only encountered a handful of people so far. We stopped near one of the large, billowing trees, and I take advantage of our break to inspect it closely. Its crown is majestic and falling like a thick curtain, some branches nearly touching the ground. I slip through the curtain, with Blake right beside me.

Instantly, the air between us charges. Maybe it's the fact that the light from the streetlamps barely reaches inside here, or that the green curtain protects us from view, but the setting is intimate. Too intimate. Heat rises to my cheeks. My neck starts to feel hot too. Actually, my entire body feels hot. A sudden gust of wind sweeps by, and a strand of hair catches at the corner of my lips. Blake pushes it away, then splays his fingers on my cheek and jaw. His thumb is pressing gently at the corner of my mouth, and I know I'm a goner. The intent in his eyes is unmistakable.

He seals his mouth over mine, and the touch is electrifying. As he feathers the tip of his tongue over my lower lip, he coaxes a moan out of me. He's demanding entry. I open my mouth, more than willing to let him in, greedy for more of what this man has to offer. His lips are as firm as they are soft, moving expertly over mine. When he slips his tongue inside, I lift my arms, lacing them behind his head, pulling him in closer. Blake not only obliges by leaning in to me, but he fists my hair, tipping my head up. His tongue is driving me insane with rhythmic moves that are jolting to life every single cell, infusing them with desire.

I'm burning for him, needing to touch, graze, and pull. I vaguely register we're moving, and then I feel a strange surface—tree bark—behind me. Blake is backing me up against a tree. He deepens the kiss, and my desire transforms into desperation. I need to touch him. Every cell in my body is buzzing, and the only thing that will calm me down is touching him. Or perhaps it's the reverse. I need him to touch me.

I slip my arms under his jacket, slowly running my hands down the expanse of his back, enjoying the feel of those taut muscles under my fingers. When I reach the waistband of his jeans, far from being satiated, I want more. So, I bring my hands to the front, slipping them under his shirt. I just need a little skin-on-skin contact. Once I have that, I become aware that one of his hands is on my waist. The other cups my ass, pulling me against him until our bodies are flush against one another. And sweet heavens, he is hard.

When we pull apart for air, we're both panting. Blake drops his head in the crook of my neck, resting there.

"You taste so good, Clara."

Feeling his heated breath on my skin makes it hard to think. I look over his shoulder to the surroundings, but the thick foliage of the tree and the dimming evening light is shielding us from view.

"What are you wearing?" he asks.

"Hmm?"

"Your underwear. Describe it."

The last two words sound unmistakably like a command, and my body reacts before my mind, pressing into him, seeking more contact. Not answering doesn't even occur to me.

"Matching set of white cotton and silk."

"Thong or G-string?"

I lick my lips. "G-string."

"How wet are you?"

"Blake...."

"Tell me how wet you are!"

The command comes on another heated rush of breath that undoes me. I'm so turned on I don't know what to do with myself. I'm almost ashamed.

I press my thighs together. "Very."

With no small dismay, I realize my hands are still under his shirt, right at the waistband of his jeans, feeling him up. But what do I do? Do I let go? No, sir, I do not. Instead, I trace the defined lines of his abdomen, the steel muscles.

His hand goes up to my hair, tugging gently, but I have the distinct impression he's barely holding back from being rougher.

"What are you doing?" I whisper as he starts breathing in deeper.

"Calming down. Trying to think about anything other than taking you somewhere private and making you come."

I lick my lips, trying to swallow a moan. I fail. It tumbles from my lips, and Blake's reaction is almost visceral. A groan reverberates from deep within his chest. It is a pure, masculine sound, and it's calling to me on a primal level. I don't know for how long we stay like this, limbs intertwined in a manner that is passionate and tender at the same time, but I like the feeling of his arms around me.

"I can't believe you backed me up against a tree." I chuckle when he finally steps back.

"I can't believe I was able to stop at that."

Well damn. I walk around him, stepping out of the tree's crown. Blake follows my lead. I'm still a little light-headed and very turned on. I need a cold shower. Stat.

My shower, which also shares a wall with Blake's. Somehow I don't think a cold shower would help all that much.

"Let's continue our climb," I suggest.

We're silent with the effort of climbing, and then we fall into an easy conversation on the way home. But when we step into the dimly lit and narrow stairwell of our house, suddenly, the air between us is thick with tension again.

"Want to walk me up to my door?" I elbow him good-naturedly, hoping to diffuse the tension. No such luck.

"Nah, I'll just kiss you against it."

"You're something," I mutter. Blake traps my gaze with his for long seconds.

I quickly step away, unlocking my door. As I step inside the apartment, I feel a tiny bit safer, even though Blake still looks all too potent and sexy.

"Good night."

"Good night," he replies, and I close the door.

I head straight to the shower, about to turn the water on, but then I hear water noises from Blake's shower too, and for a split second, I don't move at all. I'm ridiculous. We probably showered at the same time numerous times in the weeks I've been here. *Yeah, but that was before he kissed me against a tree.*

A low groan follows, which really must be a loud one, but it's muffled by the wall.

And then Blake rasps out my name. My knees buckle. The realization that he's touching himself while fantasizing about me hits me with such force it knocks the breath out of my lungs. I listen intently for a few more seconds, just to make sure I'm not imagining this, but there's no mistaking the reason behind his continuous groans. I can't help it; I join in on the fantasy. Closing my eyes, I imagine him on the other side of the wall, naked, all that lean muscle and strong build on display, his hand sliding up and down his erection fast and then faster still.

Every bone in my body liquefies. I'm beyond turned on, and I can't bear the ache between my thighs for one second longer. I slide my hand down, Blake's groans fueling me. I'm dripping with desire. I move my fingers over my opening, up until I reach my clit. Tension builds inside me until my body is tight with it. I'm right on the cusp, and I need my relief fast. I need it right now.

I imagine Blake's hands and lips on me. A thought nags at the back of my mind. Does he know I'm here? If I can hear his shower, then he must be able to hear mine too. The recognition almost sends me over the edge. Every cell in my body seems wired to my clit, and I move my hand more furiously than before. I press my other hand against the wall, seeking his skin, but encountering only the cold tiles. I want to break down this wall and reach out to him. I need him so badly. I want him to fill me up and whisper dirty things in my ear. I've never wanted anyone as desperately as I want Blake. Ever.

"Oh fuck. Clara. Fuck!" The low guttural sound reverberating on the other sound of the wall sends all my senses into a tailspin. I pinch my eyes shut and come so hard, I grip the railing of the shower for support.

"Blake!"

I'm beyond shame or caring, and I chant his name again and again until I ride out my orgasm, fully aware he must hear me. When I open my eyes again, it takes a few seconds for my vision to return. My breath is coming in pants, my desire satiated and at the same time magnified. I move my hand from the shower railing to the wall again, as if I could somehow reach out to Blake that way.

After I calm down, I finish my shower and step out. The mirror is smoked up from all the heat, and I drag my palm over it, cleaning it until I can look at myself: red cheeks, hooded eyes, ridiculously satisfied grin.

Mirror, mirror on the wall, who's the weakest woman of all?

Clara.

Even with a wall separating us, Blake and I just crossed a very dangerous line.

CHAPTER NINE

Clara

"The specials are on the front page."

I nod at the waiter, taking the menu he's handing me. I'm meeting Pippa and Summer for happy hour. I haven't seen them since the wedding almost five weeks ago, which is five weeks too long. I love being with these girls. They understand my crazy. More than that, they usually join in on it too.

Twenty pages filled with cocktails. Complete overkill. When the girls enter the venue, I wave to them, and my palms sweat lightly.

I never can hold my tongue when I'm around them. Well, I rarely can hold my tongue, but my oversharing affliction is worse around them. I don't want to tell them about kissing their brother last Thursday. I'm not even sure why, but I feel it's smarter to keep the information to myself. Big mouth that I am, I already told Kate and Penny. Penny was ecstatic. Kate, the traitor, also cheered me on.

As the girls sit down, I open the menu to the page I think has the most interesting cocktails. The two sisters resemble each other very much, even though at first sight they couldn't be more different. Pippa is tall and blonde, and Summer is petite and has light brown hair. But they both have the exact same defined cheekbones and plump lips.

"I didn't actually read the entire menu, but these seem interesting."

"Ain't nobody got time for twenty pages," Pippa exclaims, looking at the menu in bewilderment. "These sound good."

"How are the girls?" I ask Pippa after we order. Mrs. Bennett proclaimed she needed more time with her granddaughters, which is why Pippa has a free evening. Sometimes she plans girls' nights in at her house so she can keep an eye on the girls too.

"Oh, they are opportunistic little devils. They're all hugs and kisses when they're with me, and when they see Mom they jump right in her arms, and to me, they're like "we don't know you"."

"That's because Mom lets them eat chocolate in the evening too," Summer comments.

Pippa throws her hands up in the air. "They're gonna do that when they're adults anyway. I mean, look at me. They should at least have healthy habits when they're kids."

"Is Julie at your mom's too?" I ask. Julie is Pippa's stepdaughter, and about twelve years older than the twins. Pippa's husband was a widower when she met him.

Pippa shakes her head, sipping the cocktail she just received. "Nah, she's at home. Too busy warring with her father."

I grin. "Let me guess, Eric scared off another guy who asked her out?"

"Nope, but refused to let her out of the house for a date because she was wearing a very short skirt and didn't want to change. I think Julie's researching colleges in Canada right now, possibly even Europe. The farther the better."

Summer chuckles. "Eric is a tad overprotective."

"You can say that again. Anyway, I think most men are. I mean, look at Christopher."

We burst out laughing, and I nearly snort cocktail through my nose. Christopher's wife, Victoria, has a younger sister, Sienna, who is twenty and very much into dating. Christopher grills the guys so thoroughly when they show up to take her out that most don't ask for a second date.

"Sienna is a genius," Summer muses. "We really need to pick her brain whenever we need ideas to troll our brothers."

Just before Victoria's bachelorette party, Sienna decided it was time for revenge, so she teased Christopher, telling him the girls hired a stripper for Victoria. I wish Sienna had filmed Christopher because her impression of a jealous Bennett brother was beyond hilarious. Eventually Sienna told him it was a joke, but only because she legitimately feared he'd crash Victoria's party.

I sip my drink quietly, wondering how it must be to have an overprotective brother or father. I don't think I'd mind one bit to know someone has my back.

"So, Clara, what have you been up to that you don't want to tell us?" Summer asks. I choke on the mouthful I just sipped and am close to snorting it out through my nose. Luckily, I manage to swallow.

"How did you figure that out?" I ask. There's no point denying it. When the Bennett girls sniff you out, they sniff you out. They *always* sniff everyone out.

"You've been too quiet," Pippa explains. "You usually talk our ear off. How is living next to Blake?"

"He's a great neighbor."

"Unleashed his seductive skills on you already?" Summer bats her eyelashes at me, and I jerk my head back abruptly.

"He's been looking at you like he wants you for a long time," Pippa says coolly.

Now that they've straight up ambushed me, I have to 'fess up. I can't lie to them, and lying by omission is still lying.

"So, I went to this festival with him," I begin.

Summer claps her hands. "Was it a date?"

"No," I clarify quickly. "But that didn't stop him from backing me up to a tree and kissing me like nobody's business." I clamp my mouth around the straw to keep myself from volunteering more information, such as how my skin is still humming at the mere memory of the kiss, or the shower afterward. How I'm buzzing with awareness every night I go to bed because I know Blake is on the other side of the wall. The girls would read into it. Hell, *I* am reading into it.

"And?" Pippa urges.

"And nothing." There's no way I'd share details such as the dirty talk because even I know that would be oversharing.

"Wait, so you just kissed and then went home—together—and nothing?" Summer asks.

"Yep."

Summer cocks her head to Pippa. "I thought Blake was supposed to be good at this stuff. Do you think he's lost his game? Maybe he needs more help than we thought."

"No idea. So he hasn't tried anything?"

"Nope." As long as I stick to one-word answers, I'm golden.

Pippa leans back in her chair, drumming her fingers on the table. Just then, a waiter appears next to her, inquiring if we need more drinks.

"Of course," Summer says. We all order the same drink as before.

As we slurp our cocktails and then order a third round, the conversation turns to what the girls have been up to. I'm becoming more suspicious by the second. Finally, after we've finished the third cocktail, Pippa leans slightly over the table.

"So, tell us more about Blake."

"I knew it," I exclaim. "I felt like you'd let me off the hook too easy."

"We were just waiting for you to have more

cocktails," Summer explains.

"Yeah, thought that would loosen your tongue. There's not much fun in one-word answers," Pippa chimes in.

They are good; I have to give it to them.

"You like our brother," Pippa says. "We've seen you around him."

"He's a hard man not to like," I offer. "He's funny, kind, charming, has mad kissing skills and a dirty mouth."

I press my lips together, aware I already overshared.

"Hell of a kiss, huh?" Pippa asks, then turns to Summer. "Our brother hasn't lost his touch. He must have a plan."

"Girls, I'm not looking for anything but friendship."

"And hot kisses," Pippa adds with a devilish smile. Damn Pippa for reminding me of that particular detail. I swear if I close my eyes, I can call to mind every single detail of those minutes. "I personally think you two are a great match."

"Hey, I called it first," Summer says. "Right? At Alice's engagement party."

Summer sighs, a dreamy expression on her face. And that's when I realize why I didn't want to tell them. Because of course, the girls would immediately think there would be an epic love story in the making. They are the most romantic people I know. I'm not romantic, but seeing them so excited gives me hope, and I don't want that. I'm an optimistic person, but I don't like to hope for impossible things, and least of all tie my hopes to one person. That has always, always led me to heartbreak.

In the first year at the group home, I put all my hopes on Aunt Judith, my only living relative. I'd hoped she'd let me stay with her. But Aunt Judith never even visited. I went to bed every night that first year clinging to that hope. Then when I had that brief stint with a foster family I loved, I hoped again. That they'd want to adopt me or at least keep me until I was eighteen and could be on my own. That went south too. It hadn't been their fault, but I still didn't have a family. The second foster family was the final straw.

They were not particularly affectionate, but they treated me right: gave me my own room, three healthy meals, and their house was very peaceful. I prepared breakfast every morning for both of them. I tended to their garden and helped with cleaning. I was supposed to only stay with them for two months, but I'd hoped they'd want me to stay longer. I thought I was doing so well. But when the two months were up, they returned me to the group home with a pink slip in my hand for our supervisor. I begged and begged them to let me stay, promising never to be difficult, telling them I could even move into the cupboard under the stairs if they needed the room (I'd done a recent reread of *Harry Potter and the Sorcerer's Stone* and treated every word as gospel). They explained that they'd hosted me so they'd see if having children was for them and discovered it was not.

I stopped hoping afterward. It wasn't easy, but definitely less heartbreaking than waiting for someone to come and save me.

Summer's and Pippa's voices snap me out of my thoughts.

"Where did you just go?" Summer asks.

"I think someone is replaying a certain hot kiss in their mind," Pippa adds.

I smile mysteriously in return. Better they think that.

"By the way, before I forget, I talked to Sebastian today. He and Ava decided to celebrate Will's birthday at our old ranch," Pippa says. "It'll be an overnight trip. Is that okay for you? I know it's short notice, but they literally decided this morning."

"Of course it's okay. Can't wait to see the ranch."

It's where the Bennett kids grew up. They sold the ranch a long time ago to give Sebastian capital to start Bennett enterprises, but he bought it back for them a few years ago, and Mr. and Mrs. Bennett turned it into a B&B. They still live in their San Francisco home, because it's nearer to their kids, while the ranch is a few hours away.

I love that they invite me to all family events, and I make a point not to miss any unless I have an emergency. Wouldn't miss Will's third birthday for anything in the world. As I wonder what the odds are that someone else bought him the same present I did, I catch Pippa and Summer exchanging a glance.

Sweet baby Jesus, I know that look. It means they are *plotting*.

CHAPTER TEN

Clara

"I can't believe I've never been to the ranch," I exclaim one week later, on a bright Saturday morning, while I'm helping Summer unload the boxes from her trunk. I'm beginning to sweat from the effort of it, and judging by the color in Summer's cheeks, it's no picnic for her either. She filled her trunk and back seat to the brim with party supplies.

"You will love it."

We both let out a breath of relief as Daniel heads in our direction. That should make the unloading easier. He kisses both of us on the cheeks, then gapes at the car.

"Summer, the party's for one three-year-old, not ten," Daniel remarks, shaking his head. Summer grins proudly. She requested to be in charge of the party, and this is the result.

"I don't do anything half-assed. Can some of the other boys come out and help?"

Judging by the number of cars in the parking lot, everyone's here already.

"Let's take what we can inside, and I'll come

back out with reinforcements. I assumed I'd be enough."

"Well, that was just silly," Summer exclaims, shaking her head mockingly.

Daniel carries one of the heavier boxes, and Summer and I focus on the bags in the back seat.

I soak in everything as we walk the hundred feet or so from the car to the house. The ranch sits on a decent piece of land with dahlias blooming seemingly everywhere in a multitude of shades of pink, like one enormous painting. This is a *terrific* Saturday. It's barely ten o'clock, and we have the entire day ahead of us. Noises reach us as we approach the house: the chatter of adults, the laughter of kids. The front door is open and Summer hurries inside, placing the bags on the floor, and then we both head along the corridor, following the noises.

When we reach the living room, which opens to the back patio through a large door, I grin at the mayhem. Everyone's here: Sebastian with Ava and their two sons, Pippa and her brood, Logan with Nadine and their son. They're outside on the patio, chatting and chasing toddlers. I also hear Mr. and Mrs. Bennett (who have asked me numerous times to simply call them Richard and Jenna, but I'm still working on that), their voices coming in from outside, but they're out of sight.

Christopher and Max and their wives, Victoria and Emilia, are inside, sitting comfortably on the large couches. Victoria, who is five months pregnant, is currently batting her eyelashes at Christopher while pointing at her belly, and I can't help wondering what she's asking him. It must be surreal for another man to look exactly like your husband. Thank God, Daniel and Blake are not identical twins like Christopher and Max. One Blake is enough.

Speaking of Blake, where is he?

He drove here with his parents, which was how I ended up traveling with Summer instead of him. I haven't seen him in all of four hours. How can I miss him already? He's not mine to miss; I really should remember that.

"Summer's packed ten parties' worth of supplies in her car. I need help unloading," Daniel announces.

Max and Christopher immediately follow Daniel out. Still no Blake.

"You're here," Pippa exclaims, entering the house. "Come on. Let's show you to your rooms."

Is it my imagination, or are Pippa and Summer exchanging *dangerous* glances? I try not to read too much into it as I follow the girls down another corridor lined with doors on either side.

Summer opens one such door, mutters "mine," throwing in her small backpack, then resumes her walk. We stop right at the end of the corridor.

"Here's your room," Pippa announces.

Stepping inside, I smile. The room is small and quaint, with a double bed taking up most of the space and a small vanity table in one corner. I notice two doors on the wall opposite the bed. One leads to the bathroom, I assume. The other one could be a connecting door.

I nearly jump out of my skin when I hear a familiar voice behind me.

"What d'you know? We're neighbors again."

I swirl around to find Blake leaning against the doorframe, smiling broadly. He's wearing slacks and a simple gray T-shirt, looking as irresistible as always. I try not to focus on the way the sleeves stretch over his muscle-laced arms, or how he seems to fill the entire space. He oozes testosterone, every inch of him masculine through and through.

"You're in the room next door?" I ask unnecessarily.

"Yep. Had a flat tire on the way. When I arrived, only these two rooms were empty. Aside from the en suite, but that belongs to Mom and Dad."

Coincidence? I think not. I wonder which of the sisters came up with the idea to put us in adjacent rooms. My money's on Pippa, because Summer was with me in the car. But when I turn, I catch Summer schooling her expression, trying to tone down her smug grin. Pippa nods at her appreciatively. There's my answer. My gaze meets Blake's, and we both burst out laughing. His sisters look at us startled.

"You two are not subtle at all," I inform them.

"We weren't trying to be subtle," Summer comments. "Anyone else feel the sparks in the air?

No? No one? Just me?" Pippa elbows her conspiratorially.

"Just so we know," Blake chimes in, "any other things we should look out for? Maybe Clara's shower's not working, and she'll have to use mine?"

I blush at the mention of the shower. Blake catches my eye, smiling and winking. We didn't speak about what happened in our separate showers after the outing to the festival, but the tension between us has been off the charts since, and we both know why.

Summer juts her chin out, narrowing her eyes. "No, even though that would have been a great idea. Come on, Pippa. Let's get started with the decorations for the party."

With that, the two plotters head toward the door. Blake steps back, allowing them out, but then, instead of leaving too, he lingers in the doorframe.

"Want a tour of the ranch?"

"I'm helping with decorations," I answer quickly.

"It won't take long. This place isn't so big."

Truth be told, I do want a tour. This is a part of Bennett history I'd love to know more about. Besides, being with Blake in an open space is safe. At least safer than being inside here, in this small room where our hunger for each other seems to fill the entire space.

"Sure."

"Want to change first?"

"Nah, I'm comfortable like this. Let's go."

We walk side by side in the corridor.

"What are you doing?" Blake asks.

In my haste to keep my distance from him, I didn't realize I look a bit ridiculous, not to mention obvious because I'm nearly brushing the wall with my shoulder.

Swallowing, I keep my tone even. "Keeping my distance from you. I'm thinking three feet should be enough."

Blake steps right in front of me, forcing me to stop in my tracks.

"Babe, fair warning. Three hundred feet wouldn't be enough."

My cheeks heat, and I try to focus on some part of Blake that won't turn my knees to mush. I try the eyes, but they're too molten and intense.

Lips—too full.

Shoulders and chest—won't even go there. Eventually, I focus on my own hands, which are tugging at the hem of my shirt, even though it's impolite not to look at people when you talk to them.

Clearly whoever made up that rule has never been in the shoes of a woman trying to resist a very hot and determined man. Especially not one hungering for his touch and affection.

"Don't call me that. I'm not your babe."

"Yet."

Some men would sound over-the-top saying that, but Blake pulls it off and then some. And here's the thing. If I dropped the matter and walked past him, he'd drop it too, at least for now. I do the exact opposite.

"Getting ahead of yourself, aren't you?"

I know that if I push hard enough, if I challenge him hard enough, he'll break and burn, making me burn with him. I shouldn't want that, but I can't help wondering: if one kiss held so much heat, what would he do if I surrendered to him?

Blake's eyes snap fire. "I had one taste of you, and it wasn't enough. Not nearly enough. It wasn't enough for you either. Don't pretend it was." He leans in to me, bringing his lips to my ear. "You're betting on my self-restraint. You might lose."

I rise on my toes, bringing my mouth to his ear. "Here's where you're wrong. I'm betting on your lack of it. Even though I shouldn't."

His sharp intake of breath sends an arrow of heat right to my center. Sometime during this conversation, I've moved from gripping the hem of my shirt to fisting the hem of his. *You're really winning this, Clara.* Crap, I'm supposed to put a bucket of ice water on that fire lighting him up from within, not gasoline. I quickly drop my hands, sighing.

Blake steps back, looking at me as if he's seeing me for the first time. I can't believe I managed to actually catch him off guard. I only succeeded at the small price of giving myself away. Oh well, I can't even bring myself to be sorry. You know you're headed down a dangerous path when you can't even tell your own priorities. With a chuckle, he gestures for me to walk in front of him, which I do, keeping a *safe* distance.

***

"This used to be a barn," Blake says as we step farther away from the main building and toward a much smaller one. I didn't seen it when I first arrived. "Now they've remodeled it completely and it's an extra wing. I think they added an extra story. I believe it was smaller." He squints, sizing up the house. "I can't believe I don't remember. I used to come here every day. I was collecting eggs in the morning. Started doing it when I was about seven."

"Really? That young?"

"The older ones had their chores, and I was competitive. Wanted my chores too." He laughs. "That basket was almost as big as me. First time I did it, I broke half the eggs and cried. Daniel didn't let me live it down for about a decade. Hard thing to forget."

"What happened next?"

"Mom said, 'If you fail at first, you have to keep trying.'"

"Your mother is very smart."

"She is. It took about a week for me to stop breaking eggs."

I grin, trying to imagine Blake, only a few years older than Mia and Elena, wandering around with a huge basket. We spend the next half hour walking around the property, with Blake telling what used to be where, sharing anecdotes. I love that he trusts me enough to be so open with me and share a part of their childhood, of himself.

"This is the oldest tree on the property," he says about forty minutes later as we come under an enormous oak tree. It truly looks ancient—sturdy and wide. It's slowly bent forward, enough to let you know it's seen many storms and windy days. There is a swing hanging from it, and I immediately sit on it, swinging back and forth.

Blake smiles.

"What?" I ask, a little defensive.

"I knew you'd do that."

"I like swings." I feel like I'm flying whenever I'm in one. The one he ordered for the balcony arrived last week, and I spend about an hour there every evening.

"The swing has been here for a long time too." He pauses for a while, leaning against the bark of the tree. "Sebastian sat on it, with Summer in his lap, when he told us Mom and Dad would be selling the ranch."

"Oh, do tell."

Blake unhitches himself from the bark, walks over in front of me, and pushes the swing, sending me way farther back. He repeats the motion a few times, pushing harder, faster. I can feel the wind in my hair better this way. Of course, if I slipped from it, I'd faceplant straight on the ground, but I trust Blake wouldn't let anything happen to me.

"He'd already talked it through with the older gang and our parents. But he took Daniel, me, and Summer out here, explained it thoroughly. Said it's a risk, but promised to take care of us." His voice catches. "And he did."

"What did you say?"

"We were kids, and this was something new. It was exciting for us. And Sebastian is the type of person you just can't help trusting."

"So are you," I find myself saying, just as the swing comes hurtling toward him. He pushes me away again, cocking a brow.

"Which part of me spells trustworthy?"

"The one that offered me a place to stay when I needed one, then set it up just the way I wanted it so I'd feel at home." I hurtle toward him again, but instead of pushing me back, he grips the wooden board under my ass with one hand. The abrupt halt throws me off balance, and I let out a yelp. *I'm going to fall.*

Just as the thought takes shape in my mind, Blake whispers, "I've got you."

His arm is around me, firm and reassuring. And then his mouth. This kiss is so different from our first one, gentle and slow, but it has the same effect. It makes me want more. I soak in all of the warmth and steadiness that is being held and kissed by Blake.

He lets out a deep groan. I feel it reverberate through me, and the recognition that I spark that kind of desire in him turns me on. Blake eases me off the swing, still not letting me go.

"Clara?"

"Hmm?"

"Let's get back to the house."

"Okay."

I'm not sure what I'm agreeing to, but my entire body is buzzing with awareness. I like this man, and I can't fight my attraction to him any longer. The tension is palpable between us as we walk back inside the house. You'd need more than a knife to cut through it—possibly a machete or an axe.

We don't enter through the living room but through a back door, and we don't run into anybody. When we come in front of my door, he kisses the back of my hand, which is unexpected.

"I'm going to take a shower," he says. Also unexpected. I'm not sure exactly *what* I expected, but it was something more along the lines of "I'm going to back you against this wall and screw you silly" rather than kissing my hand and telling me he'll shower. "If you want me to come to your room afterward, just unlock the connecting door."

Ooooh, now I understand the shower part. We've been wandering outside in the sweltering heat and we're both sweaty. He's being a gentleman.

"It's my choice?" I ask breathlessly.

"Always your choice, and I'll respect it." With a wiggle of his eyebrows, he adds, "But if you choose to lock it, I'll just have to try harder."

"You don't give up, do you?"

"Not when I want something as badly as I want you."

Dong, dong, dong. Yep, that was the sound of my defenses crumbling to the floor. At least for now.

He kisses my forehead, then disappears into his room.

I hop into my own shower, washing off the sweat and heat. Unfortunately, by the time I step out, I've almost convinced myself that this is silly, wild, and crazy, and I don't do any of that. The key word being a*lmost*. Which is why after I dressed in my clothes for the party—a pink peasant blouse and a tight black skirt—I find myself in front of the connecting door, my hand on the key. Drawing in a sharp breath, I turn the key, unlocking the door. A sudden movement on the other side tells me that Blake was hovering in front of it.

CHAPTER ELEVEN

Clara

When he steps inside the room, I take a moment to admire him. He's wearing jeans and a tank. And he's barefoot. He's the sexiest thing I've ever seen.

Wordlessly, he interlaces his fingers with mine, kissing the back of my hand. My skin tingles at the soft brush, and my breath catches when Blake's gaze traps mine, holding it captive. So much heat and desire are in his eyes it's turning my knees weak. For a split second, I wonder what it would feel like to have his lips on other parts of my body if he's having this effect on me when he's only touching the back of my hand. I have a hunch I might not be able to take it. My body tightens at the thought.

Letting go of my hand, he leans in, and his mouth feels like liquid fire against mine. He isn't asking for permission. He's taking, and I love every second of it. Blake is relentless. We break apart for just the briefest of moments. I take a deep breath just as he runs the tip of his tongue on my lower lip, then the upper one. I swear my mouth is wired to my center because this feels as if Blake licked me *there*. A deep ache takes hold of me, and I press my thighs together instinctively.

"Fuck, it's turning you on, isn't it?"

"Yes." My voice is low and breathy. Tipping my head up, he seals his mouth over mine again, driving me crazy. I reach out for him, grateful that he's only wearing a tank. It leaves so much skin uncovered, ready to be touched and explored. I run my fingers up and down his arms, feeling the hard muscles, the veins on the inside of his forearms. I feel like he's holding back, and I don't want him to. I press my body against him. His skin is still hot from the shower, his hair damp as I run my fingers through it. Blake trails his mouth down my jaw, to the column of my neck, and lower on my collarbone.

"I want to make you come, Clara," he whispers against my skin. "Around my fingers, on my tongue."

I tug at his hair, heat pooling low in my body. "Blake."

"I want to taste your pussy. I want my mouth on you when you climax."

Oh my God. His words turn me on like nothing else. If he keeps talking like that, I will climb him right away.

"Say yes, Clara."

"Yes."

Blake smiles a sinfully wicked smile with a delicious twinkle in his eyes.

"I have to tell you though, I've never—" I

take a deep breath— "I only have an orgasm when...I'm by myself." I shift uncomfortably, looking anywhere but at him. I figure it's better that he knows from the start because he seems very keen on the *coming* part. Blake slides two fingers under my chin, tilting my head up until he's looking straight at me. His gaze is, if possible, even hungrier.

"I will change that."

I shudder at the determination and promise in his voice. I open my mouth to argue, but he slams his lips over mine, his hands working the button of my skirt. Then he changes his mind and simply pulls the skirt up to my waist, which is even better because I'm not ready to be naked in front of him yet. He leads me backward through the room, and when my legs touch the wooden panel of the bed, I sit on the mattress. Blake lets out a deep groan. It's the sexiest sound I've heard. Manly...almost primal.

"You're beautiful, Clara. I want to do so many things to you."

"Do them. All of them. Please."

"Lie back and open your legs for me."

I do, feeling more exposed than ever, even though my panties are still on.

"Take your panties off."

Licking my lips, I lift my butt slightly, pushing down the black cotton thong, feeling Blake's gaze on me the entire time. Once the panties are out of the way, he lowers himself until I can only see his head between my thighs.

I inhale sharply as he places each thumb at the

sides of my entrance, then slides them up and down my folds. I'm on fire, right until he blows a cold breath directly against my heated flesh. I shudder almost violently and my fingers dig into the mattress. Then he dips his tongue inside me exactly once, and I'm certain I'm going to break out of my skin.

"Oh, Blake!"

I plant my feet firmly onto the mattress, needing to ground myself. He pulls his tongue out, leaving me feeling empty. Then he licks up one fold, starting from my entrance right up to near my clit. He repeats the motion on the other fold, driving me absolutely crazy. Every synapse snaps to life, greedy for more.

He draws circles with his tongue, starting from my entrance, and going up, up, up, then down again. But he isn't touching my clit, never my clit. Each time his wicked hot tongue approaches it, I dig my heels deeper into the bed, anticipating the delicious—if brief—reprieve, but it never comes. Instead, my anticipation rises and rises, and it's downright killing me. I'm panting frantically, needing a release from the sweet torture. I'm so turned on I can feel myself dripping.

"Blake. Oh fuck, fuck, fuck!"

A stirring low in my body alerts me that an orgasm is building inside me. The recognition sends a bolt of heat coursing through me. When Blake finally sucks my clit into his mouth, I explode. My hips buck up and Blake greedily cups my ass, digging his fingers into my cheeks. Even lost to pleasure as I am, I can feel his desperation, his hunger for me. The intensity of his passion sends me over the edge. My climax is so intense it leaves me breathless.

He kisses my inner thighs, then comes up, resting his arms at the sides of my shoulders, caging me in. I want to tell him many things, but I'm still too high on pleasure to form a coherent sentence.

He kisses me, and I can taste myself on him. My body reacts instantly, pressing into him.

There is as much tenderness in him as there is passion, and that tugs at my heartstrings. I like being surrounded by him, feeling his chest press against my breasts, his arms at my sides. A strange thought occurs to me: *I never want him to let go.* With a shake of my head, I shove the silly thought aside, focusing on the here and now. Now that I'm not lost in the realm of lust anymore, I can see his eyes are hooded with desire—and his erection is pressing against my thigh.

"You're so sexy when you come, Clara." His voice is rough, and I inexplicably think of whiskey and honey. I want to make him happy too, so I push him off. Once he's standing, I climb down from the bed, standing on my knees in front of him, undoing the button, and lowering the zipper. I push his jeans down, but in my haste, grab his boxers too. Next thing I know, his erection springs free, slapping me lightly against my cheek. And *holy hell.* It isn't just impressive; it's about eight inches of huge.

I wrap my palm around his erection, moving up and down, then bring my mouth to the crown, licking it once. Blake's nostrils flare. Hmm...well that isn't good enough. I wonder what it would take to make his composure slip, then resolve to find out immediately.

When I clamp my lips around him, he moans out my name. *Now we're talking.* I slide my mouth up and down, running my tongue over the tip every time I come up. Then I lower my mouth, taking more in. I'll never be able to take him completely, but I want as much as possible.

"How deep can you go?" Blake asks on a deep groan.

In response, I lower my mouth more until I feel him at the back of my throat. It's comfortable, but sweet heavens, so deep. Blake takes my hand and wraps it around his base, covering the part I'm not able to take in.

In that moment, I look up at him, and I think this might be the most erotic moment of my life. I'll make this good for him. I want it to be the best he's had, just like he's made it for me. I move my mouth and fist in unison, squeezing him as tight as I can, as fast as I can.

"I like that you're so greedy."

And I become greedier still. For his sounds of pleasure, for his heated looks. Every time I look up, his face is more contorted with pleasure. His composure has been long forgotten, and I love seeing this raw side of him.

His hand goes in my hair and his fingers gently tug at my roots, moving in sync with me. In the beginning, I think it's because he wants to guide me, but then I realize it's to stop me just before I take him in too deep. When he widens inside my mouth, he tries to pull out, but I grab his ass with both hands.

"Clara...."

In response, I just dig my fingers in his ass cheeks. Blake comes the next moment, murmuring my name, and I love every second of it. I wait until he calms down and his breathing eases to let go and rise to my feet. Blake helps me, holding each of my hands in his. Instead of letting go when I'm steady on my feet, he pulls me closer and kisses me hard and hot.

"You are amazing," he says, buttoning up his jeans.

"Ah, nothing you say now counts. It's all the post-orgasm bliss. Look at you, you're practically shining."

"I think my masculinity just took a hit. Shining, really?"

"Would glowing be better?"

He holds up a hand. "Stop right there."

That's when I read the time on the grandfather clock behind him. "Oh God. I was supposed to help put up decorations."

Panicking, I push my skirt down—it was still around my waist—then look around the room for my panties. They're under the bed. I bend to retrieve them, and I'm about to put them on when I realize I should wash first. Blake's made me all sweaty and messy again.

"I have to clean up," I inform him, just as I dash past him and head to the bathroom. He's not in sight when I get out again, but the connecting door is open, and I hear the sound of running water coming from his bathroom.

I'm unsure if I'm supposed to wait for him or what the protocol for this is. Or where we stand. But right now, I don't want to overthink or analyze. I just want to feel and enjoy. Also, he left the door open, which I take as a good sign. Curious about his room, I walk over there, closing the connecting door behind me. The room mirrors mine, only the color of the walls differing—mine are lemon, his are white.

Several things happen when he steps out of the bathroom. First, he heads straight to me, pulling me into a kiss. Second, the door bursts open and Mia and Elena barrel into the room. I jump away from Blake. The girls stare at us.

"Sorry, Uncle Blake, we'll come back later," Mia says. Not many people can tell them apart, but I can.

"You're late for the *peparations*," Elena adds.

"Preparations," Blake and I say at the same time. "Come on, let's all go out, then."

Elena walks to Blake, holding her arms up. Blake lifts her without being asked to. I all but melt into a puddle when he kisses her temple. Not one to be left behind, Mia holds her arms up too. Blake easily scoops her up as well. Oh my, he looks utterly irresistible with a girl in each arm. Not only because his muscles bulge slightly from the effort, though that's a valid point too, but because he looks delicious enough to lick and climb. But what makes him most irresistible is the tenderness in him as he listens and talks to the girls.

He's still holding them as we stride down the corridor that leads to the living room. Pippa meets us halfway, looking flushed.

"Here you are. You scared ten years off my life. How many times did I tell you not to disappear on me, girls?"

"Sorry, Mommy," Mia says.

"We went to get Uncle Blake and Miss Clara," Elena adds. Blake lowers the girls, and they each take their mother's hand. "They were kissing, like you and Daddy." Elena puckers her lips, and Mia mirrors her action. Blake laughs, Pippa smiles triumphantly, and I feel my cheeks burning.

"They're great matchmaking assistants," I comment, not quite able to hide my own smile.

"Ah, not quite yet. They're barely reporting," Pippa says, lowering herself on her haunches and kissing each of the girls' foreheads. "But I have plenty of time to train them."

CHAPTER TWELVE

Clara

When we step into the living room minutes later, Summer, Nadine, Ava, and Mrs. Bennett are hard at work setting up the decorations. Lots to do, and I can't wait to jump into it.

"Where are all the men?" I ask.

"Outside," Mrs. Bennett answers. "In charge of the grill."

"On that note," Blake says, "I'm going to join them."

He smiles at me right before he heads out, and my heart soars. Silly heart. It has no business butting into all of this.

"How can I help? How much time do we have?"

Summer gestures to me to come join her. She's currently pumping up balloons. I sit on the floor next to her.

"We have two hours until the party starts officially," Summer says. "Landon just texted me. They'll arrive on time."

Summer mentioned during the drive that some of their cousins, Landon included, would be here.

"Can you give me a rundown of how many sides there are to the clan? I tried to keep track of everyone named Bennett at Alice's wedding, but it was impossible. Then there were all those people related to you who aren't called Bennett."

Summer nods. "Well, Dad was the oldest of a family of five. They each had many kids—that's the Bennett part of the clan. Mom came from a family of four. Everyone had many kids. We have good genes. Shame not to pass them on."

"My head spins. I need a family tree."

"Most of the time, so do I, especially at weddings. But only Landon and his sister Valentina will be here today from the Connor clan. They're cousins from Mom's side. You probably met them at Alice's wedding, but don't worry if you don't remember them. I think they're bringing a friend too."

Two hours later, my fingers are numb, and the room looks unrecognizable. We have covered every coffee table as well as the large table in the dining area with *Avengers*-themed plastic tablecloths. Balloons hang so tightly together from the ceiling, it looks like it's *made* of balloons. There are also figurines tall enough to reach up to my waist scattered around the room, depicting characters from the superhero franchise.

When Landon, Valentina, and their friend arrive, everyone steps inside.

"I can't believe this," Blake says, appearing at

my side. "Can a three-year-old actually appreciate all this?"

"Well, a three-year-old's party is as much for the adults as for the kid, I'll say. And I can appreciate all of this."

"You're a complicated creature."

"But I also smell nice. That makes up for it, doesn't it?"

He settles his hand at the small of my back, and even though he's done it before, the gesture feels much more intimate after this morning. "You also taste great, Clara."

This man and his dirty mouth should be outlawed. Or at the very least, he should only use unorthodox language when we're alone. I open my mouth to suggest that but forget my words at the pure heat radiating off him. With a prickle of awareness, I realize he moved his hand from my lower back up to the back of my neck and his thumb is now pressing into my skin, gently and possessively at the same time. For a split second, it feels as if there is no one but the two of us in this room. How can he do that to me? Take over all my senses, my thoughts?

"And who is the lovely lady here? I don't remember seeing you before."

The voice snaps me out of my thoughts, and I focus on its owner. The men in the extended Bennett clan are also the very definition of tall and handsome.

"Clara Abernathy." I reach out my hand, which he shakes. "Family friend. And I think we've been introduced at Alice's wedding."

"Ah, could be. Sorry, I don't remember. Weddings seem to be introduction marathons. I'm Landon Connor." His eyes zero in on Blake's hand, which is still at the back of my neck, rather possessively. Blake seems taller and larger somehow as he shakes his cousin's hand. The two men exchange a long glance. It's almost like a standoff. This is fascinating.

"See you around, Clara."

"I cannot believe all the men in your family are this good-looking," I tell Blake once Landon is out of earshot because I *cannot* pass up the opportunity. Blake sets his jaw. Jealous looks good on him. Hot. Still, I'm not heartless, so I elbow him lightly. "Relax. I was just messing with you. God, you're intense."

"You have no idea. Come on. Let's introduce you to Valentina. No messing with me. Or else."

Is it bad that I'm dying to find out what that "or else" entails? Sighing, I lick my lips.

"Stop licking your lips or I'll forget we're supposed to attend this party and lock us both in the bedroom."

I inhale sharply, nodding, even though I'm so tempted to keep pushing him. This man has the strangest influence on me.

Valentina and Landon brought gifts too, and when I glance at the presents pile in one corner of the room, I can't help giggling. I bought gifts for all of the kids, thinking that if only the birthday boy gets something new, the others will be jealous, or just plain sad. Judging by the size of the pile, I wasn't the only one thinking along those lines.

It looks like Christmas has come early.

Jenna Bennett is next to the pile, sitting on the windowsill. Some of the other kids played with Will's presents, unwrapping them before he got the chance.

"I'm going to help your mom wrap up the presents," I inform Blake.

"You don't have to do that. Will is going to rip up the paper anyway."

"Exactly. He loves that part," I exclaim, vividly remembering that, as a kid, unwrapping a present was half of the fun.

Winking at him, I take off, joining Jenna.

"I'm here to help."

"Bless you. I wasn't expecting so many gifts. It's so good to see Landon and Valentina."

I sit on the windowsill, following Jenna's lead. She's been smiling even more than usual since Landon and Valentina arrived.

"Their mother is your sister, right?"

Her smile falters. "Was. She and her husband died years ago."

"Oh, I'm so sorry. I didn't know."

"Landon and Valentina were freshmen in college. They practically kept their family from falling apart, raised their siblings."

I follow her gaze at the other end of the room, looking at the cousins in question with admiration.

"I didn't have a chance to ask before, but how

is it living with Blake?"

"He's a great neighbor. And it was awfully generous of him to help me out." I press my lips together, afraid that if I continue talking, I'll give myself away. At any rate, I'm not going to share any spicy details with his *mother*, but better safe than sorry, so I keep my mouth shut.

Jenna studies me inquisitively, and I focus on smoothing out the folded paper on one of the presents I've just wrapped. I run my thumb over it even after it's smooth as hell until Jenna looks away. Pippa might be able to smell out evasive maneuvers, but Jenna is really the master at reading people.

She's also far more subtle than Pippa, which makes her even more dangerous because she typically makes me spell out my deepest secrets before I even realize it. So, I focus the conversation on Will and the presents. Once we're done wrapping everything, Jenna pulls me into a half hug, which I return wholeheartedly.

I always have to keep myself in check so I don't lean in like a kitten starving for affection. I've always been touchy-feely, but more so with Jenna and her motherly hugs. The way I see it, I have some solid years of catching up to do in terms of hugs.

I honestly never think I'll get my fill of motherly hugs, and Jenna seems willing to dish them out often, almost as if she can sense my hunger for them. Given her ability to read people, she probably can.

Just as I pull from Jenna's embrace, Blake

catches my eye from across the room and smiles at me. I smile back, but at the same time, a small fear grips me that I'll have to give all this up—the Bennetts' warmth, and Jenna's hugs—because I can't keep my hands or lips off Blake.

CHAPTER THIRTEEN

Blake

I'm counting the minutes until someone questions me about Clara. My money is either on my sisters or Christopher. He warned me from the get-go that I had zero chances of keeping things platonic with Clara if she moved next to me.

To my astonishment, I make it through almost the entire party before Summer approaches me, smiling sweetly, which is always a bad omen, but never more than today. She keeps looking between me and Clara, who is currently protecting Silas, Logan's boy, from Mia and Elena. The twins have taken to tickling Silas as often as they can.

Summer sits next to me at the large table, which is otherwise empty. She's munching happily on a piece of cake.

"How's the newest painting coming along?" I ask.

Summer remains silent for a few seconds, as if considering my words. "It's coming along okay, but if I'm honest, I'm having more fun being a docent at the gallery than painting."

That's news to me. "Really?"

Summer nods. "Yeah. Maybe it's all the years I've spent in Rome being a docent, but I seem to like it more to tell others about paintings of great artists rather than spending days alone in my studio with just my brush and a canvas, trying to create something great, then hoping I'll find a vendor. Let's face it. I'll never be Picasso. Or Monet."

"No, you're Summer Bennett. And personally, I'd buy your stuff over that Picasso guy's anytime. His paintings make no sense. Some even freak me out."

"That's because you're not an art appreciator, Blake."

"True, you and Pippa got the creative genes and interest."

When Summer turned twelve, she started to show interest in all things art, begging everyone to take her to galleries and what-not. I was often her companion. It had been so boring I'd wanted to poke my eyes out, but I went for my sister. She drank up every word of the docents while I shut out their voice, especially when it came to modern art, which in my opinion looked as if Silas had gotten his hands on a black marker and went wild on a white canvas. Everyone else finds deeper meaning in those drawings. To me, a line is a line is a line. That's all there was to it.

"So, how's the gallery, then?"

"Oh, we just received the most wonderful collection by Van Gogh. We finished putting it up

Friday. Tickets for it are already sold out for the entire next week."

I take a guess. "Is this the guy who cut off his ear and then blew his own brains out?"

Summer narrows her eyes. "He had some issues, but he was also a genius. He used techniques, which...I see you're phasing out already."

"What? No, no, no, I'm listening." Truth be told, I'm hearing her, but not really listening. My brain is in the habit of wandering off at the first mention of words such as "technique". Almost inadvertently, I focus on Clara, suddenly wishing I could fast forward the day, so I can be alone with her.

"Let's talk about Clara instead." *Yeah, that took no time at all.* In all honesty, I haven't helped my case by eye-fucking Clara from across the room. "By the way you're looking at her, I'm gonna go out on a limb and say things are heating up? Do you need tips? She likes tacos, romantic comedies, and unusual cocktails."

Summer said all this at once, and she is now taking a much-needed breath. I take advantage of the split second of silence to turn the conversation back to her. I'm rescued by Daniel, who joins us, sitting on Summer's other side.

"This is a madhouse, and I never thought I'd say that about a three-year-old's party. What are you two talking about?"

"Clara," Summer informs him. "Our brother's been giving her hot looks for years now. I'm trying to gauge how far past looks they've gotten since she's his neighbor."

"Blake, come on. Keep your hands off her. She's sweet. Deserves better than your sorry ass."

Well, well. I hadn't anticipated this. Daniel turning against me—the traitor. He's my twin. There's an unwritten rule that he must always have my back.

"You're not helping," Summer admonishes him.

"She's a family friend. Don't make things awkward for her. Remember Caroline?"

My jaw ticks with annoyance. "Don't judge me based on your mistakes."

The two of us met Caroline during our orientation week in college. We had in common that we were all from San Francisco. One thing led to another, and we became fast friends. During holidays, she came by our house a few times, and she quickly became a family friend. She was particularly close to Pippa. Then she and Daniel started dating during our senior year. That wouldn't have been bad, per se, but things didn't work out. Afterward, she slowly pulled away from the family. She still attends weddings and major events, but isn't as close as she used to be. What a pity, especially because I suspect Daniel still has feelings for Caroline. They aren't unrequited, but it's none of my business.

"Fair enough," Daniel says.

"What are you all talking about?" Logan asks, joining us. He walks to the opposite side of the table, searching in the baby bag sitting on a chair.

"Just warning Blake off from Clara," Daniel says nonchalantly.

Logan snaps his head up. "You're hazing him? But you're always on his side. I want a front row seat at the show." Instead of taking whatever he needs from the bag, he drops into one of the seats. Lovely. Now I'm being cornered by two of my brothers.

"No, Daniel is being mean," Summer explains. "I *am* on Blake's side."

"You always are though," Logan says. "Clara's a family friend, Blake."

"So was Nadine," I remind him. "At least she was about to become one before you seduced her."

Picking on my brother is an old habit, one I've honed all my life. I also look up to Logan, but that's something I rarely say out loud. It feeds his ego, and it seriously doesn't need any inflating.

"You're not me," Logan says.

"Obviously. I have better style." On a grin, I add, "And better hair."

"You have no faith," Summer complains.

"I deal in facts, numbers, and patterns." Logan grins back. "But I actually do have faith in you. Based on the latest patterns, you're on your way to becoming an honest man."

"Just to be sure, was that an insult or a compliment?"

"Compliment."

Well, well, if today isn't full of surprises. Logan's on my side, Daniel's still pissing me off. A movement in the background catches my eye. Clara's crossing the room, carrying Silas and then handing him over to his mother. She looks good with a baby in her arms.

"You have it really bad for her," Logan comments with a shit-eating grin, and I can't contradict him.

Just then, my cousin Valentina steps in the center of the room, announcing loudly, "All right, time for Landon, Fred, and me to head out again."

"Are you sure you can't stay?" Mother asks. "All the rooms are full here, but there's a small hotel about five minutes away."

"Nah, sorry, Jenna. We have to head back out tonight."

As everyone—including my trio of interrogators—shuffles through the room to say goodbye, I scan the crowd for Clara.

I find her near where the pile of presents was—now it's just a pile of wrapping paper and cartons. She's conversing with Landon and Valentina's friend, Fred. At least she's conversing, Fred is touching her. Her shoulder. Then her arm. Down her back. Then her shoulder again.

I have the sudden urge to punch the guy, and I'm not a violent person. Stalking forward, I place an arm around Clara's shoulder when I reach them.

"I was just telling Clara she can come visit. I'll happily give her a tour."

Yeah, Fred really isn't helping his case here. The urge to rearrange his face grows stronger. *What the hell?*

"I'll let you know when I'm planning a trip," Clara assures him. She smiles up at him, and her dimples are showing. I feel punched in the gut. I thought those sweet smiles of hers were just for me. But nope, apparently she goes around handing them out freely.

When Landon calls Fred, he takes off with a nod. I step back from Clara, surveying her.

"Why do you look pissed?" she asks.

"Fred was hitting on you."

"No, he was being nice and polite."

"Showing you around town is code for trying to get in your pants."

Clara crosses her arms over her breasts, and the corners of her lips twitch.

"You were smiling at him the way you smile at me. It's messing with my head."

"Let me get this straight. You want me not to smile at people?"

"Not people. Just men. Smile at women all you want. At my brothers too, actually. The older ones are married, and Daniel knows not to mess with you."

Clara's expression opens up in a bright smile. Yeah, there they are—those dimples. They are all mine.

"You have nothing to worry about. You're the only one who is Blakealicious."

I blink. "Huh?"

"Just made that up. The love child of Blake and delicious."

"Sounds like a bad stripper name."

"Do you know any good ones?"

"What?"

"Just testing how deep your knowledge of male strippers is."

I open my mouth, and then close it again. Where were we before? Aha, now I remember.

"Are you trying to distract me from our fighting?"

"Is it working?" Grinning, she claps her hands together.

"No. So, are we clear in the smiling department?"

She places a hand on my arm, stepping closer. Rising on her toes, she kisses my cheek, then whispers in my ear, "You're not the boss of me, Blake."

This woman! She's driving me insane.

"I'm going to say goodbye to Valentina."

"This conversation isn't over," I warn.

"Wasn't dreaming it was." When she steps away, there's an extra sway to her hips. I barely resist the urge to kiss her hard, staking my claim and showing everyone she belongs to me.

CHAPTER FOURTEEN

Clara

I don't get the chance to finish my conversation with Blake at all because after Landon and Valentina leave, my phone rings. I don't have it on me, but it's somewhere in the living room. Excusing myself from the group, I follow the sound. Why can't I ever remember where I put my stuff? Eventually, I find my phone on top of a shelf. That's right, I put it up there so it would be out of the kids' reach. Glancing at the screen, I recognize the number of the head of the technical team at the studio. *This can't be good.*

"Hi, George!" I greet, putting my phone to my ear and stepping into a side corridor. There's too much noise in the living room.

"Sorry to bother you on the weekend, but we have a situation."

"I figured. What's wrong?"

"One of the sets just collapsed."

"What? Please tell me it's not the one we need from Monday to Wednesday."

"That's the one."

Groaning, I press my forehead against the

wall. "Have you tried Quentin?"

"Yes. He's in Toronto, taking the next flight, but he said to call you in anyway. Between you and me, I don't think he can handle this. He'll have a meltdown when he sees the damage."

"Yeah."

I run a number of scenarios in my mind, even though deep down I know George is right. If this doesn't get fixed this weekend, we'll delay the production by two days, and then we'll be in a precarious financial situation. No, this has to be fixed before Monday, which means spending the night at the studio and all day tomorrow.

It means no more weekend, no more Blake. Damn, and I was really looking forward to riling him up some more. That jealous streak of his is simply delicious. There is so much untapped teasing potential there. Heat flares within me just thinking about it, especially because teasing him brings up another streak—the bossy one—and that one is, if possible, even more alluring. This is my punishment for being a naughty woman. But when duty calls, it calls.

"I'll be at the studio in two hours," I assure George. After clicking off, I head straight to my bedroom and pack my bag, looking longingly at the connecting door.

"What are you doing?" Summer's voice startles me from the doorway. I explain the situation at the studio quickly, and then it dawns on me that I didn't come here by car. Fantastic.

"Oh, you can take my car. I'll just ride back with whomever."

"Are you sure?"

"Yeah."

"Thank you."

Thank heavens her car is automatic, because I can't drive a stick to save my life. Bag ready, I return to the living room with Summer. The Bennetts are a little flummoxed with my abrupt departure—one Bennett in particular—and I say my goodbyes quickly.

"I'll walk you to the car," Blake says as I head out the front door.

"You don't have to."

"I'll walk you," he repeats, his voice stronger, and I bite back a sigh. I like bossy Blake. Truth be told, I like every version of him. He's simply gotten under my skin.

Ever the gentleman, he loads my bag in the trunk.

"I wish you didn't have to go." His honesty is so disarming I can't help responding in kind.

"So do I."

He closes the distance to me, raising his hand to touch my cheek, my neck. God, it feels so good to be touched by him. I'm in danger of forgetting why I must leave; such is his power. Wisely, I step back a little. Hmm...this isn't helping as much as I thought it would.

"Yeah?"

"You think I'd rather spend my night and

Sunday working than with you?"

He offers me a smile and kisses my forehead, which is not what I was expecting.

"What?"

"We're back at forehead kissing?" I inquire. He laughs throatily.

"No, but if I kiss you—" He emphasizes the word "*kiss*" by dragging his thumb across my lower lip. "—I can promise you won't make it to the studio in time."

"Oh! Okay."

His voice is pure seduction, and combined with the pressure of his thumb on my mouth, my body tightens, my nipples peaking under my bra. This man has the most dangerous effect on me. He seems to realize what he's doing to me and drops his hand, opening the car door for me. Thank heavens for small mercies.

"See you tomorrow evening, then."

✳✳✳

I don't see Blake on Sunday because the mayhem at the studio continues. At noon, it appears everything is sorted out, so we all go home. But I barely have time to nap for a few hours before George informs me the set foundation caved in completely, and we're back to square one. The entire technical team plus Quentin and I spend the night at the studio, and all of Monday. The set isn't salvageable.

We need to rebuild its big parts, which will take the entire week. Since we can't pause shooting for that long, Quentin and I arranged for shooting to temporarily move to another of the studio's sets, which is now empty because that show is on break.

So tomorrow morning, we're all driving out to L.A., and will stay there for the week.

I drive home in a state that resembles drunkenness, parking the car in my usual spot. But then I see Blake's car, and adrenaline suddenly spikes my blood. He must be inside the bar tonight. He usually is on Mondays. I have *not* memorized his schedule, just...kept in mind some facts, purely for neighborly reasons. Ah, who am I kidding, I totally memorized his schedule.

So even though I'm dead tired, instead of going up to the apartment and sleeping like the dead, I head inside the bar. I want to see him, even if it's just for a few minutes to say hi.

To my utter shock, the place is packed. Mondays are usually laid-back. The second shock comes when I see Blake behind the counter alone. This can't be good. He usually has two bartenders on Monday. I knew my stalker tendencies would come in handy at some point. Scratch that. *Observant! That's it. I'm observant, not a stalker.*

I watch him silently, amazed by his speed. Of course, the line is something like Sisyphus's chore. No matter how fast Blake is, the line isn't getting shorter because new customers line up constantly. I elbow my way through the crowd, and instead of lining up, I wedge myself between two men who are directly in front of Blake, waiting for their drinks. They shoot daggers with their eyes at me. Ask me if I care.

"Hey, why are you alone tonight?" I ask, leaning slightly across the counter so the other patrons can't hear me.

"Clara, hey! Didn't see you. Sent both my bartenders home an hour ago. They were coming down with some bug."

"Oh."

"And I have a full house tonight." He smiles as he hands a beer to one of the customers, but I've been *observing* Blake for long enough to know when he means a smile or when it's just a pleasantry. This is the latter. I have the sudden urge to make him laugh, or hug or kiss him, but it's not my place. Blake isn't mine, despite what happened on Saturday morning between us at the ranch. I don't want to raise my hopes that it was more than a hot morning. Without asking for permission, I walk around the bar, stepping behind the counter.

"What are you doing?" Blake asks.

"Lending you a hand."

"You're tired. Don't think I haven't noticed you didn't come home last night."

I smile, beyond thrilled that I'm not the only one who is observant.

"I'm handling this."

"I'm helping you."

Blake stares me down but I don't back away,

instead holding his gaze, which is no small feat.

"Oi, still waiting for my drink," a man calls from behind the bar, cutting through the tension.

We have our hands full until well after midnight. Finally, when there are just three patrons left and it's only a few minutes before closing, I use the opportunity to use the personnel toilet.

On my way back, close to the door connecting the back office area with the bar, I hear a low, seductive female voice.

"Blake, you look sexier every time I see you."

I flatten myself against the wall. I can't see her through the open door, but if I can hear her, I imagine she either must have stepped behind the bar or is leaning across it, and they're nearby.

"Thank you, Sarah."

"You still live upstairs?"

"Yes."

My heart stops. I know it's terrible of me to eavesdrop, but I can't peel myself away, though this is one of those moments when my ability to make myself invisible is required. Instead, I'm rooted to the spot, forcing myself to breathe in and out. If Blake wants to take this woman upstairs and have his wicked way with her...

"I can wait for you to lock up," the woman says.

Stay put, Clara. Stay cool as a cucumber. Going out with women is his right, and it shouldn't be a big deal to me. It shouldn't matter at all. But it does, damn it, even though he's not mine. Yes, we kissed and had some hot fun, but it's not like we made each other any promises. Maybe it was a one-time thing, and I just didn't realize it.

"And then we can go upstairs. Like in the old days," she continues.

I feel a sharp pain in my chest as I hold my breath, waiting for Blake's answer. *Please say no. Please, please say no.*

"Don't take this the wrong way, Sarah, but it's not going to happen."

"Aww, what a pity. I'd ask why, but I don't want to hear you telling me you're off the market. It would be a stab to my ego, knowing I wasn't the one to tame you. It was good to see you, Blake."

"Take care."

I keep my ears peeled and hear the front door opening and closing, then Blake's footsteps heading away from the bar, presumably to lock the door and turn the sign to closed.

My mind is reeling, and I feel a huge wave of relief crashing over me. I take a few steps back, planning to hover around the back room for a minute or two, so Blake doesn't put two and two together. Unfortunately, Blake himself steps into the room.

He takes one glance at me and just *knows*.

"You listened." It isn't a question. I'm pretty sure he can read the relief on my face. I nod, keeping my gaze focused on the top button of his polo shirt.

"And you're avoiding my eyes because…?"

I chance a glance upward. "Why did you turn

her down?"

"Because I'm not interested." After a beat, he says, "You think I'd touch you the way I did on Saturday and then hook up with someone else?"

I can't find my voice so I just move my weight from one foot to the other, feeling like a fool. Blake closes the distance between us, raising one hand. He rests the pad of his thumb on my jawline, close to my earlobe. His other fingers go into my hair. He brings me closer, lowering his mouth to my ear. "I'm only interested in one woman. You." He feathers his lips on my cheek, sending all my senses into a tailspin.

"I feel a little silly," I admit. My voice is shaking with joy and relief.

"Don't." He kisses my temple, holding me close to him. "But I will need you to give me more credit than that." He hugs me even closer as I nod against his chest.

"I thought...maybe it was a one-time thing, and I didn't realize it."

"It wasn't a one-time thing. And just so we're clear, I don't want you just in my bed. I want you in my life."

"You're a sweet talker, Blake Bennett, and you're so good at it. Can you do it some more?"

Snuggling against him with my entire body, I soak in all of that goodness and warmth, and at the same time my fingers press into his back, feeling him up. I'm an excellent multitasker if I do say so myself.

"I mean it." He pushes me away a few inches

so he can look down at me. I swear to God, I will melt right here in his arms. "I don't share, and I'd never ask you to either."

"Okay."

"So we're clear on this front?" His eyes are full of determination and heat.

"Yes."

He seals his mouth against mine and I sigh, bracing my hands on his strong arms. Something shifted between us just now, and it fills me with a giddy happiness, so I'm going to hold on to it.

"Go upstairs. I'm going to close here and prepare everything for tomorrow," he says when we pull apart.

"I'll help."

"Nah, you're tired."

"But I won't be able to sleep right now. I'm too wired." Being held in those strong arms of his while he tells me he wants me in his life will do that to me.

"Take a hot bath and relax."

I might have done that, if not for two things. One, I'm not ready yet to say good night. And two, his voice is *commanding* again. I forgot how much I like that.

"I told you before you're not the boss of me, Blake."

"You keep saying that. I'll have to prove the opposite."

Well, he's a terrible people reader if he can't tell this is exactly what I'm aiming for. I *might* have to spell it out for him, but then he might use it to his advantage, and who knows where that might get us?

"Go upstairs."

"Or what, will you boss me around some more?"

"You bet."

"What if I don't want to go upstairs?"

Blake leans in to me, brushing his lips on my forehead, then down my temple. He stops when his mouth is inches away from mine. "Then I'm going to throw you over my shoulder and carry you there."

"You're so hot when you're bossy," I admit. He frowns.

"You gave me shit for it at the ranch, and now."

Yep, I'll have to spell it out. "I was riling you up. Get with the program. By the way, can I make you jealous from time to time? Back at the ranch...you were so hot, all possessive."

He lets out a strangled groan. "You're killing me. Killing. And the answer is no unless you want me to kiss you right on the spot, staking my claim on you."

I grin. "But that's exactly what I'm going for."

***

Blake

I cup her head, kissing her hard. Then I take her hand and lead her to the back with determined strides. There is a small office there, which I never use. I prefer to work surrounded by the hustle and bustle of the bar, often just sitting at one of the bar tables to work on my laptop. The office is too small and private for my taste, but now I appreciate its existence very much.

Once inside, I lift Clara up, propping her ass on the small wooden desk, which makes a dubious sound like it might give in.

"You're beautiful," I murmur. She's wearing jeans and a blue, strapless tank, but she could be wearing anything and she'd still be stunning. Her expression lights up, the corners of her mouth lifting in a smile. I'd do anything to put that smile on her face every day. And I will. I don't know where this urge comes from, but it feels right. She rocks back and forth a few inches, and something in her expression changes.

"Blake, not here..." She blushes, which immediately clues me in to her meaning. Obviously, I need to clarify a few things.

"Make no mistake, I will make love to you on every surface—including this desk. But the first time, it'll be on a bed. You'll need to be comfortable, and I'll need it to be solid—because, babe, it'll take a lot for me to get my fill of you. Right now I just want to kiss you...make you come once. I need to hear you cry out."

She licks her lips but has no comeback, which is a first. Instead, she parts her thighs in a silent invitation, exhaling sharply. Her eyes widen as if her own body's reaction to me surprises her.

I kiss her hard, pulling her right to the edge of the desk. She shifts even closer, parting her thighs wider. I love the way she opens up to me like she's inviting me to take all she has to give. She wraps her arms around my neck, sighing into my mouth. It's the sweetest sound, and I'm overcome by the need to lure sounds of pleasure out of her. She fists my hair, growing more desperate.

"Blake, won't anyone—"

"No, I locked the front door. Trust me."

She relaxes against me, trusting me. I won't give her any reason to regret that. Ever. I want to taste and touch every inch of this woman, but that will have to wait until she's in a more comfortable place. This—tonight, is all about her. Still, I'm a red-blooded man, and I haven't had the pleasure of worshiping her breasts. That will change tonight. I push her tank top down and Christ, she's a sight.

Red cheeks with slightly puffed-up lips, her tank top cinched around her waist. The bra is the half-cup type, pushing her breasts up. She looks so sexy, I'm tempted to leave it on. But the need to taste her is greater, so off the bra goes. She's gorgeous. I kiss down her neck, to her chest. She leans back slightly, giving me better access. Her nipples are already puckered and I haven't even touched them. I'm going to remedy that right away. I palm one and take the peak of the other in my mouth, swirling my tongue around it. Clara moans loudly, arching forward into me.

I graze my teeth lightly around her nipple, watching her. I don't want to push too much so soon. I'm going to drive her over the edge, give her pleasure like she's never had before, but I have to pace myself. She bites her lip, parting her thighs even wider. I've brought her to climax with my mouth now I want to do the same with my fingers. And I want to kiss her when she finishes, capturing the sound.

I unbutton her jeans but don't remove them, just slide my hand under the fabric of her panties, caressing slowly over her pubic bone. She's shuddering with anticipation. I kiss her when I finally lower my fingers over her opening. *Oh fuck, fuck, fuck.* She's so wet and warm, so ready, it damn near kills me not to sink into her right here on this desk. I stroke her, kissing up all her moans, greedy for her sounds. They grow more intense as I find her clit and press around it, against it, finding just the perfect rhythm for her. I wait until she becomes drenched and then slip two fingers inside her, pressing the heel of my palm against her clit. She shudders almost violently. When I arch my fingers into a come-here motion, she clenches around me.

She digs her fingernails in my arms, arching more against me, and I kiss her hard, claiming her sound of pleasure as she climaxes. Then I hold her close to me, steadying her until her breathing relaxes, whispering sweet and dirty nothings in her ear. I won't deny that knowing I was the first to give her an orgasm is a big boost to my ego. But it's also something more, beyond pride or ego. Just the thought that other men have touched her is torture for me. It's the first time I wish I'd been a woman's first in all the ways. The realization hits me like a ton of bricks. I'm experiencing many firsts with Clara, and have a hunch more will follow.

But right now, I need to take care of her, make sure she gets her sleep. She's been working the entire weekend and helped me out tonight. It's high time I took care of her. First step, covering her up, because having her beautiful breasts in my face is tempting fate and my self-control. I did a good job of ignoring the strain in my boxers when I was concentrating on her pleasure, but now I have to grit my teeth.

"What are you doing?"

"Putting your bra on." Once that's done and her nipples aren't in my face anymore, I relax as she arranges her top over the bra.

"What now?"

"Now we're going to go upstairs, and I'm going to prepare a bath for you. Which you will take alone, so you can relax and sleep. I'm sticking to that plan."

"I'm leaving tomorrow for the week. We're moving filming to L.A. until the set is rebuilt." She bats her eyelashes, then kisses my cheeks, whispering, "Does that change your plans?"

"You're going to kill me, woman."

CHAPTER FIFTEEN

Clara

I have no memory of getting upstairs, but then I do tell Blake I want to take a quick shower—alone. When I emerge, Blake is standing in my bedroom, naked. My mouth dries as I take him in, and I keep my towel safely around me until I reach the bed. Crawling backwards on the bed, I peel away the towel.

I can't wait to trace every ridge on his stomach and those oblique muscles with my tongue. He's watching me with an expression of pure male want, stroking himself while his eyes scan me, and lust shoots through me. He's scorching hot for me.

"Just so you know, tonight I'm going to take my time with you. I won't leave any inch of you undiscovered."

I swallow. Old fears rush in and I bite the inside of my cheek, searching for the right words. "Can we turn the lights off?"

Blake jerks his head back in surprise. "If it makes you comfortable, of course."

I nod and he switches the light off, then joins me on the bed, lounging next to me, propping his head in his hand.

"Clara, I know I'm so hard that I can barely see straight, but if you want to wait, or you've just changed your mind, tell me. We'll still be friends and neighbors."

I appreciate this more than he can know. But I have to open up—it's preferable to Blake thinking I don't want him. Because I do. Desperately.

"I have some marks on my back."

"Marks?"

"Yeah, scars."

For all my bravado, the first time always makes me nervous. It seems to be worse with Blake, which is ridiculous because I trust him more than anyone I've been with. But maybe especially because of that, I want him to *really* like me, to hopefully accept all parts of me.

"Want to tell me what happened?"

"One of the kids at the group home did a prank. He mixed acid in my shower gel."

Blake's body goes rigid next to me.

"I was super lucky that I accidentally hit the bottle and the contents spilled onto my back first."

"That was no prank."

Right, time to lay it all out. "No, it was an attempt to intimidate me. One of the older kids, Hank, bullied all the younger ones. He bit a five-year-old badly, then threatened everyone not to tell on him. I told on him. That was his revenge."

Hank was the resident bully at the group home. The shrink who sometimes came by the group home tried to explain that some kids took out the hurt of being abandoned by lashing out at others. But I couldn't be understanding, hard as I tried. No matter his background, he'd *made the choice* to hurt others. He kept making that choice. There was no excuse for that.

"Are you hurting?"

"No, it happened almost twenty years ago. It doesn't hurt, just looks a bit alien. But if I'm on my back, you can only see my good parts, and you can't accidentally touch anything alien."

Blake's gaze turns hard. Even with only the moonlight highlighting him, I can see the change. "Let me make one thing clear. I don't want you to hide any part of yourself from me, Clara. Ever."

He moves closer, almost half over me, and the skin-on-skin contact fires me up.

"I don't want you to feel you have to hide from me," he continues softly, trailing his mouth to my ear, then down my neck. When he nibbles at the hollow of my neck, I inhale sharply.

"I wasn't hiding, just...okay, I was hiding." Gathering my courage around me, I add, "But not anymore. Do you want to turn on the lights?"

"Don't do it for me. Only if you want to."

"Those are some fine muscles you have there, Bennett. I want to lick up every one of those excellent lines. It'd be a pity not to admire them at the same time."

Blake moves to the light switch and back so fast I have to bite back a smile. Once he's in bed, I climb over him, intending to make good on my promise. I start with his pecs, slowly working my way down licking, and touching and licking some more. Blake grips my hair, pressing his finger pads slightly against my scalp. When I lick his erection from the tip to the base, he jolts into a sitting position, pulling me right into his lap. I land with my opening right above his pelvic bone. I shudder, because my clit got a good shake in the process too. I'm dripping, which he can feel.

"Your turn."

"But I wasn't done."

"If you continue, I'll lose control, and I promised I'd take my time. I don't break my promises.

He lays me on my back, climbing over me, and sweet heavens, the things he does to me. His mouth is everywhere, as are his hands. On my breasts, sucking my nipples—twisting my them, just enough that there is no pain, just pleasure. He descends all the way to my navel, then lower still, completely ignoring my soaked slit. The bastard. He makes it all the way down to my ankles before going back up, kissing inch by inch. I'm ready to break out of my skin, but I can tell he isn't done.

He's right above me when he commands, "Turn over."

I'm so turned on and I trust him so deeply that I do as he says the very next second, fighting the age-old fear of rejection, drowning the self-doubt. I'm completely still as I lie on my stomach, listening.

I'm waiting for him to say something, but instead he does something completely different. He kisses me right there, on that skin that is proof of less happier years. The only part of me I felt compelled to keep out of sight. He touches and kisses, and not only accepts that part of me but embraces it. Soon he moves to other parts, and as he kisses up my spine, my limbs relax, every last wisp of nervousness melting.

He pulls away, parting my legs. Anticipation courses through me, and I turn slightly so I can see what he's up to.

"Don't turn. Don't look. Just feel." His voice is so strong and commanding; it sends a white-hot tingle right to my clit. I rest my head back on the pillow, simply giving in to him.

Blake parts my thighs wide, settles between them. He splays his hands on my butt, his thumbs pressing my folds together, his fingers pushing my ass cheeks together. When he swipes his tongue long and hard across the crack, my legs stiffen and my tummy contracts. I press my forehead against the pillow, breathing in through my nose. Then he parts my folds and ass cheeks, licking the space in between.

"Blaaaaaaaaaaaake." Pleasure radiates through me like a shock to my system. It's unlike anything I've felt before. He moves his hands under my pelvis, lifting me slightly so he can kiss better. With every swipe of his tongue, he brings me closer to the edge, until it feels like every nerve ending in my body is wired to my clit.

I realize I pushed the pillow away at some point and am now pressing my forehead against the mattress, fisting the bedsheet. I've never been on display like this. The sheer intimacy of this is too much. I'm going to implode if he doesn't fill me soon. The need, the *ache* for him is unbearable.

"Blake, please."

"I need to get you wet and ready, Clara."

The ache intensifies upon hearing his voice. It's in a lower octave than usual, husky and primal.

"I am ready! Please. I need you inside me."

I'm relieved when the mattress shifts.

"Condom," he says on a groan, in a tone that clearly indicates he forgot to bring any.

I have a small pack—housewarming gift from Penny. I reach for the nightstand, opening the drawer and retrieving the package, which I then hand to him.

I tremble with anticipation while I hear him rip it open, then the softer sound indicating he's rolling on the condom.

Then he lounges over me, propping his knees on the outside of my thighs, pressing my legs together. The tip of his erection is pressing up and down my entrance, and if I thought the ache was unbearable before, it's killing me now. If I could part my legs, he'd slide right into me, but I can't because his granite thighs are pressing mine together. He has the control. It's delicious and terrifying at the same time.

When he finally pushes just the tip inside me,

I hold my breath. Then he slides in, inch by inch, and I let out a loud, guttural moan. He feels amazing inside me. Amazing and huge, and he isn't even all in.

"Oh God!" Blake stills, breathing against the back of my neck. And then he pushes all the way in, and all my muscles contract.

"You're so snug and warm. You feel amazing, Clara."

My heart soars. I want this to be as out-of-this-world good for him as it is for me. He slides in and out, with measured strokes. Every time he pulls back, I feel a sense of loss, but he quickly pushes back in, filling me again. I close my eyes, overcome by sensation. Blake intertwines one hand with mine and slides the other one between me and the mattress, finding my tender spot. A sound between a moan and a whimper escapes my lips as tremors take over my entire body. I succumb to all the sinful sensations as our frantic breaths and cries fill the room. Blake moves furiously now, pinning me against the mattress, and I'm soaking in all his passion and desire.

I come hard, riding the wave of my orgasm right until he joins me too.

Afterward, he stays on top of me for a long while, and as our breaths regain a regular rhythm, I can't help thinking that this didn't feel like just sex, or fun.

It felt like everything.

CHAPTER SIXTEEN

Clara

"I need to shower," I say after a while. We're still entangled in each other's arms.

"So do I. How about we do it together?" He wiggles his eyebrows, and I can't help a grin.

"You're shameless."

"You have a dirty mind, Clara."

"So you weren't thinking about doing wicked things to me in the shower?" I pout.

"Nah, or you'll be sore tomorrow. I'm just going to help you clean up."

"Fine, let's go clean up, Bennett."

We walk to the shower holding hands, and for some reason this feels incredibly intimate. Blake starts the water, testing the temperature by bringing his hand in front of the spray every few seconds, only letting me in when it's warm enough. I love this protective side of him.

He reaches for my shower gel and sniffs through the open lid. I giggle when he recoils. "Right, no shower gel for me."

"But you always say you like how I smell."

"Yeah, I like it on *you*."

I know it smells too girly, peach and honey. When I hold out my palm for Blake to pour in it, he shakes his head.

"I'm cleaning you."

"I thought you were just going to help me out in a few spots."

"You need my help everywhere," he says seriously.

"You decided that for me, huh?"

"Yeah. Anything against it?"

"Not at all." I lean back against the cold tiles. "I'm all yours."

Blake's eyes flash as he pours shower gel in his hands, rubs his palms together to warm it up, then gets to work. I have to give it to him; he's perfectly composed as he slides his hands all over my body. He seems to particularly favor my breasts and slit, the bastard. I'm so turned on I want to climb him on the spot.

I barely register when he turns me around, soaping my back too. All of my back, including the scars. I tighten up a bit, then relax again. It's okay; this is Blake. I trust him, and I love his touch. After the warm spray washes away the soap, he turns the water off and hugs me from behind, wrapping his arms around me, resting his mouth in the nook of my neck. It feels good, and innocent... right up until I press my ass into him and feel his rock-hard erection.

"Just ignore it," Blake says.

"But I don't want to. I want to kiss it, lick it. In general thank it for the fabulous job it's done." I turn around, looking up at him. "Just putting it out there, but I won't go to sleep tonight. I have to get up in three hours anyway. Now, I have a few ideas about how we could fill those hours...."

"Are you trying to corrupt me?"

"Is it working?"

"I don't want you to be sore tomorrow."

"Clearly I need to sharpen my temptation skills."

"You're killing me, Clara. Let's get out of this shower and put some clothes on."

"Then what?"

"Then I'm going to take care of you."

I did not expect this comeback. He takes my hand again as he leads us back to the room. I slip into a robe, and Blake puts on his boxers. He looks like an underwear model, with his six-pack and wet hair. I can imagine what an uproar he's causing every time he goes to the beach. Women are probably vying for him. A pang of jealousy shoots through me, making my heart squeeze. I'm being silly, and I'm determined not to waste any second worrying. I have much better things to do until I leave. I want to get my fill of all things Blake: his smile, his touch, his humor. I'm going to miss him, and that's ridiculous, because I will only be gone for five days.

"I need to pack."

"Hell, and I thought *I* did last-minute packing."

"Not my fault. I was going to do that before going to bed, but then someone bulldozed over my plans." I elbow him, pointing to the suitcase resting on top of the dresser. "Can you get that for me?"

"Sure."

I lean against the wall, tightening my robe. Blake walks to the dresser, and he's so tall that he can easily reach the suitcase by extending one arm. The expanse of his back is ripped and as I look closely, I notice a few scratches on his shoulder blades, four on each one. I don't remember doing that. Just as I don't remember biting him, but there's a definite mark on his bicep as he flexes it to retrieve the suitcase. Heavens, what a sight this is. I should store more of my belongings at that level, ask him to reach for them. The movement makes good use of quite a few muscle groups. It's a good workout for him, and a delectable sight for my eyes.

Totally a win-win situation.

He lowers the suitcase and catches me gazing at him.

"See anything you like?"

Eh, what's a girl to do when she's caught spying? Deny or come forward. I decide on the latter, and if I'm going to own up to it, I'm going to be thorough about it.

"Make that everything. You're handy to keep around. You can assemble furniture and are tall enough to remove objects without needing an extra chair."

"That list is far from exhaustive."

"Forgot to mention your mad orgasm skills."

"That's my Clara," he declares with a grin, and

my heart soars.

Winking, he lifts the suitcase, placing it at the foot of the bed. I unhitch myself from the wall, walking to the dresser. Opening the drawers, I intend to inspect the contents so I can decide what to take with me, but I don't have a chance. Blake hooks an arm around my waist, sweeps my hair to one side, and places tiny kisses on my neck.

"You're the one corrupting me now."

"And you're enjoying it."

"I'm never going to be ready on time like this."

"Maybe that's my plan, so I can keep you here with me."

His tone is playful and raw in equal measures. I wonder if I picked up on the rawness because he's more open, or if because of everything we experienced tonight, I feel closer to him. He spins me around until I face him.

He drags his knuckles down my cheek, resting his hand on my neck, splaying his fingers wide.

"You're not just a distraction to me. I want you to know that."

I swallow in surprise, because I hadn't pegged Blake as the type to talk so openly about this.

"Thank you for being so open. You're not a distraction either, but I'm not expecting anything. I want you to know that."

"What does that mean?"

"That I don't need a label on this. I know I gave a big speech when I moved in about what I want, but I just need you. No labels."

Neither of us says it out loud, but I strongly suspect that whatever this is between us will come to a natural end by the time I move out. My heart crumbles a bit at the thought.

"Anything you want."

Well, that's a dangerous statement to make. What I want is to dote on him, learn all the things he likes, then do them just to see him happy. *Maybe he could love me,* a hopeful voice supplies somewhere in the recess of my mind. I swallow hard, chasing that silly thought away.

Blake smiles and touches his nose to mine in an Eskimo kiss. "Now, let's get you ready."

I make quick work of packing. After laying out my outfit for the road and stuffing the bag of toiletries in the suitcase, I zip it up.

"Done?"

"Yeah."

"Good. Now let's get some breakfast into you."

"I don't have anything in my fridge."

"I have some eggs and toast. I'll be right back."

My surprise must have registered on my face because he adds, "Told you I'll take care of you."

He kisses the tip of my nose again, then slips into his jeans and leaves the apartment. I barely have time to search for a pan and place it on the stove when he returns, a box of six eggs in one hand, bread in the other. I reach for the eggs, but he shakes his head.

"I'm making you breakfast."

"You can cook?"

"No, but I make a mean sunny side up."

I laugh. "That's a lifesaving skill right there."

As I watch him cook for me, I can barely contain my happiness. It might seem a small thing to some, but not to me. I hover around him, under the guise of helping him—I'm not—but I want to be as close to him as possible, touch him without being obvious. The kitchen is small, after all.

"You either have a problem with calculating the distance, or you're looking for any opportunity to feel me up."

I bat my eyelashes at him. "Guilty."

"Lucky for you, I'm an enabler. Feel me up all you want."

Well, what's a girl to do when she's given free reign? Take advantage and do so thoroughly. So while Blake busies himself with the eggs—which take a suspiciously long time, so I think they're going to be burnt to a crisp when all is said and done—I move my hands over his shoulder blades, kissing in between, then trace his spine with my mouth.

Then I step back and admire him. What I wouldn't give to snap some photos of him. I deleted those pics I took when I moved in because I know enough of the cloud and how the wrong pics could fall into the wrong hands by mistake (and anyway, they are imprinted on my retinas, no need for physical evidence).

"Eggs are ready," he announces, snapping me out of my thoughts. I do my best to school my expression so I don't give away my dirty daydreams.

Of course, Blake catches on. "Where were you just now?"

"Making a to-do list for work."

"You're a terrible liar. You had a pervy look on your face."

"Takes one to know one."

"Exactly. And you cannot out-perv me, Clara. So fess up."

Licking my lips, I try to strategize my next steps. As usual, honesty seems the best policy. But I also can't help wondering what he'd do to coax an admission out of me. I decide to find out.

"What if I don't?"

He steps away from the stove, and I peek in the pan. The eggs are not at all burnt. I really need to give him more credit.

When he cages me in against the wall, parting my legs with his knee, kissing up my neck, I barely stifle a laugh.

He pulls back. "What?

"I knew you'd do this. Unleash your seductive techniques on me to coax out a confession. See? I can out-perv you," I declare proudly, after which I proceed to tell him everything.

***

At three o'clock sharp, we leave the house.

Blake carries my suitcase to the car, placing it safely in the trunk while I type the destination address in the navigation system. I fight a yawn, dreading the trip. I had two coffees already with my breakfast, but I'm still tired. I dislike driving in the dark, but the sun will rise in two hours.

"You should've slept tonight," Blake says, startling me. I didn't see him join me. He's leaning against the open door, scrutinizing me. I fight harder to stifle a yawn.

"Nah, I'll stop on the road to buy another coffee. I'll manage to keep my eyes open until then."

"Don't you have an anti-sleep alarm? It makes loud noises when you veer off your track."

I've never heard of such a thing. Men and cars.

"Nope."

"I'm buying you one."

"You will do no such thing."

"I wasn't asking." He glares at me.

I glare back, unable to decide if he's being obnoxious or endearing. Upon seeing his glare melt into a concerned expression, I decide on the latter. He lowers himself until he's on my level and kisses me with unexpected heat. I wasn't aware you could infuse so much passion into a short kiss, but I have to give it to Blake—he's the master of passion no matter if he has to beguile me with it in small or large doses. The kiss jolts me awake. Maybe I should just ask him to join me, kiss me from time to time. That would guarantee I'll be awake, no coffee needed.

"Text me when you stop for gas and then when you arrive, so I know you're safe."

"You'll be sleeping."

"No, I won't. I'll be worrying."

I melt. I can't help it. Is it wrong that I like having someone worrying about me? If I'm wrong, I don't want to be right. I like being doted on, and that is exactly what he's doing. I can't believe this is my life. However long this lasts, I'm determined to enjoy every minute of it.

CHAPTER SEVENTEEN

Clara

"Let's call it a day, everyone!"

I haven't heard sweeter words in my life. It's been a long, long day, and I can't wait to crawl in my bed and sleep for twenty-four hours straight. Just kidding. I can only get in six hours of sleep before the mayhem begins again tomorrow.

I'm about to leave the set to head to the hotel when Quentin catches up to me.

"Clara! Have you seen the ratings?" he asks.

"Yes," I say proudly. "We ticked up nicely."

"Have you seen the jump *S&S* had?"

Oh snap. I know what's coming. *S&S* is a show on a rival network, and they've been featured on, wait for it—

"*Our Picks* featured them the week before. Talked again to Shepperd. All he wants is a rumor. He can work with that on *We See You*. In exchange, he'll shoo us in on *Our Picks*. He's hoping on some dirt on Sebastian Bennett—cheating would be best—but dirt on any of them will do."

I rub my hands down my face, itching to curl

my hands around his thick neck, give him a good shake.

Quentin is a bully, and if there is one thing I know, it's that bullies only pull back when they feel the other party is more powerful. They pounce on the weak. Obviously though, since he's my boss, I can't give him a piece of my mind, but I can make my values clear.

"Quentin, you're barking up the wrong tree. Stop with this madness. This is not who I am. I don't sell people out for ratings, and I never will. Frankly, I'm not comfortable with—"

"Don't care what you're comfortable with. All I care about is ratings. You should too, if you know what's good for you."

One of the cameramen walks up to him, asking about a take, and I leave, wondering if owning an apartment really is worth having this imbecile breathe down my neck every day.

I trudge away to the hotel, feeling like I'm sleepwalking. This is the second day on the L.A. set, but I haven't had time to sleep in, and the night I spent awake with Blake is catching up to me.

My hotel room is very small and only contains the basics, but I spend such a short time inside that it doesn't bother me. I discard my clothes, hop in the shower, then crawl into bed, all in less than ten minutes. Only when my head hits the pillow do I register something. I bolt upright in bed, turning on the light. My eyes zero in on the package lying on the small table next to the door.

That's when I remember that one of the assistants told me I'd received a package today and the receptionist brought it to my room. I hadn't been paying attention because I was focusing on an e-mail, and then I forgot altogether. Though I desperately need the sleep, there's no way I'll wait until tomorrow to open it.

I love receiving things, always feel like a kid on Christmas morning, so I venture out of the bed, shuddering. I'm naked, and it's chilly, so I take the package back to bed. There's no information as to who sent it, but that doesn't dampen my excitement in the slightest. I unpack with as much euphoria as Will attacked his presents on his birthday. Inside I discover a... gadget? Something electronic for sure. I pick up the accompanying handbook and my face cracks into a grin. An anti-sleep system for my car.

Blake sent this. I can barely resist texting him, but it's late and he could be asleep. I'll call tomorrow. I can't believe he's so sweet. His gesture warms me up, filling me with a fuzzy feeling. Aaaah, what's this man doing to me?

I startle when my ringtone fills the room, then make a grab for my phone. The one and only Blake Bennett is calling. I answer immediately.

"Hey! I was just thinking about you."

"Great minds think alike." There's background noise on his end, so he's working, as I expected.

"Thank you for the alarm."

"For a safe trip back home. Promise you'll use

it."

"Of course. I wish you were here," I say in a small voice, hoping it doesn't come across as needy. I have no idea what the rules are for "no labels". Then I break into a long yawn. "I need to sleep, I'm still exhausted."

"Oh, sweetness, you wouldn't be getting much sleep if I were there."

"Really? And why is that?"

"I couldn't keep my hands and mouth off you."

"You did a pretty good job not touching me two nights ago."

"Yeah, I was being a gentleman, and I used all my dose of gentlemanly that night."

Another yawn takes me by surprise, but I stifle it, not quite ready to say good night. I love talking to him. It doesn't hurt that his voice is pure sexiness. I hadn't realized that until now, possibly because when we're in the same room, I'm too busy drinking in his appearance to pay special attention to his voice. I really need to work on my distributive attention.

"Are you sore?" His voice is lower and huskier now. So damn sexy.

"A bit but in a good way. In a way that makes me want more."

"Clara...." He groans softly, and I bite down on my lip.

OhGodOhGodOhGod!

My name in his mouth sounds almost sinful,

and I haven't even really provoked him. I wonder what he'll sound like if I do, and settle on immediately finding out. Don't leave for tomorrow what you can do today and all that.

"I'm naked in my bed."

"I'm working."

"What's one thing got to do with the other?"

"I need to concentrate. If I have an image of you naked in my mind, I'm going to wreak havoc. Tell me you made that up."

"Fine! I'm wearing period panties and a baggy T-shirt."

"You really are naked, aren't you?" he sounds defeated.

"Yup."

"I'm a dead man."

I open my mouth but shut it again when I hear a voice calling to him from his background. "Blake, come on! Don't leave a girl waiting."

I feel my insides tighten because I don't recognize that voice. Certainly not one of his sisters. Oh man, I have to find a way to stop panicking all the time.

"I'll leave you to get back to work."

"I have a bachelorette party here. Half the women are drunk already."

"Did they hire a stripper too?"

"Over my dead body will I have strippers in my bars."

"Blake! Come on. We need more tequila," yet another woman's voice calls from his end of the line.

Many customers at the bar call him by his name. He has this approachable quality to him that instantly pulls you in, makes you feel like you've known him for ages. I've watched him with customers, and socializing comes easy to him. Almost as easy as it takes actors to slip into their characters. Only Blake isn't acting. He's genuinely a warm and funny person, and I can't get enough of him.

"Go back to the customers," I urge.

"Talk to you tomorrow? I like hearing your voice."

Those simple words fill me with joy and giddiness.

"Sure. Good night, Blake."

"Good night."

I click off the phone, placing it on the floor next to my bed. Ugh, my alarm is going to ring in five hours. But still, even though I know I should go to sleep, I allow myself a few minutes to bask in my giddiness. I can't wait to return home and pepper him with kisses, climb in his lap. I am going to make Blake the happiest man. Yes, I am. He deserves it, and ahem, *maybe* he'll even fall in love with me.

I sigh happily into my pillow, even though I should know better than to hope like a romantic fool.

CHAPTER EIGHTEEN

Blake

"Sinclair agreed to our terms," I inform Alice over the phone while I hurry up toward Ghirardelli Square, where I'm meeting Summer and Daniel.

"Thank you, thank you, thank you!" Alice's shrill voice makes me wince.

"Wow, easier on the enthusiasm, sister, or my ear will be ringing until our next call."

"I didn't make any headway on the phone, and I was sure we were going to lose him. Thank you for going to him in person."

"Well, I'm here to save the day."

"I'm so lucky I can count on you."

"Of course you can."

The business is running like a well-oiled machine, and I'm damn proud of it, but I can't turn my mind off from always thinking about ways to improve processes, cutting costs without lowering quality or squeezing our partners dry. I don't need more money. I have enough money. Too much of it, actually. More than one person would ever need. But I discovered a few years ago that there is a thrill to building businesses and making them thrive. I've always had too much energy. In my early twenties, I wasted it on parties and hanging around with people who weren't worth my time, much less my energy or affection. Then I got my head out of my ass, focused more on the family and on building something.

"You're meeting Summer now, right?"

"Yep. Daniel too."

"Can you do me a favor and put on your best entertainment show for her?"

"What happened?"

"Love troubles. Another douchebag playing with her. But don't tell her I said anything."

Just like that, I take my business hat off, slipping into brother mode.

"What? She's dating? Who do I have to kill?" Here's the thing: Logan is in *intense* mode all the time, and Christopher and Max are on the *relaxed* end of the spectrum. I'm way more balanced. But when someone threatens to hurt my family, I switch to motherfucking *intense* in five seconds flat.

"Don't be dramatic."

I can practically hear her rolling her eyes. "Okay, I'll settle for maiming."

"I have to go now, but just cheer her up, please?"

"Deal."

I arrive at our meeting point in Ghirardelli Square at the same time as Daniel. Summer is already at a booth, inspecting some gigantic red flower that looks like the stuff of kids' nightmares. A cross between a carnivorous plant and the boogeyman.

Come to think of it, *I* will probably have nightmares because of it.

Summer wants to plant some new stuff in her yard, and she asked Daniel and me to come here with her today to look at the temporary pop-up flower market and help carry the supplies. Considering the amount of planning and scheduling it takes to see my own family these days, I jump at any occasion, even when I'm practically being used as a flower mule. Mid-June strikes me as an odd period to plant flowers, but it's not like I know anything on the subject.

"Hello, fellow Bennetts," I greet.

Summer kisses my cheek, then shows me her list. Correction. Flower, pots, earth, and fertilizer mule.

"Thank you both so much for helping me," Summer says. "I'm buying you drinks for this."

"Excellent!" Daniel eyes her list with a raised eyebrow. "Can we start with that?"

"We'd better. You're gonna need sustenance. There's a booth with snacks and drinks over there." She elbows us playfully, and then we head toward the booth. Five minutes later, sodas in hand, Daniel asks me, "You going to Emma's birthday?"

"Nah, too many people I don't want to see there."

"Same for me."

Emma's cousin was the one who wanted to sell the details I told her about Pippa's divorce to the press. Emma did assure me she had no idea, but by that time, I didn't believe any of them anymore, so I stepped way back. That's what you do when you can't tell the true friends from the fake ones. Here's the thing though, always keeping your guard up is exhausting, not to mention lonely as hell. Daniel has always been the more distrustful of the two of us, kept his guard up more than I did.

"Let's make a tour and see what we find from my list," Summer suggests.

The flower market is loud and busy: vendors pulling you aside, trying to sell their merchandise; buyers questioning and negotiating. Summer keeps her list close, checking off the items she finds.

"How's the gallery?" Daniel asks her.

"We have a new Picasso collection this month. Attracting quite the crowd."

Daniel raises his eyebrows, clearly picking up something's wrong. Usually, when Summer talks about the gallery, she goes on forever. I don't think Alice clued him in, though.

"Can I ask you two something? And you'll answer honestly?" Summer asks, standing straighter.

"Sure," Daniel answers.

"Do I give off non-dating vibes? I mean, is it something I do that makes men think, *'oh, this one's just for fucking?'*"

"What?" Daniel blinks. Yeah, Alice clearly didn't clue him in.

"Summer!"

"Sorry if the word *"fucking"* offends your brotherly ears, but I need some perspective."

Daniel and I exchange a look.

"Of course you don't give off any vibes—" Daniel begins, but Summer holds up her hand.

"I asked for the truth."

Well, since she asked.

"You wear your heart on your sleeve," I explain. "And you see everything through rose-colored glasses."

"So what you're saying is I should be bitter and mistrustful?" she asks, stricken.

"No, just...more careful."

"So it is my fault," she says miserably.

"What? No, I didn't mean that."

Daniel groans. "Fantastic job, Blake."

"Come on, help me out here." I place one hand on Summer's shoulder. "It's not your fault that a douchebag played you."

"Did you talk to Alice?" She narrows her eyes to slits.

I'm really winning this, but I give it a shot, though I can never lie to Summer. "No."

"Liar."

Daniel gestures with his head toward an empty space between two booths, and we move the party there because we're standing in everyone's way.

"Can someone fill me in?" Daniel asks. "I feel like I'm missing half the conversation."

"In a nutshell, my dating life's a joke."

"Just putting it out there, but if you give us his name and address, we'll happily deck him," I offer, only half-joking.

"You know, brotherly duty and all," Daniel adds.

She shakes her head. "You both sound like Logan!"

I theatrically clutch my heart.

"No need to insult us," Daniel adds, faking offense.

"So, no glaring signs that I'm unlovable?" she insists. To my shock, I realize she's serious.

"Summer Bennett, you're the most lovable person I know."

"You say that because I'm your sister."

"Obviously. But that doesn't make it less true."

Daniel nods. "If you need help vetoing any candidates in the future, I'm at your service."

"Your Logan impression is getting scarily accurate. Come on, let's get started with the shopping or I'll never be done with it."

Fifteen minutes later, the three of us head to her car, arms loaded. This is just the first round. Summer is barely halfway through the list.

"You're really going to wear us out, huh?" I ask on the way back to the market.

"Yep. That's why I asked you to come."

"Ah, and I thought it was just an excuse because you were missing us," Daniel says.

I scan the market again. Clara would love it here. Pity the market will close before she returns. Then an idea strikes me. If I can't bring Clara to the market, I can bring the market to Clara. Sort of. I can buy her...what? I don't know what her favorite flowers or plants are, but I know she likes them. She said something about wanting flowers on the balcony.

"Summer, do you know what plants or flowers Clara likes? She said she wants some for the balcony, but she didn't get around to buying any."

She cocks her head in my direction so fast I think I hear her neck give a little snap.

"You're buying her flowers? Oh, Blake, you're finally, finally on the right track." She pokes my chest over the heart area. "And of course I know what her favorites are. What kind of matchmaker would I be if I didn't? I've done my homework."

"Good, because I have a plan, and I need your help."

I miss Clara. I haven't realized how used I am to knowing she's next door. Somewhere at the back of my mind nags the thought that her condo building will be ready in a few weeks, but I ignore it, focusing on the *now*. And the now includes a truckload of flowers. I can't wait for Clara to return and see what I've been up to.

More than once, I've been thinking about her scars. I knew she grew up in a group home, but I haven't had a real sense of the hardships she's been through. She's brave and bold, and I haven't met anyone like her. I have the overwhelming need to make sure she never goes through hardships again. Totally normal, right?

Summer talks our ears off about Clara while

we shop for her, and she's slowly reverting to her usual cheerful self.

"Shit! It's getting late," Summer exclaims when we carry the last load to her car. "I'm meeting Caroline later, by the way." She wiggles her eyebrows at Daniel.

"How is she?" I ask. "Didn't have time to talk to her too much at the wedding."

Daniel throws me a look that says, *You're supposed to have my back.*

Whenever our sisters insinuate that Daniel and Caroline should try dating again, I change the subject, even though I actually think the girls are right. Regardless, I usually have his back, twin bond and all that. But right now, I'm testing a theory. Also, payback for not having my back at the ranch.

"She's great. She talked me into taking kickboxing lessons with her. I went twice. It's actually fun," Summer says. "It's good for anger release and keeps our booty in shape. Win-win. I tried to rope Pippa into it too, but...."

"Bribe her with cupcakes," Daniel suggests.

"Tried. Failed. But Caroline's a pro at it. She's been doing it for a year, and she looks better than ever." She bats her eyelashes at Daniel. "Don't you think?"

"She's always looked great," he answers. When Summer ducks in her trunk with a satisfied smile, rearranging some of the plants, Daniel holds up his hands as if saying, *Need some help here.*

He's out of luck today because my theory is

right. If Summer's busy masterminding, she's gonna stop thinking about that douchebag, for now at least. I'm going to run this tactic into the ground, even if it means throwing both Daniel and me under the bus.

"Anyway, she's dating this gorgeous instructor," she says. "They're quite serious."

Daniel has a murderous expression. "What? She was alone at the wedding. When did she start dating him? How serious can it be if she didn't bring him to the wedding?"

"Yes!" Summer exclaims, straightening up, peeling away a leaf that caught in her hair, and grinning at Daniel from ear to ear.

It's official. Daniel's even more clueless than I am. He just dug his own grave.

"I made him up. To...err... check your level of interest."

Once again, I marvel at my sisters' talent to get what they want. The tactic is deceptively simple: subtract a helpful brother—me—add a seemingly innocent remark that's sure to bring out a reaction. Simple and brilliant, but no one except Pippa and Summer can pull it off.

My brother groans. Summer perks up, rubbing her hands in excitement. She'll be plotting Daniel's downfall instead of drowning in self-doubt because of her dating disaster. My job here is done.

CHAPTER NINETEEN

Clara

The week on set is riddled with mishaps, yet we still somehow managed to finish two hours before the deadline—Thursday at midnight. I briefly consider driving back to San Francisco the same night. I miss my bed, and a certain hot and handsome neighbor who has become so much more than a neighbor. In the end, I decide to stay the night and drive back in the morning. It's too dangerous. I'm tired, and even with Blake's anti-sleep alarm, I won't risk it.

I drive off early the next morning and wait until it's eight o'clock to call Blake. I'm just about to dial his number when my phone lights up with an incoming call from him.

"Hey! I was just about to call you."

"When will you be in town?"

Sighing, I tighten my grip on the wheel. His voice is a little rough, like he just woke up, and my insides squeeze at the sound of it. How can his voice alone affect me so much? I mean, the man's voice is sexy as all get-out, but it's still a little ridiculous.

"Lunch, but I still have to go by the studio,

drop some things off, and send some e-mails. I'll probably be there the entire afternoon."

"Can you be ready at six?"

"Why?"

"We're going on a date."

I do a little happy dance in my seat, which probably looks crazy to anyone passing by, but I couldn't care less. A date with Blake Bennett. A date!

Since I am not well versed in the art of "no labels," I wasn't really sure how this would play out.

I clear my throat, trying to sound like this is no big deal. "When and where? Why didn't I know about this?"

"I was going to surprise you."

"No, no, no. I need a proper heads-up, so I can get ready."

"Let me get this straight. I can attack and seduce you in the middle of the night, but I have to give you a heads-up for a date?"

"Um...yes."

"That makes no sense."

I smile, imagining his expression. "So, where are we going?"

"Surprise."

"Blake, come on, I need clues so I know what to wear. Help a girl out. I don't want to stick out like a sore thumb."

"You're beautiful no matter what you wear, Clara."

Well dang. This man has a dangerous way with words. "We're going to have dinner. Nothing fancy.

I'll make reservations at eight."

"No way. The earliest I can be ready is nine."

"But you said you'll be done at the studio at six."

"So? I need to get ready."

"You need three hours? Will I recognize you?"

"I'm getting fancy, not undergoing plastic surgery."

"Okay, I'll make reservations at nine thirty. I can't wait to see you."

My chest fills with warmth. "Me too."

After clicking off, I mentally go through the dresses I own. I don't want to barely make the cut. I want Blake to be proud with me on his arm.

***

Blake isn't in his apartment when I arrive at home, which is just as good, because I know him. He'd try to sneak in, and my plan is for him to see the full package at the end. It sort of works. I'm almost done when I step out of the bathroom, hastily looking around for some hairpins.

Blake is on the balcony, pacing in front of the French doors. He notices me a split second later and stops midstride, the corners of his mouth lifting up.

And that smile? I'd do anything for it. Anything.

I've made a plan that if he tried to snoop from the balcony, I'd tease him, locking the door and keeping him outside. But the moment I see him, all those plans seem extremely foolish. I need to touch him, kiss him, laugh with him. And I can't wait even one second longer. I head straight to the French doors, open them, and we collide in a hot and heavy kiss. Luckily, I haven't applied lipstick yet.

When I pull away, I'm breathless.

"Hi," Blake says. His hand is around my waist, keeping me flush against him.

"Hi back." I look up at him, drinking him in. The man is seriously gorgeous. Everything from the set of his jaw, the width of his shoulders, and the muscles lacing his arms scream masculinity. It oozes off him, making me lose my train of thought. He's leaning lightly over me, and there is something inherently domineering about his pose. Licking my lips, I feel myself liquefy in his arms. I take a step back to clear my mind and twirl around, feeling like a princess in my dress.

"What do you think?"

"I think I can't wait to get that dress off you."

My breath catches as he rakes his gaze over me. My God, he can be intense. Still, I need to make something clear before I let him have his wicked way with me—fingers crossed for *very* wicked.

I move my forefinger right in front of his nose, signaling no. "Careful. This belongs to my best friend, Penny. She loaned it to me a while ago. I have to return it intact."

"I can buy her a new one if I damage this one."

Well, well, isn't he cheeky. I start working on a sassy reply—my usual sass won't cut it; Blake requires I up my standards—but then I look beyond his shape, to the balcony outside. Mouth agape, I rush past him to the French doors, taking in the sight. Pots hang from the railing, and they're chock-full of flowers.

"Wow! What happened here?" I ask Blake, who joins me outside.

"Do you like it?"

"Of course! I love it. Dahlias are my favorite flowers. Oh, and hydrangeas. I love them."

"I know."

This catches me off guard, and I slice a glance at him. "You do?"

"Summer told me. She helped me with all this. I have a number of talents, but I don't have a green thumb, or any clue about flowers. I know you wanted to do this but didn't have time, so Summer and I did it for you."

Something stirs inside me. He's being very sweet and attentive, more than anyone has been with me. I could get used to this, and that's dangerous.

"Thank you," I say simply, proud that my voice is even.

Out of the corner of my eye, I see that Blake is watching me intensely. Being the object of his attention is messing with my senses.

"I missed you, Clara."

He tucks me into his side, kissing my temple, and my heart swells knowing he shares my feelings.

Hearing him say it first makes it easier to open up, my fears of coming across as clingy subsiding somewhat.

"I missed you too. So much!"

He wraps both arms around me, and we stay like that for several moments. Part of me had wondered if I'd built him up in my mind, but no. Being in his arms makes me feel wanted and safe, desired and respected. How can he do all this at the same time? More worryingly, how am I supposed to be without him once this runs its course? *Don't be silly, Clara.* I've been without a man for thirty years. But that was before Blake and all his deliciousness.

He's not helping my case by doing nice things for me. Doesn't he know that's my kryptonite? Obviously not, so I have to inform him. Silly man. He can't keep doing nice things for me, taking care of me, and not expect me to fall for him.

"You can't keep doing nice things for me, Blake. Why do you do it?"

He simply kisses the top of my head, hugging me tighter. "Because you're not used to it, and you should be. So I'm going to keep doing it."

"But—"

"It's not up for negotiation."

Ah, this damn man. He smiles, right before he kisses me hard. I find myself smiling back against his lips. Does he have any idea how blissfully happy he makes me? I want to do the same for him. But what can I give a man who already has everything?

Taking my hand, he leads me back inside.

Raising my hand to his lips, he kisses the back of it. I breathe in sharply, the contact zinging through me. Next thing I know, he closes the distance between us, hooking an arm around my waist, tracing the contour of my jaw with his other hand. He pushes me farther inside the apartment, kissing up my neck, my cheeks, my temple. Finally, he kisses my lips.

***

Blake

I've missed her skin, the scent, the warmth, all the things that make her Clara. Now that I have her back, I want to get my fill of her. When she laces her arms around my neck, I deepen the kiss, pressing myself against her. I'm hard, and if I'm not going to do something about it, I won't be able to get it together the entire evening.

"Shouldn't we go?" she whispers, but the corners of her mouth are up in a smile. She wants this as much as I do. I back her against the nearest wall.

"We should, but we won't. Not yet. I need to be inside you first, or I'll go crazy."

Her only response is tucking herself closer to me. I feel her hardened nipples against my chest, and nearly drive into her. But no, I need to get her ready first.

Looking her straight in the eyes, I bunch up her dress, until the fabric ends and I feel the skin of her thighs. I trail my fingers up, and then—*fuck me.*

She isn't wearing panties. I press my fingers against her opening and she drops her head back, moaning.

"You're not wearing underwear."

"I was going to put them on last."

She's wet, but I'll be fast and rough, so I need her drenched. Pressing the heel of my palm against her clit, I trail my fingers up and down each fold, coating myself in her wetness, coaxing a whimper out of her, then a moan. When I slide a finger inside her, she fists my shirt, closing her eyes. When I slide in the second one, she buries her face in my chest.

"Blake, fuck!"

My control nearly snaps. My pants feel like they're about to burst, that's how hard I am.

After inhaling deeply a few times, I wrap my other hand in her hair, keeping her forehead pressed against me while I drive my fingers in and out of her, the heel of my palm applying more and more pressure. She thrashes and whimpers, but I don't leave room for her to pull away. When I feel the first spasms around my fingers, I pull them out.

"No!" Her cry of protest is the sweetest thing. "Why did you…? I was about to…?"

She looks straight up at me, her eyes narrowed in accusation, her intent clear: if I don't give her an acceptable answer, I'll pay for it. I adore her fiery nature.

"You will climax, but only when I'm inside you. It will be more intense that way. I promise."

She tilts her head, as if considering this. "If you're not going to be inside me this very second, you'll be sorry."

I move my hand from the side of her head to her cheek, resting my thumb at the corner of her mouth.

"You don't make the rules, Clara. I do."

Dragging my thumb across her lower lip, I press it against the center, at its plumpest point. She opens her mouth, licking me. *Oh fuck.*

"This is going to be fast and quick, but when we get back, I'm going to take my time with you. I promise."

She nods, licking her lips as I cinch her dress up to her waist, then lift her up by her ass.

"Wrap your legs around me."

She does, and damn, I love how obedient she is when we're intimate. For all her sass and penchant for challenging me, she likes it that I take control in the bedroom...or against the wall.

She works on my belt, undoes the button of my pants and then the zipper, freeing my erection. She runs her palm up and down, and my balls tighten.

"Put both your arms around my neck."

She obeys immediately. Jesus! Her submission is a turn-on.

Breathing in and out through clenched teeth, I look down between us as I push forward. The length of my cock is pressing against her slit, my tip teasing her clit.

"Oh, Blake." She draws in a sharp breath, and I feel the goose bumps forming on her legs, her ass, which I'm cupping with both hands.

"One day, I want to be inside you without anything between us."

She inhales sharply. "I've ne—never done that."

"Then I'll be the first. When you're ready."

She shudders in my arms, nodding. I feel that primal instinct surge again at the thought that I'll give her that for the first time. I want to own her pleasure, her body, be the only one with the right to worship her. *The only one.* I want to earn this woman's trust, be worthy of her.

But for now, I secure her between the wall and me as I reach into my pocket, retrieving a condom—yeah, I foresaw we'd need to get our fill of each other before leaving. I hand it to her quickly before placing my hand back under her ass.

"Roll it on."

I'm pressing my fingers into her ass cheeks, parting them slightly, then pushing them together. She rips the package with shaky fingers, and I love that I can do this to her, make her tremble in anticipation. When she finishes rolling, I don't wait one more second.

I sink inside her, and it's all sweet and warm heaven. I'll never get enough of this, of her. Her inner walls are snug around me, and I'm losing my mind. She's gazing up at me, not just with lust, but also with adoration. That look is enough to bring me to my knees. What would it take for Clara to always look at me like this? To be worthy of that look?

I become faster, rougher, keeping my eyes trained on her the entire time, drinking in her pleasure and looking for signs that this is too wild for her. It is not. She takes it all, succumbs to it.

"Touch yourself," I command. She slips her hand between us, and it's a sight I want imprinted on my retinas. But at the same time, she grows a little stiff. My hunch is that she isn't used to touching herself if she's not alone.

"Relax. Enjoy this. You're so beautiful touching yourself, Clara."

I feel her relax in my arms, even as her inner muscles tighten around me. I drive inside her faster and faster, prepared to rock both our worlds. She's so tight against me, clenching again and again, that she can't possibly last much longer. I move from my heels to my toes and then back, needing to pace myself, to stave off my orgasm just a little longer, so she'll finish first.

When she cries out, rocking her hips into me desperately, I keep her close, pressed against me, climaxing too. This feels so impossibly good.

Even after we both ride out our orgasms, I'm not ready to let go of her. I'm beginning to think I never will want to. My fingers press against the skin of her sweet, round ass cheeks, and I rest my head in the crook of her neck, wanting to prolong this moment.

"Blake," she whispers softly. "We should—"

"Not yet. I want to be inside you just a little longer." I swallow, breathing her in, burying my nose in her skin. She must feel how much I need this—how much I need her, because she simply pulls me closer, keeping me in the circle of her arms. "Just a little longer, I promise."

I let her go after several minutes, and she rushes to the bathroom.

"My hair!" Clara exclaims. "I look like I've just—"

"Had a momentary slip of passion?"

"Is that what we're calling it?" she asks cheekily. I have the overwhelming need to stalk after her and kiss her long and good, but then we'd never make it out of the house, and I do have a lot planned for tonight. So, I wait for her to freshen up, only going in the bathroom after she comes out.

When I return to the living room, Clara is sitting on a chair, tying the straps of her shoes, looking dead sexy in them. She catches me looking at her.

"You like them?"

I take a moment to regain my composure, pushing away all the dirty thoughts, because if I voice them, she'd peg me for the pervert I am. She rises to her feet, strutting along the room, holding the hem of her dress up so I can see her shoes. The little vixen is testing my self-control. I close the distance, backing her against the wall—again. I have to stop doing that. Having her trapped between my arms, looking so sinfully sexy and ready to surrender, is messing with my mind. I hadn't realized just how starved I am for her, but I'll have to wait until we're back to get my fill of her.

"When we return, I'll keep you up in bed until morning. Until then, you're not allowed to tempt me. Do you understand?"

"You don't get it, do you? You're not the boss of me."

A sassy grin spreads on her beautiful face. Yeah... I'm a dead man.

CHAPTER TWENTY

Clara

Come on, Clara, you can do this!

It's seven o'clock on Saturday, and I'd usually be in my bed this early in the morning—that goes double now that there is a hot man in it. But I woke up half an hour ago to drink water and had a stroke of inspiration to finish an illustration. So, I slipped out of Blake's bed and took refuge in my apartment, working at the large desktop I have installed on my kitchen table. I'm at the last stage of the process with this one. I start all of them by putting pen to paper, and then I import the rough sketches to my computer and use various programs such as Illustrator and Photoshop to finish them.

From time to time, I lift my head to give my eyes a break, focusing them on the explosion of colors—pink, reds, yellows—on the balcony. The dahlias and hydrangeas love the end of June weather.

With a bit of luck, I'll finish this before Blake even wakes up.

"Early bird, huh?"

I jump out of my seat, heart thundering in my chest. "Jesus! Don't sneak up on me like that. You'll give me a heart attack." Blake is standing in the doorway to the balcony, which I left wide open. I glance at the clock. Damn, when did it become nine? No wonder he's awake.

"Another illustration ready?" he asks.

"I was just adding the final touches."

"My offer still stands. I can ask my contact to take a look at your work anytime."

"No, no, that's really not necessary."

Blake cocks a brow. "You don't want anyone to ever see your work?"

"I'd love to share it with others, but I'm not ready yet."

"When will you be?"

"I don't know." I shrug, turning off my desktop monitor. "Coffee?"

"Yes, please."

Minutes later, I hand him a cup. He pulls me in for a soft kiss, and I have the overwhelming desire to pinch myself to make sure I'm not dreaming about all of this. We've spent almost every night in the same bed since I returned from my trip last week.

"How did you sleep?" I ask.

"Someone slept on my arm the entire night. I woke up thinking it fell off."

I smile sheepishly. Yes, I have the habit of sleeping on his arm, on his chest. At some point Blake seems to have realized there is no shaking me off, so he spoons behind me, keeping an arm under his head, the other around my waist. I've never slept better than when feeling Blake's chest pressing against my back...and the inevitable morning wood, but that's an entirely different story. That's the bonus.

"It's your fault. You kept an arm under me instead of your head. You're quite the spooner."

"It makes you happy," he states with a smile. I swear my toes curl all on their own. Does Blake know how swoonworthy he sounds when he says those things? Evidently not, because he's not using his seductive voice or his playful voice. There is no secret agenda; he genuinely means it. Which makes it all the more swoonworthy.

"Go take a shower. We have to pick up the girls in half an hour."

Tonight he's taking me to see the Bennett Enterprises show. It's the first time we'll attend an event *together*, together. And before that, we're taking Pippa's girls, Mia and Elena and Julie, out for ice cream. Blake often takes the little ones out for walks or an ice cream, but he's never invited me over. I'm not sure he kept me out on purpose, but I was thrilled when he asked. I think it means he's letting me in a little more. Maybe I'm building this up in my mind to be more than it is, but I can't help myself.

"I'm so happy you asked me to go to the Bennett show with you. And to take the girls for ice cream."

"Thank you for saying yes."

"Who can say no to you?"

He gives an exaggerated wiggle of his eyebrows. Right, the amount of confidence this man possesses first thing in the morning is astonishing. Most people I know, myself included, need a good few hours to build up that trust. Makeup and coffee help, not to mention drop-dead-sexy shoes. Blake rolls out of bed with one hundred percent confidence.

"Shouldn't have said that. Boosting your ego first thing in the morning is a dangerous move."

Blake smiles, and without taking his eyes off me, brings one of my hands up to his mouth, kissing my wrist. It's just a light feather of lips, but a shudder zips down my spine. I catch my breath. When I feel the tip of his tongue on my skin, heat zings my center. I attempt to withdraw my hand but Blake pulls me flush against him, one hand still holding my wrist, the other securely on my waist. We look like we're about to dance, a beautiful and innocent pose.

Hold that thought!

He slides the hand from my waist farther down, lifting my nightgown and palming my bare ass. Uh-uh, I should have known better. Blake doesn't do innocent. Goose bumps form on my ass right away. He runs his thumb up one ass cheek, then down the other, then up the crack between them. I involuntarily roll my hips against him, then take a large step back.

"You are a terrible man. I need to get ready."

While I shower, Blake steps inside the bathroom. I point a menacing finger at him.

"No tempting me or we'll never make it out of the house."

"No tempting." That's when I notice he's holding my phone. "Penny's calling. Third time in a row. Must be urgent."

My heart in my throat, I turn off the water, step out, and dry my hands on a towel. Blake leaves after handing me the phone. *Please, please dear God, don't let anything have happened to her.*

"Hey, sweetie," she says. "Your boss is downstairs."

"What?"

"He's at the interphone. Says he needs to drop off some documents for you. You have this address listed as your work address right?"

"Crap. Yeah, I do. Sorry about that."

"You want me to send him over to Blake's? Or just take the documents from him and you'll pick them up later?"

The last thing I want is for Quentin to come over here, realize I'm living above Blake's bar. My clearing the air when we were away on set only made his nagging more incessant.

"Take the documents, please. I'll drop by today to pick them up. Sorry for this. I'll make it up with cocktails, I promise."

Said documents must be the contracts from a new sponsor. I was supposed to go over it as soon as he got them, which I assume was yesterday evening.

"Nothing to be sorry for, but I won't say no to a cocktail."

"Thank you, Penny."

Damn, that was a close call.

***

"Wow," I exclaim that evening when we step inside the location for the Bennett show. I've been to a number of galas and events for my job, but this is something else entirely. It is elegant but not over the top, rich but not opulent, and despite the size of the venue and the number of people in attendance, it maintains an air of familiarity. It's almost cozy. Stretching from the back wall to the center of the room is a long runway. On either side of it are small tables, with two to six seats around them, all facing the runway. I'm no pro, but I suspect that the seating arrangements contribute a lot to the intimate atmosphere. Fashion shows usually have rows upon rows of chairs, but this arrangement is far better.

"There are so many people."

"After it's over, we're going somewhere, just the two of us. I want to show you something."

"Already saw that today."

Blake narrows his eyes, and I can't wait for his comeback. Would it be witty, sexy, both? He surprises me by not saying anything, instead pulling me behind a black panel. From the cables and tools strewn on the floor, I suspect this is a backstage of sorts for the technical team, which is not here at the moment. Blake either knew this or suspected it, because he leans into me like a man with a plan. He kisses my neck, biting me gently. We're shielded from everyone's view, but still. This man has no shame, or mercy. And I love every second of this, even though

I shouldn't.

"Blake!" I intended to work severity into my tone, but it sounds wanton even to my own ears. "You can't touch me like that in public."

"Keep talking like that and I'll kiss you against this wall, just so you know who's in charge."

"Is it bad that now I'm thinking of ways to provoke you?" I lick my lips, shaking my head.

Blake steps back. "I'm making an effort here."

I wiggle my eyebrows. "This is what makes it more fun."

He's reckless, but hot damn, whenever I'm with him, I want to throw caution to the wind.

"Come on. Let's sit before I do something crazy like throwing you over my shoulder and walking out of here."

Taking my hand, he leads us back into the room. If possible, the place seems even fuller than a few minutes ago.

For the first time, I focus on the people and not the decor. All men are wearing suits, and the women have exquisite dresses. As is always the case with such events, I feel out of my depth. It's not that I feel inferior to everyone else, because I don't. But I just feel like I don't belong, like this is all just make-believe. In a way, it is.

We walk up to one of the tables nearest to the runway, where Christopher, Max, Daniel, and Logan are sitting. There are two empty chairs. The brothers look up, and their reactions when they see me are almost comic. Daniel and Logan mask their surprise more skillfully, only a slight jerk of their head giving them away. Christopher and Max—I can't tell who's who—rise in unison. One claps his hands; the other opens his arms wide, as if thanking the skies. I can tell they're about to roast Blake. I've been around the family often enough to know the dynamics. But I never can tell *how* they'll choose to torment Blake, and I dearly wish I could pick up on it faster so I can join in on the fun.

"I never thought I'd see this day," one of the twins says. I make a concerted effort to tell which one he is. Judging by the way he winks, and the cocky smirk, it must be Christopher. I have a fifty percent chance of being right.

"Watch it, Max," Blake warns. Okay, so I failed one hundred percent.

"Clara, please give us the rundown. Is he treating you well? Should we kick his ass?" the actual Christopher asks.

"Or give him pointers?" Max adds.

"Anything you two want to add?" Blake points at Daniel and Logan.

Logan drums his fingers on the table, narrowing his eyes in mock concentration. Then he perks up, as if he has the right answer. "No, I think Max and Christopher about covered the range of scenarios."

Daniel flashes a grin, pointing with his thumb at Logan. "I agree with him."

"I'll have you know he's being a swoon-worthy gentleman."

Logan cocks a brow. Next to me, Blake nods.

"He bought my favorite flowers and planted them on the balcony."

Christopher and Max both feign shock. Teasing is an art in this family. I can only hope I'll be as good one day.

"'Atta-boy," Logan exclaims.

"I think he's giving all of you a run for your money in the charming department," I add for effect. The brothers look slightly affronted at this, and Blake smiles proudly. Too proudly. Hmm, my wicked side rears its head. Having Blake's back is good. Riling him up is even better.

"But he's also very inappropriate."

He cocks a brow at me. "You'll pay for this."

"I'm looking forward to it."

The four brothers guffaw just as a waiter appears with a tray of glasses filled with a fizzy drink. I take a sip from mine. It's champagne, as I guessed, and it's delicious. As the waiter leaves, the lights turn dimmer, and the screens at the side of the runway light up.

"Where's Sebastian?" I ask.

"See that mirror at the back of the room?" Logan asks. "It's a see-through glass. A room is behind it, and Sebastian watches from there. Too much press around here for him. He did attend at some point, but I swear the reporters have only become nosier over time."

"I can imagine that," I say, my stomach twisting as I remember my conversations with

Quentin.

"Ava will be here. She's backstage with Pippa now," Daniel adds.

Everyone sits down, Blake and me included. As an energetic, upbeat song replaces the soft background music, I realize this is the first time we're together in front of the family, or at the very least the brothers (Will's party doesn't count since we were still on shaky ground). But I know how this works. Everyone will know about this by the time the evening ends.

Ava joins us, sitting in one of the two remaining chairs. She grins at me, giving me a thumbs-up.

"How come you're not watching with Sebastian from the back room?" I ask quietly.

"I like to tease him." Even in the dim light, I can tell Ava's blushing. "Besides, I need to concentrate on the show, put out any fires if needed, and Sebastian is very good at distracting me."

"Oh yeah, the Bennett men should come with a warning sign."

When I turn to face the runway, out of the corner of my eye I see Ava furiously typing on her phone. Correction: everyone will know about me being here within an hour.

Blake takes my hand, kisses my knuckles, then puts our interlinked hands on the table as the show starts.

I watch with rapt attention, not wanting to miss one detail. The girls strutting up and down the runway are gorgeous. They're all wearing simple clothes so the jewelry stands out.

I have to admit, I have a hard time seeing the jewelry on the runway, so I glance at the screens often, but many in the audience appear to do the same.

At midpoint, there is a break, and I excuse myself because I desperately need to go to the bathroom. As I walk away, I catch two women sitting a few tables away watching me. They have their heads together, and one is pointing at me, but she quickly withdraws her hand when I look her way. I rack my mind, wondering if I've met them before. Maybe in passing at work? I really can't place them, and considering they pretended to look away when I caught them staring, I don't care about placing them. If people lack manners, I won't spend any of my energy being pissed and annoyed about it.

To my surprise, the toilets are empty. Thank goodness. I practically sprint to a stall.

When I dress up minutes later, I have to rearrange my boobs. It's the type of dress that has the unfortunate tendency of sliding up from too much movement, and now the tight part of the fabric meant to highlight my waist is squishing the underside of my boobs. I remain in the stall, one hand in my neckline, when I hear the bathroom door swing open.

"Oh please, Blake's lowered his standards. That woman is so insipid she's practically invisible. All I'm saying is he'd better not expect me to jump in his bed once he's done with her. Once standards drop, I'm out."

My hand freezes in the act of rearranging my breasts. My blood, on the other hand, is starting to boil. I'm not sure that the glass of champagne I had is helping.

"She seemed to be friendly with everyone in the family." This is another speaker. "He never asked you to sit with his family at the shows."

"Maybe she wanted to snag a Bennett and realized Blake and Daniel are the only ones left. As if anyone's gonna make those settle. Goodness knows I tried."

"You should switch brothers. Daniel's here tonight."

"Nah, they talk. The one thing they're not sharing is women."

"Why would you want to marry into that god-awful family anyway? I mean, they're rich, but they're all over each other all the time. I can't understand how anyone can live like that."

Try living without a family for a change.

My hackles rise. I can't believe anyone would trash Blake and his family like this. Then there's also the small fact that they insulted me. I feel like punching the door, but then again, the poor door hasn't done anything to upset me. These women, on the other hand...

"Rich trumps annoying. Blake was always generous. Maybe I'll give him another go after he stops running around with that twat. If I can't get a ring, at least I'll get myself some more jewelry. You're right about the family, though. And now so many of them have kids. It's a nightmare. Blake was spending time with them almost every weekend. I think he was hoping I'd join him, but he never straight-up asked. I think my eye rolls were a dead giveaway. Like there aren't a million better things to do in a weekend than waste them with brats."

What the hell? Who talks like that about kids? What kind of person picks on innocents? Bullies, that's who. Now I understand why Blake waited a while before asking me to join him during his time with the kids.

Right, it's time to step out and face the music. I quickly rearrange the dress over my chest and open the door of the cubicle. The two women smirk when they see me, then return to refreshing their makeup. Since they're silent, I can't tell who's who. Time to find out.

"So, which one's the bitch and which one's the sidekick?"

Their faces fall simultaneously, and I don't feel one ounce of guilt.

"What did you just call us?"

"Ah, you're the bitch. I recognize the voice." I have to admit, Blake has exquisite taste in women. This particular one could stride down the runway herself. Leggy, blonde, huge boobs. What the hell am I thinking? He has terrible taste in women. She's a viper.

"You don't talk to me like that."

I'm not catty often, but when I am, I have a damn good reason. I'm pissed.

"I talk how I want to anyone who insults the Bennett family and me. They're good people. The best people. And you don't pick on kids. Anyone with a shred of decency knows that."

"Please," the bitch says with a smirk.

The sidekick tilts her head to one side. "Insipid *and* potty-mouthed. My, hasn't Blake gotten himself quite a deal."

"You two must have very sad lives if you're wasting such a beautiful evening gossiping about others instead of enjoying yourselves." I cross my arms over my chest. "Blake is a great man. If all you've wanted from him were presents and money, you missed out on the best."

Both women snort, and then I realize I'm stooping to their level. Instead of wasting my time here, I could be chatting and laughing with the clan. Without another word, I leave the bathroom, feeling a lot calmer. I have to admit, letting out the anger is a good thing. It brings relief.

I walk at a brisk pace to my place. The table is empty because everyone is mingling during the break. Our glasses have been refilled with champagne, and I immediately attack mine.

Blake drops in his seat a few seconds later, kissing my forehead.

"What took you so long?"

"Ran into some unpleasant people."

"Are you okay? Do I need to punch

someone?"

"No. You just have terrible taste in women."

"What?"

"Look over my shoulder, two rows back and three tables to the right."

I saw them return to their table shortly after I did. Blake looks and groans. Then he focuses on me again.

"Yes, I've made some questionable choices in the past."

"Questionable implies there might be some chance of redemption."

He smiles. "Bad choices. That was one of the worst."

"Now we're talking."

He slides a thumb under my jaw, shifting to the edge of his seat, closer to me.

His smile grows more pronounced. "I've never seen you mad. It's a good look on you. You're fierce. Maybe I should get you mad more often."

I huff, pulling away. This man is clueless, but I'll show him the right ways. "Don't. I don't like to get mad. It's a waste of energy. Then I get mad at myself for being mad. Like now. Instead of enjoying this evening, I'm—why are you laughing?"

"Your monologue is adorable. You ramble even more than usual."

"Thanks, you're really winning points right now."

"I didn't know I was supposed to win points."

I sigh. "You weren't. I'm still rambling.

Just...how could you be with that woman?"

"Loneliness. I used to think that bad company is better than no company."

I have no comeback to that. It had never occurred to me that Blake could get lonely. Not with his large family or his social skills. It seems that whenever I see him, he's in the midst of a crowd, either chatting or entertaining the group.

"But I was a jackass for a long time, so I got what I deserved. Sorry you ran into Vivian, though."

"That's her name? Sounds like a villain, which fits, I guess. I would've pegged her for a Cruella or something."

"I can't believe you're sassy even when you're pissed."

"I do what I can. She was really bitchy, about you, me, your family. I can't believe anyone would pick on your family—even the kids. I gave her a piece of my mind."

He cups my cheek, kissing the tip of my nose. "You defended my family?"

"Yeah. You too. She said some things. Never mind. Don't really think I set her straight, but at least I got it off my chest."

"You're amazing, Clara. Can I keep you?"

My heart flips, and I simply lean in to him, hungry for more contact. But then his eyes grow hard, startling me.

"What did she say about you?"

"Eh, standard bitchy stuff. That I'm insipid, invisible. Shouldn't have let it bother me."

He pulls back a notch so he's staring directly at me, eyes hard. "Just so we're clear, you're never invisible. I see you. I've always seen you."

"You say the sweetest things," I murmur.

"I mean every one of them."

"That's what makes *you* sweet."

"We really have to work on your compliments, darling. Might want to use some more masculine ones."

"Nope. Sweet about covers it."

Cocking a brow, he rests his hand on my shoulder, moving his thumb on my collarbone. Shit. That's not a sweet spot for me, but right now, having his hand there feels so good. Too good.

"You're also sexy." I lick my lips. "And intense."

He slips his thumb under the strap of my dress, his eyes never leaving mine. Holy bejeezus.

"Very intense. Keep your hands to yourself, mister." To drive the point home, I push his hand away from my shoulder, inching back with my chair. "We're in public."

Which I almost forgot until I mentioned it. People are milling around, socializing. We're surrounded by the buzz of their voices and the background music, but Blake made me forget everything. The table fills, and as Ava sits, she leans in to me.

"By the way, at the next girls' outing, you're spilling every detail," she whispers.

I grin sheepishly. "Don't worry about that. If

there's one thing I'm not good at, it's keeping my mouth shut."

She nods happily. "You have that post-hanky-panky glow that only comes from excellent hanky-panky."

"Glow? I'm so far past glowing, I'm practically a neon sign."

The lights dim again and the show starts back up. We all watch in silence, and I'm in awe once more.

Once it ends, a number of people crowd in on us, congratulating the family on the excellent show. One such person is Caroline. I know her from the various Bennett weddings, and she even joined us for the odd girls' outing. Such a pity she and Daniel broke up, and then she drifted away from the family.

With chagrin, I realize that seems to be my own story, minus the *over* part and the *drifting away* part. No, no, this is different. I went into this with eyes wide open. Blake and I are enjoying each other while we're neighbors, and that's it. I'm not harboring any secret dreams of happy ever after. Okay, so I am harboring secret dreams; sometimes they're so secret, I manage to convince myself they don't exist.

"Caroline, long time no see," Ava says.

"Not that long. I was at the wedding."

Ava makes more small talk with Caroline, but I'm busy observing Daniel—specifically the way he looks at Caroline. With *longing*. Well, well.

My meddling tendencies are rearing their

head, but pffffffft...I'm a little fuzzy from the champagne. This might be a task for the master meddler, Pippa. Or at least a sober Clara. Before I can whip a coherent plan here, Caroline's gone again.

***

I'm unsteady on my feet as Blake and I leave the venue a few minutes later.

"Can we walk a few blocks and then grab a cab?" I ask Blake, needing some fresh air.

"Sure."

"How can I be so light-headed?" I ask, holding on to him for dear life. I'm *really* unsteady on my feet. "I just had two glasses."

"Three. You drank mine too," Blake exclaims.

Oh crap. Well, that explains why my glass wasn't getting empty even though I kept drinking.

"Don't worry, I'll take care of you, my drunk girl."

"Tipsy," I correct.

"Got it."

"But I'll pretend I'm drunk if it means you'll take care of me."

We come to a halt between two Jacaranda trees, and he pulls me flush against him.

"I thought you didn't want me to take care of you." He nuzzles his nose against mine in an Eskimo kiss. *Ah, damn it, Blake*! He has to turn down the charm, right now, or I might say some things I shouldn't.

I put a finger to my lips. "Shhh, it's a secret, but I actually love it that you're so protective and attentive."

On a whim, I kiss his cheek lightly.

"What's that for?"

"Bringing me to the show with your family. I didn't know how 'no labels' works exactly. If it meant just fun under the covers, or...."

Damn champagne. It loosens my tongue, and I really need no help in that department. I speak too much as it is, and one is not supposed to say these things out loud.

Blake wraps an arm around my waist, cupping my cheek with the other hand, and holds my gaze captive in his.

"I want to make one thing clear. There's going to be rough fucking and sweet lovemaking and everything in between. But it will always be more than fun under the covers. Okay?"

I shudder involuntarily as I nod. "Okay."

"When I said I want you in my life, not just my bed, I meant it. And here's a label for you—mine. You're mine."

"You're being sweet again. Just thought I'd point that out." I inform him. Lucky he's holding me tight, because I'm swooning a little. A lot, actually. "I know you had plans for us tonight, sorry. I don't think I'm up to anything."

"Let's get you home, drunk girl."

"Tipsy. Just tipsy."

CHAPTER TWENTY-ONE

Blake

Daniel and I used to stick around for the show after party, give press interviews, but not anymore. It doesn't help Bennett Enterprises, but it does attract people like Vivian.

"We're going too fast," Clara mumbles. She's adorable when she's had too much to drink. By the time the cab pulls in front of our building, she's steadier on her feet, but something in the way she moves gives her away. Doesn't matter. She's safe with me. I'm here to look after her, every step of the way.

"Would you like to come in?" she asks once we're in front of her door, batting her eyelashes in an exaggerated way.

"Are you trying to flirt?"

She pouts. "If you have to ask, I'm failing miserably."

"I was going to come in anyway, make you sure you get into your bed safely."

She nods eagerly, turning around and unlocking the door with surprising ease. Once inside, I take her in my arms and kiss her like I've been meaning to ever since we left. Christ, I can't get enough of this woman. She got under my skin, and I want her to stay there. In fact, I'm determined to get under *her* skin and stay there. The recognition startles me because this is another first for me. I'm out of my depth when it comes to this, but I'm determined to make this woman the happiest she's ever been. I can't go wrong with that.

"What are you thinking?" she asks when I kiss down her neck. "I can *feel* you thinking."

"I'm thinking that I can't get enough of you. This was just an apartment before, but now it's home. You made it home. You're real, open, honest." I kiss back up the side of her neck, then her cheek.

"Especially when I'm drunk."

"I thought it was just tipsy."

We both laugh.

"Right, tipsy. I'm much better now, though." She steps back and twirls around as if to make her point. Okay, I'll give her that, she's steady on her feet. "This dress is so pretty. It's the kind of pretty that makes me feel pretty."

Her words slice through me. "You are beautiful, Clara. Never doubt that."

"Not like you, though. Not in your league."

"What?"

"You're Blakealicious."

"That's not a word."

"It should be. Blake and delicious combined. You're so hot, you're down right lickable," she explains seriously, "and I'm—"

"Mine. You're mine."

"I really like that label," she whispers, her eyes wide and uncertain, like she just confessed a deep secret. I meet her admission with one of my own.

"Me too."

She's still not one hundred percent sober because she wouldn't talk so freely. Despite being a chatterbox, Clara keeps her cards close when it comes to her feelings. Except after drinking. Lucky me. And I know exactly how I will convince my woman that she's fucking beautiful. I will show her.

I kiss her hard, tasting her frantically. I need her—now, all night. But I want to take my time and pace myself. Then again, I set that goal every time we're together, and I end up being rough and demanding with her. We're a tangle of limbs as we head to her bedroom, and once we're inside, I pull her to a wall, turning her around.

"Put your hands against the wall."

She does just that, and I lift her dress inch by inch until my fingers feel her soft and smooth skin. I skim my hands between her legs and she immediately splays them wider, giving me access. I drag my thumb along the scrap of fabric covering her entrance, rubbing her over her panties in a slow, lavish movement. Pushing her hair to one side, I kiss the back of her neck as I continue driving her crazy with my thumb. Her soft moans fill the silence, and I lower my other hand to cup one ass cheek. Her skin turns to goose bumps under my grip. I love how responsive she is to me. When I feel her soak through the fabric, I take my hands off her. She swirls around, eyes wide and pleading.

"Blake," she protests. I scoop her in my arms, drowning her protests with a long and hard kiss, and she laces her arms around my neck, deepening the kiss. She tastes sweet, and for a moment, I consider simply kissing her the entire night. Then I lower her on the bed, and we share an accomplice smile before ridding each other of their clothes.

"Careful with the dress." She smiles up at me. "But don't worry. You can be rough with me all you want."

That smile is my undoing. My plan to take it slow just went out the window. Having her naked in front of me isn't helping my case either.

She flicks on the light switch at the side of the bed, and I love that there is no hesitation in that action. She is damn beautiful, every single part of her, and I'll make sure she knows that. I'll remind her every day and every night, worship her.

"That's it, I want to see you, babe. You're so damn beautiful."

Clara sits on the bed, and my erection is in front of her. She licks once across the crown, and energy strums through me, settling at the base of my spine. Then she leans on her back on the bed.

"You think you're the only one who can tease?" she asks.

"You can tease me all you want. But you don't make the rules, Clara. I do."

I move over her, and she spreads her legs to her side, opening up for me. I close in, fist my erection at the base, and slap one of her folds with it, then the other. When I push the tip over her clit, she digs her nails in my arms.

"You like this?"

"Yes. I like everything you do to me."

"Fuck, Clara. Grip the headboard."

"But I want to touch you."

"Grip the headboard," I repeat, and she lets go of me, doing as I instruct. "Good. If you don't keep them there, I'll tie you up."

Her eyes widen and her breathing intensifies. I pull back, lowering myself on the bed until my face is between her legs. Then I cup each ass cheek in one hand, pushing her ass high in the air until I have access everywhere I want.

I lick her from her crack to her clit. She digs her heels deeper in the mattress, her toes twitching and curling. Oh yes. I want to bring her right to the cusp before I slide inside her. I dip my tongue into her opening and feel the muscles in her ass contract under my fingertips as her inner muscles spasm around my tongue. She's gripping the headboard tighter, pushing herself on her heels like this is too much for her. I like seeing her like this: unrestrained, feeling and enjoying, reveling in the pleasure. Pulling away, I run my hands over her ankles, then kiss the same spots, first lavishing one leg with attention and then the other.

"You're gorgeous, Clara." I continue upward

until I reach her navel. Her breathing is frantic, and I have a perfect view to her breasts moving up and down. Christ, she's a sight.

"Let go of the headboard."

She obeys immediately, possibly thinking she's finally allowed to touch me. I have other plans. I flip her on her stomach and then kiss her everywhere, including her scars. Especially the scars.

"Every inch of you is beautiful. These scars right here, they just show you're brave, that you stand up for what you believe in."

She sighs softly, and I can't hold back anymore, so I grab a condom from the nightstand and pull it over myself, then flip her on her back again.

I'm so hard, I can barely think straight. Her flesh is glistening, and just the thought of those soft inner walls closing in on me is enough to drive me crazy.

"Blake," she whispers, almost begging.

I position myself at her entrance and slide inside in one swift move, entering her all the way to the base. She cries out beautifully as she clenches around me, fisting the sheets. She is so tight and snug and fucking perfect.

I lift her ankles, placing them on my shoulders and move fast, watching myself slide in and out, her chest rising up and down in quick succession. She's not just fisting the sheets, she's pulling at them.

"This feels so good, so deep," she rasps, writhing and moaning as I drive inside her faster.

"You're amazing, Clara. Fucking amazing, you know that?"

Her nipples are puckered, calling to me as her breasts move with every one of my thrusts. In a matter of seconds, I change positions. I lower her feet back on the bed and lounge over her. As much as I like watching her, tasting her is even better. I kiss her chest, take a nipple in my mouth, then skim my lips up her chest and neck, her jawline. I pepper her cheeks with kisses before feathering my mouth over hers. She parts her lips, allowing me to kiss her deep and hard.

Every time we're together, she gives more of herself to me, and I do the same. Not because she demands it, but because opening up to her feels natural and right. I want to make her feel all the things I feel and don't know how to voice.

Squeezing my eyes shut tightly, I breathe in through my nose to stave off the orgasm for just a while longer. I'm close. I can feel it in the tightness at the base of my spine. But when she starts clenching around me, I know I'm a goner. I move my hips so I grind against her clit, and she explodes underneath me.

We climax as one, a tangle of messy and sweaty limbs, our cries mingling together, her fingers tugging hard at my hair, my nails digging in her thigh. After regaining my composure, I sit up. Clara pushes herself on her elbows, and we both look at the state of the bed. The sheets are completely torn out of their corners. I can't remember who ended up pulling

them out altogether. It might have been her. It might have been me. We might have done this together.
She laughs. "We're such a mess."
I kiss her forehead. "We're fierce."

CHAPTER TWENTY-TWO

Clara

Quentin: In my office. Now.

I leap from my chair, staring at the words on my phone. Not a good omen, and not what I expected. I just received the confirmation that the stars of our show will be on a famous late-night talk show, and I'm damn proud of that. It took a lot of hard work to obtain that, but it will give us a big boost. Since I just forwarded the e-mail to Quentin, I was expecting praise, and this smells fishy.

When I enter Quentin's office, his face is set in grim lines. The man usually looks like he has a stick up his butt, but today that stick must be extra-long and thick.

"What's the matter, boss? Did you read my e-mail about the talk show?"

He nods, gesturing me to sit in the chair opposite him, which I do, the back of my neck prickling with unease.

"I remember you telling me you don't know the Bennett family well." He turns his computer monitor toward me, and my entire body goes cold.

It's a celebrity gossip website featuring photos from last Saturday's Bennett show. I appear on a number of those, laughing with Blake, talking to Logan or Ava. One in which Blake is clearly kissing me. My mind begins to spin. How could I have been so careless? I knew there was press there.

Then I mentally slap myself. Why should I be hiding? I didn't do anything wrong.

"You lied."

Deep breath, shoulders straight. "It's my private life. I don't have to lay it out for you."

"Damn right you do if I ask you to." Quentin is a short, thick man, and behind his desk, he looks even shorter and thicker.

"As long as my private life doesn't interfere with my work—"

"Spare me the bullshit. I asked you for dirt on the family, and you lied to my face, telling me you're not close to them."

"I also told you I don't sell people out for ratings. You asked me to betray the trust of people I care for. That's not part of my job description. Or yours."

"I've been at this job longer than you, girl. Everyone does what they can to get forward, including stepping on bodies."

"Not how I operate. And Nate got at the very top without trashing anyone."

"Saint Nate." He scoffs. "Please. If I hear anyone else in this goddamn network singing his praises, I will throw up."

"What is the point of this? I'm doing my job very well, and you know that." Another deep breath. I can't lose my shit, no matter how much I want to.

"Guess what? Very well isn't enough."

"I got us on the late-night show. That is a million times more important."

"I decide what's important, not you. And when I ask you to cooperate, you cooperate."

"You consider backstabbing cooperation?"

"Maybe I didn't make myself clear enough. If you're not willing to cooperate, I will let you go."

"You will let me go," I repeat blankly.

"Yes, and I'll make sure you don't get another job in this network, no matter how many phone calls Saint Nate makes for you."

"I see." Well, that makes my path very clear.

"You do?" He clasps his hands, his nasty smile making an appearance for the first time today.

"Yes. I quit." I am not going to come to work every day with this slimy man breathing down my neck, asking me to do things after which I could never look at myself in the mirror, just because he isn't capable of hard and honest work. No more. I am worth more than this. There have to be more options than this.

His smile freezes on his face. "What?"

"I quit."

***

You never know how dispensable you are until faced with the fact. One hour later, as I walk out of the studio building, all my belongings in a box, HR termination contract on top, the enormity of my decision hits me, and my knees nearly buckle from the weight. I barely make it to my car, and once I climb in, I'm in a stupor. *What have I done?* I blink back tears, trying not to panic, but panic I do. My chest feels so tight and my eyes sting so badly, I can almost feel a panic attack coming. Or a stroke. I'm about to research stroke symptoms before I realize I'm in the garage of the building. No reception or Internet here.

This deep breath technique doesn't work jack shit when you're panicking. Could I have handled this better? Maybe.

Jesus, what have I done?

The right thing. I did the right thing. It's just that doing the right thing sometimes has the habit of biting me back with a vengeance. Almost unconsciously, I touch the marks on my back.

Okay, this is obviously not how I pictured my career change happening. Ideally I would have already had a job lined up before quitting this one because I have a mortgage to pay. My best skill is that I get shit done, and I don't feel I'm too good for any job. Hopefully, that will be enough for my unemployment to be short.

***

"You have the biggest balls ever," Penny exclaims. When I arrived at the apartment, I realized I'd work myself into a frenzy if I spent too much time alone with my thoughts. On a whim, I asked Penny if she could have lunch with me. So now she's wolfing down a shawarma, sitting on the swing on the balcony, while I rid my flowers of dry bits. I can't eat. I feel a little faint just at the smell of shawarma.

"Or I'm stupid."

"No, you're not. You're loyal to a fault. That's very rare. You have no idea how many back stabbings I see on a daily basis, and it usually happens over petty things, not a job."

"It was just all too much, and I acted impulsively."

"If you ask me, this was a long time coming. You weren't happy there."

Shifting my weight from one foot to the other, I snap a dry bit with a little too much gusto. "Well, the point of a job isn't to be happy, but to receive a pay-check. Have some stability. I wanted to transition out of TV, but I wanted to have a plan for it."

"You can't plan everything."

"That coming from the person who wakes up at five o'clock every morning to run? You're the master planner."

"Yeah, and it's zero fun. Look at this as an opportunity to figure out your next steps without a slimeball breathing down your neck. Use it. Also, you have a *fine* man to fill all those spare hours with."

I swallow hard at the thought of Blake, unsure how he'll take the news of my unemployment status, especially because it will be accompanied by a huge request. I'm going to ask him if I could live here a while longer than I intended.

My building developer informed me that they're handing over the keys soon...and I can't afford my mortgage anymore. Renting it out so I can finance the mortgage until I get a job is my only option. Staying here *free* would be a big help. *Ugh*...I already feel like a leper about it, and I haven't even asked Blake yet.

"Have to go. Sorry I can't stay longer," Penny says.

"Thanks for coming."

"Hey, you're here early!" Blake exclaims, appearing out on the balcony, scaring us both half to death. He and Penny met a few Saturdays back when she dropped by for breakfast. "Hi, Penny."

"Take care of my girl. I have to go."

"Short day?" he asks after she's gone.

I decide to rip it like a Band-Aid. "Nope. I quit."

"What happened?"

Sitting on the swing, I tell him everything quickly, trying not to make a big deal out of it. Blake grows angrier by the second.

"I can't believe this," he explodes, pacing around the balcony. "Why didn't you tell me this before?"

"Didn't see the point. I didn't want to worry you, and I was dealing with it."

"Clara..." He stops pacing, training his eyes on me. "Being part of my family doesn't mean just attending birthday parties and weddings. A whole lot of shit comes with the territory too, and people like this Quentin are at the top of the shit list. I've dealt with this kind of people for a long time. I'm not going to let you fight my family's fights. That's what I'm here for."

"Oh, sorry I didn't tell you. I promise I will if it happens again. Honestly, I thought he'd eventually drop the whole thing."

"I want you to tell me everything—not only if it affects my family. Anything that bothers you. Anyone who makes you uncomfortable. I want to know. Okay?"

I nod, too overwhelmed by the intensity of this moment to find my voice.

"There's something else on your mind," he states.

"Yes, I received an e-mail from my building's developer. They're handing the keys over this week."

Blake's expression turns blank. "You're moving out?"

Hugging my knees to my chest, I shake my head. "Actually, I meant to ask if I could stay here until I find a new job? I thought about renting the condo so I can make the mortgage payments. I know there's a lot of interest in that building, and I was hoping to swing it by not paying rent here."

Blake sits next to me on the swing. "That's not even a question. You're staying, and I'm taking care of you. Anything you need. Anything you ask for. Actually, it'll be more than what you ask for because you have the lousy habit of not asking for nearly as much as you deserve."

"Thank you, Blake. You're a lifesaver."

"You quit your job without a second thought rather than blab about my family. Do you have any idea how much that means to me?"

The vulnerability in his eyes startles me.

"It was the right thing to do."

"People usually do what's right for *them*. You're different. Loyal and sweet, and—"

Without warning, Blake takes my hand, leading me inside his apartment. He kisses me softly. My lips, my cheek, descending to my jaw and my neck.

"You're so precious to me, Clara, you have no idea."

This closeness between us right now is unlike anything I've experienced with him. With a startled gasp, I realize his chest is shaking slightly. He kisses me anew, deeply and slowly.

I am so lost in him, soaking in all his warmth and deliciousness that I don't even realize he's ridding me of my clothes until I'm buck naked in front of him.

He lowers himself on his haunches, gaze focused on me. The glint in his eyes is a mix of wicked and yet even more vulnerability. Maybe he feels this change between us too. All I can do is hold my breath and watch him. He lifts one of my legs, and I wobble for a split second before he places my thigh on his shoulder. He kisses my inner thigh, inching closer and closer to my pubis. When he runs his thumb along the rim of my opening, following the movement with his tongue, I bite back a moan. Oh damn, he's sexy. So unbelievably sexy. He's so good with his tongue, and his hand.

He's teasing me again in that delicious way of his, dragging his tongue up one fold, then down the other, so close to my clit, but without touching it. Oh God, I can't take this anticipation. I—

Fuck.

He nips at my clit, and I buck forward, out of breath. Out of everything. For a split second, my vision turns black. Every muscle in my body tightens, absorbing the shock of pleasure.

Maybe it's that I have a direct view of him nuzzling my clit with his nose while his tongue probes me on the inside, or maybe the vulnerable moment we shared before he opened me up intimately, but I feel my orgasm building inside me faster than ever before.

"I can't...I'll fall...I'm...*Oh God, Blake.*" I know I'm not making much sense, but I have to warn him. "I'll fall."

"Hold on to me."

I grasp his shoulders, but the leg I'm standing on wobbles. "I am, but"—I breathe in sharply—

"don't let me go," I rasp, and I'm not talking just about this very moment.

"I won't. Trust me. I won't let you go, Clara. Promise."

I come apart in his arms, and Blake keeps his promise, holding me until I'm steady on my feet.

Rising to his feet, he cradles my face, his thumbs pressing at the corners of my mouth, the rest of his fingers splayed on my cheeks and neck. I feel adored, safe, and treasured. I have no idea how he can do that with a simple touch, but he does.

I want to reciprocate—he might not need the kind of reassurance I do, but he does need it in other ways, like knowing with absolute certainty that I will not betray him or his family.

"I didn't know it would feel like this," he says, catching me off guard. "Sharing every day and night with someone. *Wanting* to share my life."

"I didn't know either," I whisper, too stunned to come up with a better reply. Slowly I gather my wits around me, fueled by his admission. "It feels right."

"It feels perfect." He kisses my cheek, my temple. "Fucking perfect. This is more real than anything I've had."

"Blake," I reply softly, pressing my hands over his, then bringing one of his palms to my lips, kissing it. The air charges between us, and a strange energy strums through me. I can tell Blake feels it too, because his eyes widen. This, right here, is more raw and intimate than anything we've experienced before.

I'm falling for this man.

CHAPTER TWENTY-THREE

Clara

Free time does not agree with me. After working straight out of school for more than a decade, you'd think I could use a breather. But two weeks into my unemployment, I feel restless and guilty. I must have sent about eighty applications for various organizational and operational jobs, and I'm still waiting to hear from most. In the evenings, I help Blake at the bar, and I fill my mornings by working on my illustrations. The one I'm working on right now is giving me headaches, but I have nothing but time to figure it out. Too much time.

I startle when my phone rings and leap to my feet, glancing around. It's ringing somewhere around me, but I can't find it for the life of me, and this is not a good time for me not to be reachable. It could be a call for an interview. Finally, I find the darned thing under the couch—ask me how it got there.

Glancing at the screen, I see it's Blake, who is currently down at the bar, going through the inventory before opening in a few hours.

"What's wrong?" I ask, phone pegged to my ear as I rise to my feet.

"Can you come down for a few minutes?"

"Sure."

On that cryptic note, he clicks off. *Huh, what's all that about? I'd better go check on him.*

I step inside the bar, expecting to find Blake alone, but instead he's at one of the high tables with a man in a suit. He's dark-haired and looks like he's in his early fifties.

"Clara, you're here," Blake exclaims upon seeing me. "Great. I want to introduce you to someone."

I join the two of them and shake hands with the man, exchanging names.

"Charlie here publishes children's books," Blake says, and I feel like I just downed a glass of cold water.

"Our largest imprint specializes in illustration books. Blake tells me you have a large portfolio," Charlie continues. The back of my neck prickles. "I could look at it, if you want some feedback."

I don't dare look at Blake. He set me up.

"Great idea," Blake exclaims. I'm still not looking at him. Instead I try my best to keep a polite smile.

I clear my throat. "I don't think my portfolio is quite ready to be seen."

Charlie waves my words away. "Nonsense. It's never too early to get feedback."

Biting the inside of my cheek, I nod, because I

don't see how I can get out of this without offending Charlie, or Blake. On second thought, Blake can shove all his hurt feelings up his ass. He deserves it for putting me on the spot like this.

"I'll be right back," I tell Charlie. Whirling on my heels, I strut out of the bar, and then I break into a run as I round the corner of the building, climb the stairs, and enter my apartment. I barely have time to take a few deep breaths, let alone process all this, when I hear footsteps behind me.

"Clara."

"Don't even talk to me right now."

"You're angry."

At least he has the good sense not to put a question mark at the end of that sentence. I whirl around, facing him, holding my chin high, my shoulders straight.

"Yes. So angry that if I had a pointy object now, I'd poke you with it repeatedly."

"Machete or knife?"

"What?"

"The pointy object, would it be a machete or knife? I need to know how bad this is."

"This is not a joke, Blake," I say, deflated.

"You started with the pointy object," he points out. He's so calm, so collected, whereas I'm simmering with anger.

I shift my weight from one foot to the other. "Why are you doing this? Putting me on the spot? Pushing me?"

"Because you need to be pushed."

"Wrong answer. This is not your call to make. I am not ready."

"Bullshit. You've been working on this for more than ten years. The best things happen when you get out of your comfort zone."

"Gah." The nerve of him! "You say that because you always had a cushion to fall on."

Jesus, I didn't mean to raise my voice.

"I know that. Don't think I ever take my privilege for granted."

"I'm sorry. I didn't mean to attack you. I just...I'm not ready," I repeat.

Blake closes the distance between us. Brave of him, since my anger is still alive and simmering—coming close to a boil.

"You don't see what I see." He puts his hands on my shoulders, looking me straight in the eyes.

"Enlighten me. What do you see?" I challenge.

"A strong, hardworking woman who is afraid to put herself out there. You think your dream is safe as long as you keep it to yourself. You're afraid that you'll lose your safe haven if you get criticized."

Wow. Wow. I couldn't have put this into words any better.

"So, if you know all this, why push me?"

"Because you want to make this step, you're just afraid. What's the worst that can happen? Charlie says you still need to sharpen your skills. Your confidence will take a hit, maybe you'll even stop illustrating for a while. But then eventually you're going to start it again. If you don't, I'm going to nag you until you start again just to shut me up."

Poof, there's my anger. Vanished into thin air. My current predicament revolves around having a knot in my throat, and if I try to form words in spite of it, they might come out mushy and emotional. Blake moves his hands from my shoulders to hold my face.

"You have no idea how amazing you are, Clara. But I do." He presses his thumbs gently against my temple, the rest of his fingers splayed wide at the sides of my head. "If you really don't want to show him your work, I'll go down alone and make up an excuse."

"Look at you, all democratic. Giving me a choice."

He smiles, kissing my forehead.

"I'll show it to him. I feel particularly brave. Will you stick around while he's looking over them? Just in case my bravery deserts me and I try to make a run for it?"

"I'll be there. Told you I have your back. I believe in you."

***

A few minutes later, the show is on. I shove what I think is the collection of my best works under Charlie's nose, and he's inspecting every page, *hmming* and *aaaahing*. I can't tell if they're good or bad sounds, but if he doesn't form actual words soon, the tension rising inside me will choke me.

"Charlie, how about voicing some of that feedback?" Blake asks eventually. The two of us are standing around one of the small round tables, and Charlie is the only one sitting. Kind of wish I'd perched up on a seat too because my knees feel like they're about to give away, and not in a good way. As if sensing this, Blake brings his hand at the small of my back, moving it in small, soothing circles, as if saying, *I'm here for you, and I'll be here no matter what Charlie says. I'll have your back, always.*

Charlie snaps his head up. "Sorry, I tend to lose myself in illustrations. These are very creative. What's your background?"

"I took a class at a community college, but mostly I'm self-taught."

Charlie nods. "How many illustrations do you have in total?"

"Lost count a few years back, but the number is in the hundreds."

"No better way to hone your craft than by continually using it. Our imprint is company-fresh talent. We're looking to bring on board three full-time illustrators, with a two-week training period right in the beginning. The recruitment process is just about to start. Would you be interested?"

Wooooooooot! Hell yes! *Breathe in, breathe out, Clara. Sound polite. Do not let your crazy come out right now. You can do a happy dance later. It might involve Blake, and we might be naked.*

"Yes, very interested."

"Excellent. I think you'd be a match for us. Go on our homepage, you'll find the job posting there. Apply and you'll hear from us. Best of luck."

I'm still dizzy when Charlie leaves, which is when I unleash my crazy, smothering Blake with kisses.

"Congratulations, babe," he says when I give him the chance to breathe. Then I attack him again.

"Thank you. Thank you. Thank you."

Oh snap. I'm in love with this man. Head over heels in love, earth-shattering love, and any number of euphemisms are appropriate to describe what I feel. The more exaggerated the more appropriate.

I jump into his arms, kissing him even more energetically than before. Blake stumbles backward until we arrive at the counter. He lifts me onto it, pulling away a few inches.

"Clara, wait. I'm losing control here."

"Where's the problem?" I ask wickedly. "Your team won't arrive for eons."

"Babe, I have a dangerous effect on you, and I plan to take advantage of it."

Lifting me off the counter, he leads me into that tiny back room where he did wicked things to me that night right before we made love for the first time. Since I was hanging around the apartment, I'm wearing a rather loose dress, which Blake seems to find particularly amusing. The second we're in the small office, he pushes me against the closed door, cinching my dress up, then pulling it over my head, leaving me in my underwear only.

His eyes darken as his gaze slides down to my see-through bra, then lower to the silk thong.

"You're fucking sexy. I want you to keep these on."

"Whatever you say, boss." I'm not entirely sure how keeping my panties on will work, but I trust the master.

He cocks a brow. "Thought I wasn't the boss of you."

"Not in general, just in the bedroom, or the office."

Staring me straight in the eyes, he lowers his hands, stroking my slit over the silk once. I'm slick the next second, my knees buckling from the unexpected burst of pleasure. He smiles wickedly as he strokes again, and a new wave of heat rushes through me. My nipples press against my bra, bringing pleasure and torture in equal measures. Watching me, he repeats the movement, until my panties are so soaked through that I'm almost ashamed. But shame doesn't keep me from coming hard. My hips swivel against his hand. *Sweet baby Jesus on a unicorn.* He made me climax by only touching me over my panties.

"How can you do this every time?" I whisper, lacing my arms over his shoulders, because my legs are shaking.

"What?"

"Bring me to your mercy?"

"It's the easiest thing in the world because you're so responsive to me. We're doing this together."

Eyeing the bulge in his jeans, I undo the button and lower the zipper, relieving some of the pressure. I want to take care of him. When I slip my hand in his boxers, he lets out a deep groan.

"Fuck, if I'm not going to be inside you in five seconds I will explode. See? I'm at your mercy too." He moves us from the door to the desk, then opens a drawer, retrieving a small pack of condoms.

"Brought these here after our first night. Knew we'd make it back here eventually."

"Let me put it on."

With shaky hands, I undo the foil, then roll it on, feeling him pulse under my touch. I want this to be good for him.

I want to make this so good that he won't want to let me go.

It's crazy, I know, but I've never wanted anything more than I want Blake. Pushing the fabric of my thong to one side, he hoists me up on the edge of the desk, then slides inside me in one fierce move.

"Fuck, I love how tight you are after you come."

Feeling him stretching me out all at once nearly whips my breath away. Drawing circles around my nipples over my bra, he pushes in and out with deep, measured strokes, sending pleasure rippling along my nerve endings. Light-headed, I cling to him at first, then perch my hands on the edge of the desk, grounding myself so I can meet his thrusts with my own. Nothing is fast enough. Nothing is deep enough. My craving for this man is insatiable.

A faint crack has us both stopping, listening intently.

"What was that?" I ask. Blake pushes the desk a tad, and another crack follows.

He grins. "The table's gonna give out."

Well, first time I'm having furniture-breaking sex, that's for sure.

"Let's not make this poor desk crumble," he says, helping me off it, leading me to the chair of all places. How on earth will we—

"Perch one foot on the seat. Keep your hands on the backrest."

Ah, but of course. My imagination can't keep up with his expertise.

"Lose the panties first."

"But I want to keep them on like you said," I challenge, throwing him a seductive look over my shoulder.

In response, he gives me a light smack on each ass cheek. My muscles contract instantly as I exhale sharply.

"Do you like that?"

"Yes. I like everything you do to me, Blake. Everything."

With a knowing smile, he pushes my panties down, lowering himself on his haunches. I turn my head, fixing my gaze on my hands, bracing myself. I have a feeling I'm going to need it.

He cuffs my ankles with his hands briefly before rasping out, "Step out of your panties."

I do as he says, shuddering in anticipation.

"Do you want me to take off the bra and shoes too?" I ask shyly.

"No. Keep those."

When he rises to his feet, he licks me right where the thong was seconds before between my cheeks. I grip the chair so tight that my knuckles pale.

"How close are you to climaxing?"

My entire body is tight, buzzing like a livewire.

"Very."

He slides inside me, bringing one hand in the front.

"I'm just going to touch your clit. I won't move. I want to feel you come while I'm inside you once."

His words alone nearly send me over the edge. Feeling him so deep inside me while he touches my clit is too much. It's all too damn much. So much tension. So much pleasure. So much Blake.

I cry out when I climax, and Blake starts rocking in and out of me while I'm still riding the wave, spasming around him. The heightened sensations send me onto another wave. I don't know when the first orgasm ends and the second one begins.

As Blake rasps out his own relief, I allow myself to wonder for the very first time, what would it be like if Blake fell in love with me? What would it take to make him fall for me?

CHAPTER TWENTY-FOUR

Blake

"Mr. Evans, follow me. Mr. Shepperd and Mr. Meyer are waiting for you in the meeting room."

I follow the secretary down a narrow corridor, then step through the door she opens for me. I made an appointment with Clara's ex-boss, Quentin Meyer, and Ryan Shepperd, the head of that trashy gossip segment *We See You*, using a fake name.

I suspected that Shepperd imbecile would not give up on his goal just because he doesn't have a story or a source. I know how these people work. If they don't find anything, they start making shit up. Which is why I had a detective dig deeper. Turns out I was right. They concocted a story 'revealing' Sebastian's double life. They plan to run it as their lead segment next week, to kick off August with a bang. They're going to change that plan drastically after this meeting. I'm making them change it.

The second I'm inside the room, their faces become ashen. As head of that trashy gossip segment, I was sure Shepperd would know exactly who I am, but it's a nice surprise that so does Quentin Meyer, judging by his wide eyes.

"What is the meaning of this?" Shepperd asks, standing.

"You're Blake Bennett," Meyer comments, rising to his feet too.

"We've got that out of the way, then. Excellent. Let's begin."

"Wait a minute!" Meyer exclaims. "No one will begin anything. You entered this building using lies—"

"Lies! Yes, let's talk about that." I sit at their meeting table, making myself at home. "I happen to know you plan to run a false story about my oldest brother."

Shepperd narrows his eyes. Meyer jerks his head back.

"I'm going to make this simple for you, gentlemen." Both gape at me as I push two stacks of papers in their directions. "You're going to sign these, and if you ever talk or write about my family, you're going to pay for it."

The two men look too stunned to speak for a few moments, then Shepperd starts.

"Freedom of the press—"

"Does not give you free reign to lie," I say coldly. "Do libel and defamation ring a bell?"

Shepperd smirks, but Meyer starts reading the document in front of him.

I have a team of lawyers who can build a solid case of libel and defamation on short notice, which is how fake stories usually die. Some have a very wrong idea of what freedom of the press means compared to what the law actually states.

If all that fails, good old threatening and bribing shuts people up, at least for a while. It's my least favorite mode of operation because not only does it feel like rewarding those bastards, but it also leaves the door open for them to try to extort us later down the road. That's why bribing usually comes with some solid threatening and intimidating.

Right now, they are both reading the documents in front of them, and I can practically see the color drain out of them. Good.

"You can't—this is insane," Shepperd mutters. "I run a gossip segment—"

"So glad you brought that up. You aren't running it anymore."

"What?"

"Ring up Sheldon," I say, referring to the person right above him in the hierarchy. "You'll find out he's waiting for your resignation." Turning to Meyer, I say, "The same is true for you."

"Are you insane?" Meyer exclaims. "Horowitz—"

"Hates your guts, as does half the network." As do I. Just imagining this slimeball making Clara's life hard is enough to make me want to punch him. His willingness to sell out my family only adds gasoline to the fire. "So, don't let the door hit you on your way out. But before, you'll both sign those documents, or I will make your lives very hard."

I pull myself to my full height, glaring at both of them. My bet is they will cave within thirty seconds. They cave after twelve.

***

"Hello, fellow Bennetts," I say two days later, stepping inside Sebastian's office.

He sits behind his desk, while Logan paces around. They both look at me curiously. I asked them to meet me for lunch today, which is why I brought burgers for everyone.

"Double cheese." I put one brown paper bag in front of Sebastian, then hand the other to Logan, saying, "Extra pickles."

"Why did you want to meet?" Logan asks as we start on our lunch.

"To give you a heads-up about a few things. I got wind that the slimebags from *We See You* plan to trash Sebastian."

I start by telling them everything I know from Clara and then everything I found out through my own digging.

Logan swears; Sebastian just leans back in his chair, drumming his fingers on the desk.

"These people never give up, do they?" Logan asks through gritted teeth. "If they don't have fodder for tabloids, they make it up."

"Exactly," I confirm. "But I killed the entire story. Just wanted you two to know in case anyone contacts you about it."

"Blake," Sebastian says slowly, "I appreciate this, but I don't want you to get caught up in this fight. You can waste your life fighting the tabloids, but there's no winning here."

"Sebastian, you're too cerebral for your own good," Logan says. "I'm with Blake on this one."

"It's the reverse of the medal," Sebastian continues. "The press spent years building me up to be some kind of superhero, now they want another angle. After all, there are only so many articles you can write about the success of a company and its founding family. After a while, you want some dirt, something to prove their life isn't perfect either. People like a success story, but they love a scandal and tearing others down more."

"Lucky I like tearing down people who try to tear down the family," I say dryly. I lost count on how many stories I've killed over the years. Daniel and I started doing this to stop our own stupidity from damaging the family. In our early twenties, we went from one wild party to another, and that's fodder for tabloids. As the years went by and Daniel and I appeared less in public, the type of stories the press was after changed. They wanted dirt especially on the oldest trio—Logan, Sebastian, and Pippa—since they're the pillars of Bennett Enterprises.

In the beginning, we mostly had to kill facts that leaked out, such as details about Pippa's divorce, which leaked because of my own big mouth. But as Daniel and I became more careful, the press was fabricating stories—one in particular was a painstakingly detailed fake account of Logan making deals behind Sebastian's back with the goal of seizing control of the company. I remember feeling sick to my stomach about the lengths to which people would go. Finding out about these things and killing them before they reach the public is a tedious and relentless job, but someone has to do it. Daniel and I are up for it. We owe Sebastian so much; this is the least we can do.

Most of the time, we didn't even tell our eldest siblings. They had enough on their minds without having to worry about such imbecilic attempts to discredit them. Now I'm thinking that might not have been the best approach, because I don't think Sebastian actually realizes the extent to which some people would go, and the damage they can do.

"Look," Sebastian continues, "these types of stories hurt only as much as you allow them to. As long as you and those you care about know the truth, nothing else matters."

Groaning, I drag a hand down my face. I can see his point, but what he doesn't seem to realize is that if your name is dragged in the mud often enough, people start doubting you, and doubts are the hardest to fight or disprove.

Logan raises a skeptical eyebrow. "I for one would rather not read accounts of you having a double life, even if they're fake."

"Exactly." Agreeing with Logan so thoroughly on a topic happens so rarely that this is almost weird.

Sebastian shakes his head, shrugging. "In that case, heads-up—it's possible a story about me trying to take back everyone's shares will be published next week."

When he set up Bennett Enterprises, Sebastian gave every single one of us shares in the company—one of the many reasons I'll owe him for the rest of my life.

"What the fuck?" Logan exclaims, mirroring my thoughts. How did I miss that?

"I want all the details," I say at once.

Sebastian hesitates, then spills it all out, and I already make a fight plan.

"I'll handle this," I assure him, even though it's a bit late in the game to kill a story.

"Blake—" Sebastian begins, but Logan puts his hand up.

"You go ahead with whatever you're planning," Logan tells me, interrupting him. Then he points at Sebastian with his thumb. "This one needs saving from his own too-democratic ways."

I grin. "Consider it done."

"By the way, since you're here, we also wanted to talk to you about something else," Logan says. "Clara."

"What are your intentions with her?" they ask in unison. I choke on nothing at all, then cough up a lung. This took an unexpected turn.

"You've got to be kidding me," I exclaim once I stop coughing. They are not. That's the Bennett clan, versatile as ever, effortlessly jumping from planning our attack on the press to cornering me, because why not kill two birds with one stone?

"She's practically family," Sebastian insists. "And you two have been going at it for a while now."

"Going at it?" I ask blankly. "Who says that? You're getting old, Sebastian."

Sebastian looks at me sternly. I know for a fact this is his boardroom stare, and it would intimidate a lesser man, but not me.

"Stop messing with us." Logan's tone is hard. I could explain it all, but hazing them is more fun. Besides, this is between Clara and me.

"Easy, Logan. I was getting used to you not riding my ass anymore. I need some time to get back in the saddle."

Logan gives me his own boardroom stare. What is it with these two today? Did they have a drink or ten and forgot this stare has zero effect on me?

"Where do you see this going?" Sebastian insists.

"This is between Clara and me," I placate him, flummoxed to be getting *the talk* from my own brothers. "My own blood cornering me. I can't believe it."

"Being our brother means we get to give you advice even when you don't want it," Sebastian says.

"Don't feel much like a brother right now, more like a barely tolerated neighbor."

"Look," Sebastian interjects. "When you find a good woman, you do everything to keep her."

"Clara's a good woman." That was Logan, helpful as ever.

"She's the best woman," I correct him. "And that's all I'm saying on the subject."

Logan looks as if he'd like to say more, but through some miracle, remains silent. So does Sebastian. Then they both grin.

"Our job here is done," Logan says.

Sebastian nods. "Yeah, that's as good a confession as any."

I groan. Can't believe I fell for their good cop, bad cop routine. Come to think of it, they both played bad cop today.

"Right. Next time you corner me, be good lads and make sure there's at least beer around. Whiskey would be even better."

"After the fallout with her boss, I assume she's looking for a job," Sebastian says. "We can always find a place in Bennett Enterprises for her."

I shake my head, telling them both about her possible career in illustrating children's books. She applied for the position Charlie told her about and is waiting to hear from them.

"You've made it clear to this Charlie that *not* hiring Clara isn't an option, right?" Logan asks. I grin. Clara explicitly asked me not to interfere because she wants to receive the job only if she's good enough. Logan usually tries to solve everyone's problems even when they don't want his help, which got him in hot water with Nadine before they were married.

Privately, I agree with his mode of operation, but I already pushed my luck by arranging the meeting with Charlie in the first place, and I also empathize with her desire to succeed on her own.

"When you get between a woman and her independent ways, prepare for a tsunami-sized blowout. I learn from other people's mistakes."

"Don't worry, you'll make your own," Logan deadpans. Sebastian chuckles.

"Take that back." I point a finger at him. "Your words have the nasty habit of being prophetic."

CHAPTER TWENTY-FIVE

Clara

Straight or undulating?

After blinking hard several times, I shake my head, then decide to call it a night. You know you've been working on an illustration too long when you can't even tell if a line you drew is straight or undulating.

Stretching, I tilt my head to the left and to the right, attempting to dislodge the stiffness in my neck. No such luck. I'll need a hot bath for this, using my favorite bath bomb—vanilla and lavender. I barely form that thought when there is a knock at the front door.

"It's me," Blake's voice states, sounding surprisingly down.

"Come on in."

I wasn't expecting him for another hour or so. He said he's on family duty today, but he didn't give me details—and I'll admit being a *little* jealous for not being part of whatever he was up to.

The second he steps inside, I know something must have gone south. Defeat and disappointment are written all over him, from his battered expression to his hunched shoulders. Wordlessly, he slumps on the couch, tilting his head on the headrest, closing his eyes and pressing the heels of his palms against them.

"What's wrong?" I ask, scrambling to put together a plan to cheer him up. It'll have to be a great one. My usual shenanigans will not suffice. Tentatively, I sit on the couch, trying to assess how to best help him, to understand what he needs so I can give him just that. I wish he would look at me, but he's still in the time-out position, eyes closed. Finally, he looks at me.

"Read any news today?"

"No, was too lost in my illustrations. What happened?"

Blake pulls out his smartphone, taps it twice, then hands it to me.

Bennett Enterprises: Will greed disintegrate the empire?

I read the entire article, which claims to have insider info that Sebastian is trying to take control over all shares. By the time I finish it, I feel cold.

"I don't understand."

"Remember I told you a lot of people are like Quentin and that idiot from *We See You*? Well, these are some of those people."

"But this article is a lie," I exclaim.

"Yeah, the press has a way of inventing dirt when they don't find any. That's what Shepperd was going to do on *We See You*."

I wince. "What?"

"Did some digging after you quit because I suspected he wouldn't give up just because he didn't have a story. He was planning to make up one."

"Was?"

He smiles a little. "Let's just say he and Quentin are no longer a threat. Actually, they no longer have a job, but that's another story."

"What did you do?"

"I've got my secrets."

Clearly, because I would never have pegged Blake for one to employ mafioso tactics, but then Quentin and Shepperd deserve whatever they got.

"This is what you meant when you said you fight your family's fights," I say in amazement. I find the family dynamics fascinating. The older ones protect the young ones, but the reverse is also true, so it all comes full circle.

"Yeah, but I didn't do that for them. I did it for you."

A knot lodges in my throat. "For me?"

He nods, and I suddenly become a bit misty-eyed. Pointing to the phone, I ask, "What about this?"

"I met with Sebastian and Logan last week to give them heads-up about Shepperd, and Sebastian said he'd caught wind that this would come out." He points to his phone. "I pulled all the strings to keep it from being published, but I couldn't stop it, damn it."

"I'm so sorry. How is Sebastian taking this?"

"He doesn't care at all what is being written

about him. Says as long as the people he cares about know the truth, nothing else matters."

"That's a great approach."

I inspect Blake, trying to gauge exactly what's upsetting him, especially since Sebastian himself isn't bothered.

My people-reading skills aren't worth jack shit, but he has *something* on his mind. Since I can't guess, I'm gonna need words. Tucking my feet underneath me, I inch closer to him, then stand higher on my knees, facing him.

"Talk to me, Blake. What is eating away at you? Don't keep me out." The five-o'clock shadow grazes my lips as I kiss down his jaw, then back up on his cheek. I want to be helpful to him, but I can't do it if he doesn't open up. I want him to know that it's safe to show me his vulnerable side too, that he doesn't have to always be in his fun or strong or seductive mode for me. I nibble at his earlobe, then trace a straight line down his neck. A low grunt reverberates in his throat. I pull away, looking him straight in the eyes.

"Tell me, Blake," I beckon.

"I don't like letting my family down."

Ah, so this is the crux of the issue.

"You didn't," I say gently. "You gave your best, but sometimes even our best can't change the course of things." And then the real crux of the issue hits me. "You let yourself down, am I right?"

Surprise flickers in his eyes, but he nods. I place one hand on his chest without saying anything.

I need to choose my words carefully.

"You're a good man, Blake. You're a great man. But some failure is inevitable, even when you have the best intentions."

His jaw tightens almost imperceptibly. It might not be noticeable to anyone else, but I've learned him intimately enough to pick up subtle changes. I hit a nerve with my failure comment. I think back on the day he introduced me to Charlie, how terrified I was of failure too. Blake's reassurance that he'll be next to me no matter what was exactly what I needed. It strikes me that on some level everyone needs this, reassurance that even if we fail and we're stripped bare of our successes, the person at our side will still respect us, love us.

"And I want you to know that you don't have to always be in a fun, strong, or seductive mode for me. It's safe to show me your vulnerable side too." I drop my voice to a conspiratorial whisper. "I promise I won't tell. You're my knight even when your armor's pierced."

"Yeah?"

He peppers kisses up and down my neck, nipping at my skin. Lowering his hands to my ass, he pulls me closer to him until our groins touch.

"I need you, Clara."

"I'm yours. Whatever you need."

My pulse skitters as Blake kisses me. He does nothing else except kiss me, and yet desire pools between my legs. Then he leads me to the bedroom, pushes me on my back on the bed, lying next to me.

In the light streaming from above, I have a clear view of the desire etched on his features. He pushes down my skirt, and I make quick work of undoing the buttons of my blouse. Thong and bra go next, and then I'm naked in front of him.

Discarding his clothes, he pulls out a condom, gloving up. I am turned on just from watching him. Won't volunteer the fact out loud, but the man would make an excellent stripper.

I'm reminded of a feline on the prowl, shoulders moving in a rippling pattern as he moves on the bed. His eyes lock on my center.

"Beautiful, you're so ready for me, and I haven't even touched you."

Licking my lips, I part my legs wider. He moves between them.

"Put your hands under your knees. Lift your legs."

Heat trickles down my inner thighs at his command. Oh my. Lying on my back, I place my fingers behind my knees, lifting one leg, then the other.

He settles between my open legs, my calves rubbing against his granite forearms. A shudder courses through me when he slides his crown up and down my folds, coating himself in my arousal. He pushes in, just an inch, and it's like he lights a fire inside me.

"Pull your legs closer up."

He slides in at the same time I move my legs, and—

OhGod OhGod OhGod... The angle changes the closer I bring my thighs to my torso, and the deeper I take him in.

When he's inside me to the base, his balls slap along the crack between my ass cheeks, making my legs quiver. Pleasure strums through me, sharp and unexpected.

"You like this, Clara?"

"I love it. Please move."

Since my legs are suspended, I can't move myself, or I'd be rocking against him. He smiles wickedly, and I realize how completely he owns me right now. My pleasure is all in his power. Slowly, he rocks in and out, and I moan in relief.

Keeping his hands at the base of my inner thighs, Blake loves me deeper and more urgently by the second. Each time I think my bliss can't ratchet any higher, he proves me wrong. I feel on display more than physically right now. No one's ever known me the way Blake does: intimately, sentimentally, in all ways. When an unbearable pressure takes hold of my lower body, I need to touch my clit more than I need my next breath. I let go of one leg—

"Don't move your hands."

"Then touch my clit, please. Blake, I need this so badly," I pant, the force of his thrusts no longer bringing me pleasure, but more intense longing. I desperately crave my release. Blake brings one hand to twist one nipple lightly, then the other. My breasts move with each thrust, and as a drop of sweat from his forehead lands above my navel, he lowers his hand to my clit. I spoke too soon—

He circles his thumb *around* my clit. Oh, God no. I can't take more build-up. Every breath comes out shaky. My entire body quivers.

"I need to come Blake, please."

"I like hearing you beg."

He strokes directly over my clit once, and I erupt. Blake leans over me, covering my mouth with his, intertwining his fingers with mine. I come so hard I nearly fade out, but I cling to this moment for dear life because I don't want to miss even one second of this incredible closeness, and I want to watch Blake come. As he pulls away from my mouth, his handsome face contorts with pleasure, a blue vein bulging along his throat. I press my heels against his ass on every thrust.

When I feel him widen inside me, I push myself up a tad, kissing him, muffling the sound of his climax like he did to me seconds ago, keeping my eyes open and soaking in all the goodness of this moment.

After he removes the condom and we clean ourselves, we lie in bed on our sides, watching each other.

He grips my right hip in that deliciously possessive way of his. "I needed you so badly: your voice, your warmth... and that's so new to me. You make everything right. Thank you for being here for me tonight."

"I'll be here for as long as you want me to.

Let me be your anchor tonight, Blake."

Blake makes a rushed sound, like a sharp intake of breath. He locks his gaze on mine, his fingers pressing into my flesh a notch deeper.

"What if I want you to be my anchor for more than tonight?"

My pulse speeds up, my chest filling with warmth, and hope floods me. Hope for so many things: a life together, going to bed next to him every night, waking up with him still by my side. Raising a family together—maybe one as numerous as his own. Damn, what's wrong with me? The man is not proposing. But he is putting himself out there, giving me a piece of himself he was holding back.

"Anytime you need me to be." My voice catches at the end, and I bite down on my lip as I make the decision to go out on a limb, even further than he went. It feels like I'm putting my heart on a platter and handing it to him, like I'm giving him complete power over me. But I feel brave, and I think he needs to hear it.

"I am going to tell you something, and I don't expect you to say it back. I don't have any expectations at all, but I want you to know. I love you, Blake. Truly and deeply, and these feelings I'm having...they won't go away. I know we agreed on "no labels", so...."

He gently cups the side of my face, his thumb tracing my lips, as if he can barely believe the words that came out. He opens his mouth but I cover it with my hand. I don't want him to feel pressured, or to think this is an ultimatum of some sort.

"Don't say it back or I'll think you're saying it because I said it."

I feel his lips curl in a smile against my palm, and I drop my hand.

"What's the appropriate time to wait so you don't think I'm saying it because you said it?"

Nope, totally not imagining how our kids might look. Also not imagining how cute his dimple and rich hair would look on a boy. *Keep your feet on the ground, Clara.* Easier said than done when the rest of my body feels airborne.

"I don't know. A day? A week?"

"Have I told you how amazing you are?"

I swear my heart doubles in size. It will explode soon. "I believe you have, but feel free to tell me that again. You can add smart and cunning while you're at it."

"How about chatterbox?"

"Only if I can make free use of Blakealicious."

"Ouch. Fine, waving the white flag here. We'll just be silent, and I'll hold you until you fall asleep."

He nods, opening one arm, beckoning me to snuggle up to him.

"You like to spoon. Admit it."

"Never."

CHAPTER TWENTY-SIX

Clara

"Please take a seat, Ms. Abernathy. We'll call your name when it's your turn."

I drop in a plastic chair at my gynecologist's practice, pulling out my phone and checking my e-mails. Job hunting is a stressful endeavor, and I honestly hadn't thought it would last so long. I went to more interviews than I could count, and still have a ton scheduled. But the cherry on the top? I applied for the illustrator job Charlie talked about, and after reviewing my portfolio, they asked to meet me face-to-face next week, and as part of the process, I have to do a custom illustration for them. I am really trying not to get my hopes up, but I'm failing miserably. I'm also working tirelessly on said illustration. If I'm fighting for my dream, I'd better do it at full speed.

"Ms. Abernathy, you can go in."

Right. It's high time I switched to pills for birth control. Blake was absolutely enthusiastic when I told him. I stride into her office with a big smile. After all, today I'm here just for a prescription for birth control. I'm not up for my yearly checkup yet. It's mid-August now, and I got my who-ha checked in April. Visits to the gynecologist are my least favorite. I mean, going to the doctor is never pleasant, but something about having someone look into my who-ha is unnerving.

"Clara, nice to see you." She shakes my hand, welcoming me into her practice, pointing to the seat in front of her desk. She's a petite woman in her forties with a sweet and calming demeanor.

The one thing I love about her practice is that it doesn't smell like a hospital. I can imagine I'm in an office, right until I have to drop my panties and spread my legs, but with some luck, I won't have to do that today.

She sits behind the desk, looking at my file. "You were here four months ago. Anything wrong?"

"Oh no. I just want some birth control. I've only been using condoms until now."

She smiles sweetly, closing the file. "Sure. Do you know what you want? Or should we go through all your options? There are pills, IUDs. I have to tell you right off the bat that none of them is one hundred percent certain, but then again, neither is the condom. You get about ninety-nine percent certainty."

I laugh nervously. "I think that's enough. I want pills."

She nods, picking up a pen and pulling a small notebook from under a stack of papers. I make a mental fist pump. This will be a record short visit.

Then she puts the pen back down. Damn it. So close.

"We need to do a urine test before."

"Oh, okay."

Fifteen minutes later, she looks at the results of the test and smiles.

"Oh!" she exclaims, startling me. Crap. A surprised doctor is never a good thing.

"Looks like you won't need that birth control after all."

I frown, not quite understanding. "Why? Am I—am I sterile?" That couldn't be, right? It would have come up sometime in the past twelve years or so of controls.

"No, of course not. You're pregnant."

My mouth goes dry, and my vision clouds for just a split second. I must have misheard her. "Pregnant? With...a baby?"

She laughs softly. "Yes."

"But I don't understand. We've used condoms every time. I mean, we've been at it like bunnies because that man can fuck me silly on a daily basis. He has quite the stamina—" Shit. Here comes my verbal diarrhea again. The good doctor doesn't need to know so much. "But that shouldn't matter as long as we used protection, right? We used a condom every time. And it didn't break. Not once."

"Sometimes a break isn't obvious."

My mouth goes dry as I breathe in and out, euphoria and panic warring inside me. There is a baby growing inside me. A baby! I place my hand on my belly, not quite ready to believe there is a tiny human there. The panic pushes away the euphoria for the moment.

"Are you sure?"

"Yes. Let's do a transvaginal ultrasound, and I'll tell you exactly how far along you are."

A few short minutes later, I climb on the examination bed, and she proceeds with the ultrasound.

"We have a heartbeat," she says triumphantly, pointing to the screen next to the bed and emotion clogs my throat as I watch the tiny blip. "By the looks of it, you've been pregnant for about six weeks."

"But six weeks...I drank coffee every day."

"Just make sure you adhere to the restrictions from now on, and you'll be just fine. I'll give you a full list."

"Okay." I draw in another deep breath. "Okay."

"Since you came in here for birth control, I'm assuming this was unplanned. You have options if this isn't what you want. Abortion, adoption."

It takes me a second to register what she means.

"No, I want it. Of course I want it. I'm just...I wasn't expecting this."

"Sometimes the best things in life happen unexpectedly."

I'd agree with her, but almost everything in

my life so far has been unplanned. I was hoping to do better than that for my baby, at least be married or employed.

My mind spins while the doctor gives me instructions, recommends vitamins, and whatnot. Still, I'm overcome with joy, and I place both hands on my belly. It's silly, I know. There's nothing to feel. It'll be months before he or she starts to kick. But it's growing inside me. Someone tiny to take care of and shower with love.

I can already picture it: the nursery, the adorable clothes. Me sitting in a rocking chair, singing a lullaby until the baby falls asleep. I can practically smell that sweet and sugary scent of a newborn.

There is just one question mark. How will Blake take this?

My heart begins to thrum faster again, the panic barreling back in as I leave the building. I'm happy I didn't come by car because I couldn't concentrate on driving. The walk will do me good. Maybe by the time I get home I'll have my thoughts together.

Except I want to keep thinking about the baby because that seems safer. With Blake, this could play out too many ways. I distinctly remember him telling me that starting a family right now is the last thing he wants. We've been growing close, but a baby is a huge and *permanent* thing, and I am starting to panic for real.

Sweat breaks out of my forehead, and I stop

at a kiosk to buy a bottle of water. I gurgle down the ice-cold liquid, and it helps me calm down somewhat. Blake is a good man through and through. Still, the prospect of talking to him sends my mind into a tailspin, again.

What if he won't want me for good...or the baby? My eyes sting at the mere thought that he'd push me—us—away. One would think that at this point in my life, I'd be a pro at dealing with rejection, but I am far from it. Every time I deal with it, I feel like that eleven-year-old again, who was dropped at the orphanage with a pink slip of paper in her hand. I guess some wounds never really heal.

I'm ridiculous. I've seen Blake with his nieces and nephews. He adores them. I don't doubt that. He plays with them, spoils them, never ever loses his patience. Whether he wants me for good or not, he'll do right by the baby. I know he will.

But I really hope he'll want me too.

CHAPTER TWENTY-SEVEN

Clara

"Thank God they're feeding us at least," Theresa exclaims. She's a fellow candidate for the illustrator position. They called in thirty candidates from the pool of two hundred who applied, and we were all asked to come here at eight o'clock this morning. We're interviewing with different people. So far, I've had six interviews and my head is spinning. The whole thing will last until five o'clock.

"Amen!" I say as we head toward the buffet lined up in the entrance area of the waiting room. "But I have to be quick because my next interview starts in ten minutes."

"Mine in twenty. No matter the outcome today, I'm going to have a bubble bath tonight."

"I love bubble baths too." But I won't be taking one tonight. I have a very important thing to do, namely tell Blake about the baby—yes, I'm that much of a coward. I've known for an entire week, and I haven't worked up the courage to tell him. Not only that, but I kept to myself as much as possible, afraid that Blake would see right through me otherwise. I've been using the interview and the custom illustration I had to do for today as an excuse, but I'm not sure he's buying it.

Tonight is the night, though.

I bought a pair of baby shoes, which I plan to use as an introduction. It's a bit cheesy, but I'm feeling very cheesy these days. I'm blaming the hormones. I've been carrying the shoes in my purse since I bought them. Sometimes between interviews, I look through my bag so I can see them.

I've prepared an entire speech. Actually, I've prepared quite a few variations, depending on how Blake will take the news. A big part of me hopes he'll just take me in his arms, overcome with joy, and say we'll figure this out together. The rational part of me is making contingency plans.

"Sushi!" Theresa exclaims when we reach the buffet. I look at the selection wistfully. The food selection includes other goodies too, thank goodness, because I'm not allowed to eat sushi. So instead, I load my plate with everything else. This week has been a bit terrible. I've had to give up coffee, and I feel permanently jet-lagged. On the bright side, I have zero morning sickness.

"Why aren't you eating sushi? Not a fan?" Theresa asks as we walk away from the too-crowded buffet area and sit in the chairs in the waiting area by the elevators.

"I love sushi, but sadly I can't eat it right now."

"Pregnant?"

I wince, and I can feel my eyes widening.

Theresa's eyes widen too. Crap. She was just stabbing in the dark, but I gave myself away.

"Yeah, I'm pregnant." The corners of my mouth lift up in a smile all by themselves as I say this. I realize I haven't said it out loud since the doctor gave me the news. I haven't told anyone. I couldn't possibly tell any of the Bennetts before talking to Blake, and Penny has been buried in deadlines all week. "Six weeks."

"Wow, how will this work if you get the position?"

I'm about to say I haven't thought that far when a familiar voice booms from behind me.

"You're pregnant?"

I literally leap to my feet, whirling around. Blake is standing just outside the elevator, feet planted wide, a bag of takeout in his left hand. My stomach rumbles at the smell. Something from Blue Moon, by the package. I don't even care what it is. Everything from there is delicious. I cleared my plate, and I'm still hungry.

"Clara?" Blake's voice snaps me back to the matter at hand, which is far more important than my all-consuming hunger.

"I'll leave you two," Theresa says, right before she scurries off with her plate.

"What are you doing here?"

"Wanted to surprise you with lunch. Roast beef. Your favorite. Thought it would bring you luck." He places the takeout bag on one of the chairs. "You're pregnant?" he repeats, frowning now. My entire body tenses. I've seen Blake frown maybe a dozen times since I've known him. I was hoping this wouldn't be an occasion for frowning.

"Yes, I have...I mean I am...." Jesus, why can't I whip two words together in a coherent sentence? Sweat dots my palms, and I wipe them both on my jeans. I wish he'd crack a joke. I wish I'd crack a joke, but my brain isn't cooperating. The grim set of his mouth really isn't helping. I could use a smile. I'd be grateful even for the hint of a smile.

"Six weeks? Why didn't you tell me?"

"I haven't known for six weeks. I went to the doctor like we talked about, so I could get birth control. And that's when I discovered."

"You went to the doctor last week," he points out. There's still not a hint of smile on his face. "Is this why you've been so distant?"

A knot lodges in my throat. "I didn't know how you'd take the news."

"What do you mean you didn't know how I'd take it? Why are you so nervous? You don't want the baby?"

"I'm—" My voice catches. I shake my head, closing my eyes. The image of the tiny shoes pops up in my mind. "I can't believe you asked me that," I finish weakly.

"Clara Abernathy!" a voice resounds from deeper inside the waiting room. "Your interviewer is waiting."

"I have to go."

"I can wait until your next break."

"Don't."

"Clara—" he tries again.

"Please don't. I have a gazillion more interviews, and I want to have a clear head."

Without waiting for his reply, I turn my back to him and head straight to my interview room.

***

They start triaging us in the afternoon. By four o'clock, just six of us are left from the thirty. Theresa didn't make the cut, which is a pity. I liked her. They'll only hire three though, so the game is still on. I'm dizzy and hungry by the time they call me in for the last interview. A woman with a short, graying bob welcomes me inside. My portfolio is to her right, my custom illustration for them on the left.

"I'm Sheila Radcliffe. Take a seat, Ms. Abernathy. You're pale. Are you feeling all right?"

Yep, just confused and broken-hearted. And what with the lack of caffeine in my system and the general drowsiness the doctor warned might hit me in the first trimester, I feel like I'm wading through a particularly thick cobweb of thoughts.

"Just been a long day, but I'm excited to be here."

She scoffs. "Please, between the two of us, I can be honest. This process has been a nightmare. Our HR really needs to get their act together. Who's got time for ten interviews?"

I smile weakly. "This is my twelfth."

"Pffft, see what I mean? I wanted you on my team since I saw this."

She holds up an illustration from my portfolio. It's two years old, and I did it on a whim, in one crazy night. It's a little strange and a lot colorful.

"Wow, really?"

She nods. "Really. This tells me you have creativity. Technique can be learned, but creativity comes from within. So yeah, that's what convinced me. But HR insisted on a million interviews to see if we're a good fit and whatnot." *Ah yes, that does sound like HR bullshit.* "I told them the only thing I care about is the illustrator's work, not which personality type they are, but alas, I don't make all the rules. So, Clara—can I call you that?"

"Yes, please."

"Brilliant! You're available to start immediately, right?"

I can barely believe this is happening. "I am."

"Good. Because I want to change the plans. I do get to make some rules, thank goodness. All of the remaining six candidates are my favorites, and I don't want to narrow it down yet. What I do want is for all of you to go through with the two weeks of training, and at the end of it, we'll see who we're keeping."

I nod, a little disappointed that the process will stretch out even more.

"Would you be able to start the training tomorrow instead of next week? There's a plane flying out this evening—we're paying for all expenses, of course—and I really want to get the ball rolling."

Oh snap. The training is at their headquarters, which is in Boston. If I take off this evening, it means I get a very short time to talk to Blake, and I was hoping to at least get a good night's sleep before tackling that. But there's no way I can say no. Friendly as Sheila is, it's clear that saying no is an exclusion criteria.

"Sure, no problem. I'm your girl."

She claps her hands, smiling brightly. "Excellent. I think you'll like it at Ayaks Publishing, Clara."

CHAPTER TWENTY-EIGHT

Blake

Hi, Blake. I got to the next level!!! Which is not being hired. They'll decide which of us they keep after the two-weeks training. They changed the schedule and want to start the training tomorrow, so I have to fly out to Boston tonight. I'm home now, packing, but you're not here, and I can't wait any longer or I'll miss the plane. Maybe this is for the bes,t though! You'll have two weeks to think about everything. We'll talk when I get back. I understand this was a shock to you, but I hope you'll do right by the baby, even if you don't want me. Please don't call. I don't want to talk about this on the phone.

I read the message for the twentieth time. She thinks I don't want her. Jesus, out of all the mistakes I've done in my life, this takes the cake, by far. Yeah, it was a shock, but that was a knee-jerk reaction.

I planned to apologize last night, but that went nowhere. While she was here, packing, I was running around setting up our big dinner. I'd planned on this being a big dinner even before I screwed up. This was going to be the night when I told her I loved her and officially asked her to move in. I wanted to wait until after the whole Ayaks business was over because she spent the week before in a frenzy working on their custom illustration. It was my "go big or go home" moment. I thought she'd love a great, romantic gesture. Screw great gestures. This is what you get for waiting for the right moment. There is no right moment. There is just right now.

And right now, the morning after, she isn't answering her phone. Yeah, I respected her wish last night about not calling, but after spending most of the night awake, I broke down and called. Zip. Nada. No answer.

My phone rings, and I desperately hope it's Clara. It's not. My baby sister's name appears on the screen.

"Hey!" she greets cheerfully. "What are you up to?"

I debate for a moment telling her what happened, then decide against it. It'll open a can of worms.

"Not much."

"Do you want to have a late breakfast? Pier 39? I'm in the area."

"You got the day off from the gallery?" I ask in confusion.

"Something like that."

"Sure, I can be there in twenty minutes or so."

Twenty minutes later, I'm heading toward Pier 39, making my way through streams of tourists who've gathered around the docks to see the sea lions roasting in the sun.

Summer waves at me from one of the tables. I almost do a double take when I see Pippa with her too. Somewhere at the back of my mind, a little voice tells me something's gone awry. I mean, my family is up for impromptu get-togethers often. But both my sisters just happen to want to have a late breakfast on a workday? Smells like dead fish to me.

"Hey, baby bro," Pippa says, as I sit on the third chair around the table.

"Didn't know you'd be joining us too."

She stretches her arms, closing her eyes. "The morning is too beautiful to spend it inside the office. It's good to be in the sun."

She's not fooling me one bit, but I go with the charade. "Right. Let's order."

After the waitress writes down our order—I just want coffee, my sisters order half the menu between them—and takes off, both my sisters train their eyes on me.

"You look a bit tired," Summer comments. "Slept badly last night?"

"Nah, everything's peachy."

Summer's eyelid twitches, and Pippa's eyebrows climb up to her hairline. The girls definitely know something. I don't know why this surprises me. I should accept the fact that the women in my family always have the upper hand, an ace up their sleeve. Any day now, I'll come to terms with it.

"How's Clara?" Pippa asks. The waitress arrives with our drinks, and the three of us are silent until she leaves.

"In Boston." That much is true.

The girls fidget more, exchange glances. And even though I could torture them for hours—I'm a pro at this after so many years—I'm impatient today.

"We can do this all day," I inform them, pushing my coffee cup away and setting my elbows on the table. "Or we can cut right to the chase. Did you talk to Clara?"

"Before we choose sides, how about you tell us what's going on?" Pippa suggests without answering my question.

The waitress appears again, this time with the food, which she lays out in front of my sisters. They don't even glance at it. Bad omen. My sisters can't resist food when it's in front of their nose, unless it's for a good cause. Or a lost cause—which I suppose I am.

What's a man to do when his sisters shoot daggers at him with their eyes? Confess all of his sins.

They both listen with rapt attention as I recount everything that happened yesterday. And damn it, saying everything out loud makes it a million times worse.

"Let me get this straight. A woman tells you she's pregnant, and the first thing you ask is if she doesn't want the baby?" Summer looks like she wanted to punch me. Pippa just pinches her nose but remains silent, which is the surest sign I've fucked up so badly, she doesn't even have a comeback.

"Not my finest moment, okay? She was all

jerky and couldn't look me in the eye, and I couldn't understand why she'd keep it a secret from me when she had no problem saying it to that woman she'd just met between interviews."

I know how much Clara wants a family; she told me the day she visited the apartment. But she also described her ideal partner as someone who's the polar opposite of me. So, for those decisive moments, I thought maybe she was all jerky and hadn't told me because she didn't want a family with *me*.

"Here's a thought—maybe she was nervous about telling you?" Pippa says, opening and closing her hand. I have a hunch she'd like nothing better than to close that hand around my neck, squeeze a bit.

Summer nods. "You guys aren't married or engaged. She was in between jobs. And then she found out she was pregnant. It's no woman's ideal situation. Maybe she was afraid you'd react badly."

I press my palms against the socket of my eyes. I can't *believe* myself. She is everything to me. Everything.

"Jesus, all of you men have the tendency to put your foot in your mouth, but you're in a league of your own," Summer exclaims.

"Tell me something I don't know."

"Did she hit you?" she continues.

"She's not a violent person."

"Neither am I, but my palm's twitching. I badly need to hit you for her."

Words I never thought I'd hear from my baby sister.

"Let's concentrate on the issue at hand. I need to talk her."

Pippa scoffs. "How about what she needs?"

"What do you mean?"

"Her message said you'll talk when she's back, right?"

"Yeah," I say hopefully. Pippa seems to understand far more of the situation than I do.

"To me this just reads like she needs some distance from your sorry ass."

"Distance? How's that helpful? She's pregnant, for God's sake. What she needs is for me to take care of her and pamper her and make sure she's not overworking herself."

Pippa's mouth twitches. "You're aware Clara has been living thirty years of her life without you, yes? She's very self-sufficient."

"But she doesn't have to be, that's the point. What if she's sick? The first trimester is the one with morning sickness. I've read about it."

"Did you now?" Summer asks. For some reason, she seems to be having a field day with this.

"Yes, I did. I had a long night with no Clara to read just about everything. This isn't the time for her to be alone. I want to take care of her, and the baby."

"So you're happy about the baby?" Pippa asks.

"Of course I am. Last night, before everything

blew up in my face, I planned to ask her to move in for good, make this official. I love her, and I love that baby too."

"Your heart is in the right place," Pippa concludes. My sisters exchange another glance, and something in their expression sets me on edge.

"When did you talk to her? What did she say?" I ask them.

"She didn't say much," Summer says quickly.

"You're lying." I'm looking straight at Summer now. Pippa has a good poker face, and she can stick to her guns if needed, but Summer has never been able to resist spilling information to me when she had it. Until now.

"Not lying. Just withholding information," Summer says weakly.

Pippa groans. "She told us that in confidence."

"Girls," I warn. "I need to know what she told you."

A moment of silence, and then Pippa shakes her head. "I'm usually not a fan of breaking another woman's confidence, but I do think you need to know. She called me yesterday, and I was with Summer. It took her a while to get to the point. I think she was trying to test out if we'd be happy about the news or not. She was...well, from experience I can tell you pregnancy hormones aren't a joke. It's like PMS on steroids. Once I burst out crying during a commercial for baby cough syrup because I suddenly thought how awful it must be to have your baby die from a fit of coughing."

Summer and I stare at her, stricken. Pippa is oblivious to our horror.

"But back to Clara. When she finally did tell us, she said she hoped we'd love the baby too, accept him or her as part of the family, even if Clara wouldn't belong to it. She told us that she'd manage being a single mother, she'd come through for her baby, and she wasn't worried about the money, but that she really hoped the child wouldn't grow up without an extended family, because it would be a lonely childhood. I suspect she was thinking back to her own childhood."

Jesus. I lean back in the chair, running my hand through my hair in frustration. Clara is amazing, and I've never felt more grateful for something as I am for having her in my life. I have no idea what I've done to deserve her, but I'm madly in love with her, and I want to shout it from the rooftops. For now though, I want to tell her. She needs to know.

"I need to talk to her," I repeat for maybe the hundredth time today.

"Wait for her to return, like she asked," Summer insists. "I think she really wants to focus on the training so she makes the final cut."

Tapping my fingers on the table, I start whipping up a plan. I'll need it to be solid, and it will involve textbook groveling. I will not lose this woman.

CHAPTER TWENTY-NINE

Clara

The training is a ten-hours-a-day deal. They put the six of us together with a dozen candidates for their children's nonfiction department, since most of the techniques the trainer teaches can be applied no matter the illustration type. We receive a lot of individual feedback. It's intensive as hell, and even more competitive than I thought. Since everyone knows they're only going to hire three out of six for the fiction illustrator positions, tensions are high between us. Everyone's polite, of course, but the negative vibes...*yikes*.

"Ms. Abernathy, these lines could be sharper. Focus on them," the trainer says. He's a tall man, maybe a few years older than I am. The trainer's feedback motivates me to do my very best and kick ass. What doesn't go with ass kicking? Lack of coffee, moderate consumption of sugar, heartbreak, visions of Christmases where I'm the only one putting presents for Beanie under the tree—I'm calling the baby Beanie until I know the sex; it's sweet, but not emasculating, and it only *vaguely* sounds like *Blakie*.

On the second day, I add morning sickness to

the mix. The hotel is just a block away from the headquarters, but if I don't head out soon, I'm going to have to miss breakfast so I'm not late. Since I had no morning sickness until now, I was hoping to go through the pregnancy unscathed. After spending fifteen minutes with my head in the toilet, all those hopes go to hell in a handbasket.

After calming down, I wash my face and return to the room with small, tentative steps, sitting on the bed, sniffing myself, because I have a suspicion I still stink of vomit.

Sniff. Sniff. Blech. Suspicion confirmed.

I'll have to hop in the shower. Judging by the nausea at the back of my throat, I'll have to skip breakfast anyway.

I'm halfway to the bathroom when there is a knock at my door. Reluctantly, I change direction. One of the receptionists is in front of my door, carrying a huge bouquet of sunflowers.

"Ms. Abernathy, we had these delivered for you," she quips, jerking her head back in alarm when I lean in to take the flowers. My fabulous E*au de Vomit* must have reached her. Poor woman.

She scurries away and I shut the door, bringing the flowers to the small desk in a corner. I itch to read the card that came with them. I can see it, wedged between the green stems of the sunflowers. The second I put the flowers on the small table, I snatch the card from them. The writing on the card belongs to Blake.

I am proud of you. You'll kick ass and get the job. I know it.

Blake

I turn the card. No more words. Was there a second card and it got lost? One that said I'm sorry? And possibly *I love you and Beanie*, but I'm working on not getting my hopes up too much. Hint: it's not working.

I look between the flowers, but...nothing. Right. Grabbing my phone, I call Blake right away. He answers after the first ring.

"You got the flowers?"

"And the card. I'm thinking there were two and one got lost."

"Nah, it was all a ruse."

"What?"

"I wanted to talk to you, but you asked me not to call you. Knew you'd call me right away if I sent that card."

My heart hammers so fast, I need to sit down. "You're being sneaky again."

"Always for a good cause."

"I don't know what to say."

"That's good because I have a lot of talking to do. Just listen. I'm sorry for my knee-jerk reaction. I didn't mean it. I am thrilled about the baby and I love you and—"

"Wait." As much as I want him to love me, I need to get something out of the way. "Don't say it if you don't mean it. I—we can work everything out with the baby so you're part of its life. But don't say you love me just because of the baby. Don't get my hopes up if you don't mean it."

Well, too late anyway, because I can feel hope swelling in my chest already, desperately wishing he means it.

"I do mean it, Clara. I love you. That evening I was planning a big dinner, asking you to officially move in, make a love declaration."

"You were?" I whisper.

"Yeah. I was waiting for you to have the interviews behind you, thought it was the right moment. But there is no right moment, just right now. This is our moment. I love you, and the baby."

"You love Beanie," I whisper, my heart all but bursting out of my chest.

"Huh?"

"That's what I'm calling the baby until we know the sex." I touch my belly in round circles.

"Terrible, even for a nickname."

We both laugh, but then our chuckles fade into a long and heavy silence.

"Blake, I need time to process this," I say eventually.

"I thought as much. Look out for a delivery tomorrow too."

"Why?"

"I can do better than flowers, but thought I'd start small."

My smile reappears. "Blake."

"I want to see you, Clara. There is nothing I want more. But I won't come until you ask me to.

Now go and kick ass."

I do just that, starting my training day with renewed energy, and my heart significantly less heavy. The next day, Blake sends me a box of crystallized ginger with a note that says *Ginger is supposed to help with morning sickness.*

Wow, I'd read about it, but what with the fabulous training taking up every waking hour, I didn't even have time to run to the pharmacy for any cures. And speaking of time, I'm dangerously close to running late, which is why I head straight out of the hotel, munching on the ginger. *Ah, these are going to make my life so much better.*

On my way, I thumb off a message to Blake.

Clara: How did you know about my morning sickness?

He answers a few minutes later, just as I enter the building.

Blake: I have my methods. Any time you want me to fly over there and take care of you, let me know. Any time.

Grinning, I slip my phone in the front pocket of my jeans, joining my group.

***

"All right, everyone! Let's order in lunch, and maybe it's time for a round of introductions, get to know each other better," the trainer suggests. I think the competitive vibes are becoming unnerving even for him.

The introductions reveal I'm the only one to have passed the three-zero mark here in the room. Everyone else ranges from college graduates to midtwenties, but I don't mind. It might have taken me a long while to get here, but I'm not going anywhere except forward. Still, some of the looks the recent graduates gave me when we introduced ourselves this morning were downright comical. I forgot that when you're twenty-two, thirty seems ancient.

All this I owe to Blake, for pushing me, for believing in me. If it weren't for him, I'd still be getting ready. I'd still be waiting for the right moment. Blake put it right. *There is no right moment. Just right now.*

The first thing I do once training is over for the day is call him.

"Hey!"

"Hey back. Wait a second," he says softly. I recognize the voice of Blue Moon's location manager in his background. A sound of a door follows and then silence. "I can talk now."

"I realized I forgot to say two very important things when we spoke."

"I'm listening."

"Sorry for not telling you about Beanie right after coming home from the doctor." I only have half a block to walk to the hotel when I stop and head for the small park on the adjacent street instead. I don't want to go back into the stuffy hotel bedroom just yet. "I got all wound up because I remembered that conversation when I first visited the apartment when you said how you weren't even thinking about starting your own family, and—"

"And I wasn't. I was happy being everyone's favorite uncle. But falling in love with the right woman changed that."

Swoon level dangerously high!

I sit on a bench in the almost empty park, the wood backrest a little too hard under my skin. It's a fine end of August evening. Blake continues, as if he didn't just make my insides melt.

"But your search for someone 'safe' and 'non-argumentative' didn't pan out, huh?"

I wave my hand dismissively, even though he can't see me. "Oh, about that. I was dead wrong. Apparently I want a man who doesn't back down from an argument when he thinks I'm standing in my own way. You make pushy sexy as all get-out. And if it weren't for that, I wouldn't be here, so thank you. That was my second point."

"Yeah?"

"Yeah. And Blake? You do make me feel safe with your reckless, furniture-breaking-sex style of approaching life."

"Is that your long-winded way of asking me to fly out to Boston?"

I grin. "Nope. Not at all."

***

When Blake said he could do better than flowers but was starting small, I assumed he was talking about cutesy stuff like more flowers and ginger cures. Boy, was I wrong. He pulls out the big guns the next morning when the receptionist hands me a small rectangular package. Inside, I find a key to his apartment, and no note. But I don't need more words.

I just need him.

The day after, I receive yet another package, just as small. Inside it, I find another package, and my heart skips a beat. It's a jewelry box with the Bennett Enterprises logo on it. My palms instantly become sweaty, and excitement bubbles in my throat. I swear even Beanie gives a tiny leap behind my navel. On second thought, maybe it was just my stomach.

"Beanie," I whisper, hand on belly, "I don't know if you realize the momentousness of this, but your dad is proposing to your mom. Just thought I'd spell it out for you." And for myself. I stare at the lovely box, admiring the delicate and classic velvet, the craftsmanship of the logo, working up the courage to open it.

It takes me so long to gather my wits that it's almost time to head out to training when I finally take off the lid.

There is nothing inside. It's absolutely empty.

Confused and apprehensive, I call the culprit.

"Blake Bennett, you do not play with the emotions of a pregnant woman this way. What is the meaning of this?"

"Hey, not my fault. Not the best idea to send jewelry through delivery services, because it could get stolen. I'm going to have to bring the ring in person."

I break into a fit of laughter. Genius. Pure genius.

"You're taking sneaky to a whole new level, Blake."

"What was that? Reception's not good. Sounded like you were asking me to fly out to Boston."

"On the next plane, please."

CHAPTER THIRTY

Clara

Six hours—length of the flight from San Francisco to Boston.

Twenty minutes—driving time from the airport to the hotel.

By my calculations, Blake arrived at the hotel about five hours ago, which is how long I've been glancing at the clock on my computer every ten minutes or so. Only two hours to go. I'm as jittery as can be, completing every task, taking the instructor's feedback in stride, applying it dutifully. Twice I stop myself from blurting out some excuse to leave early.

When the day is over, I practically fly out the door. Run down that one block. There's a commotion in front of the elevators, so I take the stairs. My room is on the second floor. The climb doesn't do anything to wear out my energy. On the contrary; by the time I enter my room, I worked myself into a frenzy.

"Blake," I whisper, taking it all in, vases upon vases of flowers spread around the small room. Candles in between, casting a warm and romantic glow. And the man. *Oh, the man.*

He meets me halfway, hooking an arm around my waist, pulling me flush against him, kissing me hard. Oh God, how I missed him. His scent, the feeling of being held in his strong arms, being pressed against his granite chest. I can't get enough of his warm, determined mouth.

"I missed you," he whispers when we pull apart to breathe.

"I missed you too." That's when I realize I'm level with him, and my feet are dangling in the air. The man lifted me off the floor. Now that's what I call strong.

When he puts me back down, I stand on my toes, but since I'm wearing flats, I still only reach up to his chin. Honestly, I love that he towers over me. It gives me a sense of safety, as if nothing can happen while this mountain of a man has his arms around me. His solid build also has other benefits. There's a lot of Blake to kiss and caress.

"As far as big, romantic gestures go, this is...wow."

He kisses the tip of my nose, smiling before lowering himself on one knee and opening his fist. I shiver lightly as my heart seems to grow in size and then grow some more as I take in the clear-cut diamond and the intricately braided pattern of the white gold band.

"Clara, we've had many firsts, and we'll have many more. But I also want to be your last. Your only. I want to be with you always. When you need someone to believe in you. When you need someone to love you. I'm yours, no matter what. I want you to go to bed with this certainty, and wake up with it too. Will you marry me?"

My tongue sticks to the roof of my mouth, and all I can do is nod. This reckless and totally adorable man is mine. All mine. And I can't wait for the entire world to know it.

I soak in every second of this, to memorize every single detail. I want to look back on this moment years from now and remember everything. I've never been more certain of anything in my life. It's exhilarating.

"Yes, yes, yes!" I say when I find my voice, watching as he slides the ring on. Then I cup his face with both hands and kiss him.

Still on his knees, he takes control of the kiss, descending until he reaches my belly, rubbing his cheek against it, then whispering, "Beanie, I promise you'll have a great name. Don't mind your mom, she's just being hormonal. Nicknames don't count."

He holds my hips in that wonderful way of his, which is both possessive and protective. When he looks up at me, his gaze is molten and wanton. I lean into his touch, closing my eyes. He guides me to the bed, gently laying me on it, removing my clothes one by one while I do the same with his until we're both naked. I can't stop touching him. His broad, strong shoulders, the ridges on his chest marking the defined muscles, and the V-shaped lines leading downward. He's hard already, and kissing me everywhere. My neck, my shoulders.

"My nipples are too sensitive," I whisper, hating to break his stride, but they've been unbearably sensitive for days now. The friction with any kind of fabric is excruciating.

Blake nods, kissing along the top of my breasts, then the underside. I roll my hips against him, and the tip of his erection touches right next to my navel. The hot point of contact sends a wave of shudders through me.

With a wicked smile, he moves, rubbing his erection along the length of my opening. I part my legs wider, needing him, but he doesn't slide in, though I'm ready for him. Any readier than I already am and I will break out of my skin. I'm hot and bothered, and I need him inside me.

He pushes just the tip inside before pulling back out, gripping himself at the base, and circling my clit with the crown.

"Blake. Oh God. Oh God. I will—"

Words fail me as he circles around my clit again and again, working me into a frenzy until every cell in my body strums with energy, every nerve is connected to my center. I cry out his name when the first spasm rocks through me. And then he slides inside me, every inch of him, while I'm coming so hard I'm afraid I will pass out. My inner muscles clamp around him, and the sensation of being so full of him while I'm still riding my orgasm sends my vision into a tailspin.

When I come to myself, his arms cage me in

at my sides.

"You feel amazing, Clara." He's shuddering lightly, as if he's barely hanging on to his control. "This moment here is everything, and I want to make you some promises while we're connected like this."

Oh, this wonderful, charming man. He'll never cease to surprise me. If I loved him any more, my heart might burst. I fight to calm my racing pulse because the rush of blood and adrenaline causes my ears to buzz, and I don't want to miss one word of what Blake has to say. But the more I fight, the more frantic my pulse becomes, the louder the buzz in my ears. I swallow hard twice, and there is a tiny *pop* in my ears. Then Blake's voice reaches me.

"I promise to take care of you, and love you. I promise to be the man you need and deserve, every day. I want you to have the best of everything, Clara, and I want to be the one to give you all that. I'll be a happy man to spend my life fulfilling every single wish you have, raising a family. It'll be my honor to grow old next to you. I love you."

I've never heard anything more romantic, and my eyes are stinging.

I swallow yet again, preparing to make some promises of my own. Oh, I have so many things to say to him. Though I've always been a chatterbox, when it comes to matters of the heart, I've always tried to employ a filter, but not anymore. There is not one part of myself I haven't given Blake already.

"I love you, Blake, and I promise to make your life better, in the small things and the big things.

I love you more than I can say, and I'll show you. Every day."

He touches my nose in a sweet Eskimo kiss and moves inside me.

"Hey," I admonish. "I'm not done."

"We have all the time for words later. Now I want to make love to my future wife."

CHAPTER THIRTY-ONE

Clara

"That was hands down the best proposal," Pippa exclaims.

"An empty box?" Summer taps her manicured nails on her cocktail glass, as if assessing the merits of the tactic.

"Creative." Alice nods, fighting a yawn. She and Nate flew in yesterday from London, and she's still fighting jet lag.

"Oi, stop comparing how amazing your men are. We single ladies here are starting to get jealous," Caroline says. Penny and Summer clink their glasses with her. "Hear, hear."

Ah, this is one hell of a bachelorette party. All the Bennett women, whether by birth or marriage, are here, plus Caroline, Penny, and Kate—who flew in yesterday too. We started with a lazy spa day, which was lazier for the girls, because I received the head-to-toe bridal treatment, complete with foot massage and pedicure.

Right now, we're in a lounge bar in the Marina district, sitting on a round, comfy couch. Behind us, the glass wall of the establishment offers a clear view of the city lights blinking in the night, the Golden Gate Bridge in the distance.

I'm listening intently to the girls' chatter when Beanie kicks me hard. *Whoa.* Hand on my huge belly, I gently rub where I felt the kick. Since neither Blake nor I wanted a quick, shotgun wedding, we took our time, and now at seven months, I look like I'm going to have a baby elephant. Nope, no twins here, though I am asked that question about twice a week. I just eat a lot and Beanie is huge. Soon, Bean Bag will be more appropriate. We're having a boy, and choosing a name is still an ongoing fight. At this rate, Beanie might go on his birth certificate.

When we went in for the ultrasound, Blake kept his eyes eagerly on the monitor, but his smile faltered for a split second when the doctor pointed to the heart. After a thorough interrogation—I might have resorted to underhanded techniques and a little emotional blackmail, but I'm not even sorry—he admitted he was hoping we'd have twins.

"Maybe we'll get lucky next time. If not, we can practice until it happens. With my family genes, we're bound to get lucky eventually."

I agree one hundred percent with his plan. After Beanie is born, I will take a few months off from my job, and then I will work from home almost exclusively. At the end of the training period, I was one of the three illustrators the Ayaks team chose. So, surreal as it might sound, I—the woman whose middle name was practical, and didn't put much stock in dreams—illustrate for a living. Then again, taking a leap of faith and fighting for my dream is much easier with a glorious man who believes in me by my side.

"I wonder what the guys are up to," Pippa says, bringing me back to the present.

"I'm surprised Blake didn't want to have his bachelor party in Vegas," Alice comments, "considering how hard he lobbied for it for everyone else's parties."

I smile to myself. When I asked Blake why he's not flying out to Vegas for a weekend, his exact words were "No way in hell am I going to be away from you and Beanie for a weekend."

As we order a new round of drinks, Summer touches her earlobe, and Pippa nods almost imperceptibly. Aha, we're entering the *meddling* part of the evening. Our target: Caroline. The operation shouldn't be too complicated because we're only looking for a confession—though a hint would also suffice—about her feelings for Daniel, see if there's still something there. Summer and Pippa said that a bachelorette party is the perfect occasion for getting the scoop. Alcohol is involved, emotions are all over the place, secrets might be spilled...or lured out.

Of course, since I love meddling, I was completely on board with their plan. Gives me a chance to see the sisters at work on someone other than me, and sharpen my own meddling skills. Who knows when they'll come in handy?

Plus, I've picked up a few tricks, and this is my moment to shine. While sipping on our drinks—just orange juice for me—I do my part, guiding the conversation toward everyone's college days. Nostalgia should kick in any second now. As soon as everyone brings up fond memories, I stir them to college flames, since Caroline and Daniel were together during their senior year.

Caroline holds up her hand. "I say we talk about the wedding."

Aha, that's an evasive maneuver if I ever saw one. She also narrows her eyes at me, which pretty much means she saw right through my tactic.

Ahem, I still have a lot of sharpening to do when it comes to my meddling skills. Summer winks at me, as if saying, *Don't worry. We have a plan B.*

I'm pretty sure the girls have as many plans as there are letters in the alphabet, and if not, they'll make one up on the spot, because they're creative like that.

Speaking of creativity, there's something I meant to ask them, and I seize my opportunity, moving next to Summer.

"One question: Did you two have something to do with my building not being ready in time?" I'm still renting out the condo, and Blake and I broke down the wall between our apartments. We'll keep living there until our little family becomes not-so-little.

Summer forms an O with her mouth. "Of course not. We're matchmakers, not mean girls."

I elbow her playfully. "Hey, I was just curious, that's all."

Just as I wonder what their plan B implies, Pippa turns to Caroline. "Speaking about the wedding, we still need to put someone in charge of handing out the thank-you gifts to the guests at the end. Daniel's on it, but he needs assistance. Could you help him, Caroline? Or would it be too uncomfortable for you? You'd be doing us a huge favor."

"When you put it like that, how can I say no?" Caroline sighs, a dreamy expression on her face. Pippa smiles triumphantly, and I bow to the master.

EPILOGUE

Clara

"No, you can't come in. You're not allowed to see the bride before the ceremony." Jenna Bennett is employing her most stern motherly voice, talking to Blake through the cracked door.

"Mom, I don't give a rat's ass about antique traditions. I'm coming in."

Jenna steps back, muttering about how he can't respect rules even on his wedding day. I grin, beyond happy he isn't one to respect traditions because I was hoping I'd get to spend a few minutes alone with him before everything kicks off.

"Fine, I'll leave you two alone, but just for ten minutes."

I admire my asymmetric, braided bun in a sideways mirror.

"Thanks, Mom."

Once we're alone, he closes the distance to me, slowly looking me up and down. My dress is magnificent, a princess-style white gown with a satin and lace bodice, and a voluminous skirt—satin only. I won't deny I feel a bit like an elephant, what with my middle looking as if I swallowed a football, but that doesn't keep me from grinning like a lunatic. I understand what Alice meant at her own wedding about not being able to stop grinning. Too much excitement and happiness bubble inside me for a simple smile to do them justice.

"You look beautiful, Clara." Taking my hand, he lifts it, kissing my knuckles. "I wanted a few minutes alone with you."

"Great minds think alike."

"Mom driving you crazy?"

I shake my head, whispering, "Not at all."

Biting the inside of my cheek, I fight against the wave of emotions...and lose. Everyone warned me not to cry because I'll ruin my makeup, but I'm a pregnant woman getting married. It'd be weird if I *weren't* crying. Still, I'm determined to keep the tears at bay for as long as possible.

"You know how much I love your family, and I'm very lucky to have all of them in my life. I like being smothered and loved, and everyone meddling in my business."

Blake smiles, resting his hands on my bare shoulders, his thumbs pressing gently just where the fabric of the bodice meets my skin.

"You've lucked out, because I'm going to smother and love you for the rest of our lives, and my family will meddle for that long as well."

"Ah!"

"What's wrong?"

"Beanie kicked hard. I think he loves

romantic promises."

Taking Blake's hand, I put it exactly where Beanie kicked, on my lower left side. He's still now, but then....

"You make me the happiest man, Clara. The happiest. I can't believe I'm so lucky to have you. I promise I will take care of you, of our family. Any fears, I'll be right here, fighting them with you. Any dreams, I'll fight for them next to you." *Tap, tap, tap.* Beanie kicks almost every third word, until I get misty-eyed and Blake's voice becomes hoarse with emotion. "This is my promise to you, and to our son."

"And I promise to always be all the things you need, even those you don't know you need. The partner in crime, the shoulder you lean on. The one person you come to and open up to no matter what. I will take care of and spoil you. Both of you."

Beanie kicks harder, right where his dad's hand is on my belly, as if he knows we're talking about him. Blake lowers himself on his haunches, kissing my belly.

"Don't worry, buddy, I'll teach you all the tricks about how to marry a great woman."

"What would you have said if we'd had a girl?"

"I'd have told her no man will ever be good enough for her."

"That's a double standard if there ever was one."

Blake rises, touching my nose with his. "I

can't wait for you to fight me on it."

There is a knock at the door, and Nate's voice reaches us. "Clara, it's time."

"Come on in, I'm ready."

Nate steps inside, beaming, offering me his arm. He's the one walking me down to the altar and giving me away to Blake, who leaves the room as someone calls his name in the distance.

***

My heart pounds so hard during the ceremony that I have trouble hearing everything the minister and Blake are saying, but of course Beanie sets me straight as soon as my husband speaks his vows, because he kicks like nobody's business. Even though we're in a church full of people, and though we're only supposed to be holding hands during the vows, I place Blake's palm on my belly so he doesn't miss all the tap-dancing Beanie's doing. By the time the ceremony ends and Blake kisses me, we're both teary-eyed.

The party stretches until the early hours of the morning. The guests leave in small groups, until there's just very close friends and family left. The sheer number of cousins the Bennetts have is mind-boggling. So far, I've been able to chat only with the Connor clan—mostly with Landon—but I can't wait to get to know the rest better too.

"Well, I think Beanie's gonna be a tap dancer," I say, dropping in a seat at one of the large round tables where most of the family gathered. "He's been active all night."

"You two still haven't decided on a name?" Sebastian asks.

"No, but we really don't need your assistance," Blake informs him. Then raises a finger in warning toward Logan, who just opened his mouth. "Or you, Logan. You named your son Silas. You don't have a right to vote."

"Ours are named Will and Audrey," Sebastian remarks.

"Don't think I forgot you wanted to name poor Will, Seamus. I have a good memory, brother."

"Hey, that's news to me. And I really, really like that name." I sit straighter in my chair. Blake whirls to me, eyes hard and determined.

"Babe, we're not naming any offspring Seamus. Don't fight me on this."

Ah, well...I'm going to bide my time. I found over the past few months that the larger my belly becomes, the easier he caves in to my requests. Not about names so far, but I still have two months to work on that.

"Say, how did Caroline and Daniel end up being in charge of giving thank-you gifts to the guests?" Blake asks, taking me out on the dance floor again.

"Ah, a little nudge from your sisters, and me. Thought I'd start officially meddling, now that I'm a Bennett and all that."

Blake kisses me softly, then pulls back,

nodding. "You like to meddle, and you have terrible taste in names. I think you're more of a Bennett than I am."

THE END

Other Books by Layla Hagen

The Bennett Family Series

Book 1: Your Irresistible Love

Sebastian Bennett is a determined man. It's the secret behind the business empire he built from scratch. Under his rule, Bennett Enterprises dominates the jewelry industry. Despite being ruthless in his work, family comes first for him, and he'd do anything for his parents and eight siblings—even if they drive him crazy sometimes. . . like when they keep nagging him to get married already.

Sebastian doesn't believe in love, until he brings in external marketing consultant Ava to oversee the next collection launch. She's beautiful, funny, and just as stubborn as he is. Not only is he obsessed with her delicious curves, but he also finds himself willing to do anything to make her smile. He's determined to have Ava, even if she's completely off limits.

Ava Lindt has one job to do at Bennett Enterprises: make the next collection launch unforgettable. Daydreaming about the hot CEO is definitely not on her to-do list. Neither is doing said CEO. The consultancy she works for has a strict policy—no fraternizing with clients. She won't risk her job.

Besides, Ava knows better than to trust men with her heart.

But their sizzling chemistry spirals into a deep connection that takes both of them by surprise. Sebastian blows through her defenses one sweet kiss and sinful touch at a time. When Ava's time as a consultant in his company comes to an end, will Sebastian fight for the woman he loves or will he end up losing her?

AVAILABLE ON ALL RETAILERS.

Book 2: Your Captivating Love

Logan Bennett knows his priorities. He is loyal to his family and his company. He has no time for love, and no desire for it. Not after a disastrous engagement left him brokenhearted. When Nadine enters his life, she turns everything upside down.

She's sexy, funny, and utterly captivating. She's also more stubborn than anyone he's met…including himself.

Nadine Hawthorne is finally pursuing her dream: opening her own clothing shop. After working so hard to get here, she needs to concentrate on her new business, and can't afford distractions. Not even if they come in the form of Logan Bennett.

He's handsome, charming, and doesn't take no for an answer. After bitter disappointments, Nadine doesn't believe in love. But being around Logan is addicting. It doesn't help that Logan's family is scheming to bring them together at every turn.

Their attraction is sizzling, their connection undeniable. Slowly, Logan wins her over. What starts out as a fling, soon spirals into much more than they are prepared for.

When a mistake threatens to tear them apart, will they have the strength to hold on to each other?

AVAILABLE ON ALL RETAILERS.

Book 3: Your Forever Love

Eric Callahan is a powerful man, and his sharp business sense has earned him the nickname 'the shark.' Yet under the strict façade is a man who loves his daughter and would do anything for her. When he and his daughter move to San Francisco for three months, he has one thing in mind: expanding his business on the West Coast. As a widower, Eric is not looking for love. He focuses on his company, and his daughter.

Until he meets Pippa Bennett. She captivates him from the moment he sets eyes on her, and what starts as unintentional flirting soon spirals into something neither of them can control.

Pippa Bennett knows she should stay away from Eric Callahan. After going through a rough divorce, she doesn't trust men anymore. But something about Eric just draws her in. He has a body made for sin and a sense of humor that matches hers. Not to mention that seeing how adorable he is with his daughter melts Pippa's walls one by one.

The chemistry between them is undeniable, but the connection that grows deeper every day that has both of them wondering if love might be within their reach.

When it's time for Eric and his daughter to head back home, will he give up on the woman who has captured his heart, or will he do everything in his power to remain by her side?

AVAILABLE ON ALL RETAILERS.

Book 4: Your Inescapable Love

Max Bennett is a successful man. His analytical mind has taken his family's company to the next level. Outside the office, Max transforms from the serious business man into someone who is carefree and fun. Max is happy with his life and doesn't intend to change it, even though his mother keeps asking for more grandchildren. Max loves being an uncle, and plans to spoil his nieces rotten.

But when a chance encounter reunites him with Emilia, his childhood best friend, he starts questioning everything. The girl he last saw years ago has grown into a sensual woman with a smile he can't get out of his mind.

Emilia Campbell has a lot on her plate, taking care of her sick grandmother. Still, she faces everything with a positive attitude. When the childhood friend she hero-worshipped steps into her physical therapy clinic, she is over the moon. Max is every bit the troublemaker she remembers, only now he has a body to drool over and a smile to melt her panties. Not that she intends to do the former, or let the latter happen.

They are both determined not to cross the boundaries of friendship…at first. But as they spend more time together, they form an undeniable bond and their flirty banter spirals out of control.

Max knows Emilia is off-limits, but that only makes her all the more tempting. Besides, Max was never one to back away from a challenge.

When their chemistry becomes too much to resist and they inevitably give in to temptation, will they risk losing their friendship or will Max and Emilia find true love?

AVAILABLE ON ALL RETAILERS.

Book 5: Your Tempting Love

Christopher Bennett is a persuasive man. With his magnetic charm and undeniable wit, he plays a key role in the international success of his family's company.

Christopher adores his family, even if they can be too meddling sometimes... like when attempt to set him up with Victoria, by recommending him to employ her decorating services. Christopher isn't looking to settle down, but meeting Victoria turns his world upside down. Her laughter is contagious, and her beautiful lips and curves are too tempting.

Victoria Hensley is determined not to fall under Christopher's spell, even though the man is hotter than sin, and his flirty banter makes her toes curl. But as her client, Christopher is off limits. After her parents' death, Victoria is focusing on raising her much younger siblings, and she can't afford any mistakes...

But Victoria and Christopher's chemistry is not just the sparks-flying kind...It's the downright explosive kind. Before she knows it, Christopher is training her brother Lucas for soccer tryouts and reading bedtime stories to her sister Chloe.

Victoria wants to resist him, but Christopher is determined, stubborn, and oh-so-persuasive.

When their attraction and connection both spiral out of control, will they be able to risk it all for a love that is far too tempting?

AVAILABLE ON ALL RETAILERS.

Book 6: Your Alluring Love

Alice Bennett has been holding a torch for her older brother's best friend, Nate, for more than a decade. He's a hotshot TV producer who travels the world, never staying in San Francisco for too long. But now he's in town and just as tempting as ever... with a bossy streak that makes her weak in the knees and a smile that melts her defenses.

As a successful restaurant owner, Alice is happy with her life. She loves her business and her family, yet after watching her siblings find their happy ever after, she can't help feeling lonely sometimes—but that's only for her to know.

Nate has always had a soft spot for Alice. Despite considering the Bennetts his family, he never could look at her as just his friend's little sister. She's a spitfire, and Nate just can't stay away. He loves making her laugh... and blush.

Their attraction is irresistible, and between stolen kisses and wicked-hot nights, they form a deep bond that has them both yearning for more.

But when the chance of a lifetime comes knocking at his door, will Nate chase success even if it means losing Alice, or will he choose her?

AVAILABLE ON ALL RETAILERS.

The Lost Series

Lost in Us: The story of James and Serena

Found in Us: The story of Jessica and Parker

Caught in Us: The story of Dani and Damon

***

Standalone USA TODAY BESTSELLER
Withering Hope

Aimee's wedding is supposed to turn out perfect. Her dress, her fiancé and the location—the idyllic holiday ranch in Brazil—are perfect.

But all Aimee's plans come crashing down when the private jet that's taking her from the U.S. to the ranch—where her fiancé awaits her—defects mid-flight and the pilot is forced to perform an emergency landing in the heart of the Amazon rainforest.

With no way to reach civilization, being rescued is Aimee and Tristan's—the pilot—only hope. A slim one that slowly withers away, desperation taking its place. Because death wanders in the jungle under many forms: starvation, diseases. Beasts.

As Aimee and Tristan fight to find ways to survive, they grow closer. Together they discover that facing old, inner agonies carved by painful pasts takes just as much courage, if not even more, than facing the rainforest.

Despite her devotion to her fiancé, Aimee can't hide her feelings for Tristan—the man for whom she's slowly becoming everything. You can hide many things in the rainforest. But not lies. Or love.

Withering Hope is the story of a man who desperately needs forgiveness and the woman who brings him hope. It is a story in which hope births wings and blooms into a love that is as beautiful and intense as it is forbidden.

AVAILABLE ON ALL RETAILERS.

***

Your Fierce Love
Copyright © 2017 Layla Hagen
Published by Layla Hagen

All rights reserved. No part of this book may be reproduced or transmitted in any form, including electronic or mechanical, without written permission from the publisher, except in the case of brief quotations embodied in critical articles or reviews.

This is a work of fiction. Names, characters, businesses, places, events, and incidents are either the products of the author's imagination or used in a fictitious manner. Any resemblance to actual persons, living or dead, or actual events is purely coincidental.

This book is licensed for your personal enjoyment only. This book may not be re-sold or given away to other people. If you would like to share this book with another person, please purchase an additional copy for each person you share it with. If you are reading this book and did not purchase it, or it was not purchased for your use only, then you should return it to the seller and purchase your own copy. Thank you for respecting the author's work.

Published: Layla Hagen 2017
Cover: http://designs.romanticbookaffairs.com/

***
Acknowledgements

There are so many people who helped me fulfil the dream of publishing, that I am utterly terrified I will forget to thank someone. If I do, please forgive me. Here it goes.

I want to thank every blogger and reader who took a chance with me as a new author and helped me spread the word. You have my most heartfelt gratitude. To my street team. . .you rock !!!

Last but not least, I would like to thank my family. I would never be here if not for their love and support. Mom, you taught me that books are important, and for that I will always be grateful. Dad, thank you for always being convinced that I should reach for the stars.

To my sister, whose numerous ahem. . .legendary replies will serve as an inspiration for many books to come, I say thank you for your support and I love you, kid.

To my husband, who always, no matter what, believed in me and supported me through all this whether by happily taking on every chore I overlooked or accepting being ignored for hours at a time, and most importantly encouraged me whenever I needed it: I love you and I could not have done this without you.

<<<<>>>>

YOUR FIERCE LOVE